SELECTED POEMS OF
W. B. YEATS
葉 慈 詩 選

SELECTED POEMS OF
W. B. YEATS
葉 慈 詩 選

SELECTED & TRANSLATED BY FU HAO

傅浩 編譯

國家圖書館出版品預行編目資料

葉慈詩選＝Selected poems of W. B. Yeats /
　傅浩編譯. 一版. -- 臺北市：書林.
2000〔民 89〕
　　面； 公分

　　ISBN 957-586-862-5（平裝）
873.51　　　　　　　　　　　89002920

欲利用本書部分或全部內容者，須徵求書林出版公司
同意或授權，請洽書林出版部，電話：2365-8617。

葉 慈 詩 選
Selected Poems of W. B. Yeats

定價：390 元

編　譯／傅　浩
編　校／陳慧雰・黃嘉音
出版者／書林出版有限公司
　　　　台北市新生南路三段 88 號二樓之五
　　　　電話：23687226　傳真：23653548
　　　　http：//www.bookman.com.tw
發行人／蘇正隆
郵　撥／15743873・書林出版有限公司
印　刷／優文印刷廠
登記證／局版臺業字第一八三一號

2000 年 4 月一版，2001 年 7 月二刷

ISBN 957-586-862-5

葉慈詩選

Contents

目 錄

The Wind Among the Reeds (1899)

In the Seven Woods (1904)

The Green Helmet and Other Poems (1910)

選自《在那七片樹林裡》(1904)

選自《綠盔及其他》(1910)

Responsibilities (1914)

The Wild Swans at Coole (1919)

Michael Robartes and the Dancer (1921)

The Tower (1928)

The Winding Stair and Other Poems (1933)

選自《旋梯及其他》（1933）

譯者序

一

威廉・巴特勒・葉慈（William Butler Yeats, 1865-1939，又譯葉芝），係愛爾蘭詩人、劇作家、散文家。少年時興趣廣泛：曾在都柏林藝術專科學校學過繪畫；很早就顯露出詩歌創作的天賦；醉心於東方神祕主義，組織和參加過祕術研究社團；關心民族自治運動，一度加入愛爾蘭共和兄弟會。1896-1904 年與劇作家葛列格里夫人和約翰・辛等共同籌建愛爾蘭民族劇院，發起了愛爾蘭文學復興運動。1922 年愛爾蘭自由邦成立，當選爲參議員。葉慈一生創作不輟，其詩吸收浪漫主義、唯美主義、神祕主義、象徵主義和玄學詩的精華，幾經變革，最終熔鍊出獨特的風格。他的劇作多以愛爾蘭民間傳說爲題材，吸收日本古典能樂劇的表演方式，開創了現代西方戲劇中東方主義和原始主義風氣。1923 年，「由於他那以一種高度藝術的形式表現了一整個民族的精神、永遠富有靈感的詩」，葉慈被瑞典學術院授予諾貝爾文學獎。他的代表作品有詩集《葦叢中的風》（1899）、《塔堡》（1928）、《旋梯及其他》（1933），劇作《凱瑟琳・尼・胡里漢》（1902）、《庫胡林之死》（1938），哲學散文《幻景》（1925），短篇小說集《隱祕的玫瑰》（1894）等。

葉慈誕生於愛爾蘭首府都柏林，是一位畫家的長子。雖然他的家庭傳統上說英語，奉新教，祖先是英國移民，他本人所受的也是正規的英國教育，但他自小就有很強的民族意識。這也許與他在倫敦上小學時受英國同學歧視和欺負的經歷不無關係。作爲

英裔愛爾蘭人，他對宗主國英國的感情是愛恨參半的；他恨英國
人在政治上對愛爾蘭的殖民統治和壓迫，同時又愛使他得以直接
學習莎士比亞等大師並且使他自己的作品得以更廣泛流傳的英
語。正是處於這樣一種尷尬地位，才使他在從事文學創作伊始就
感到確定身分的迫切需要。

　　作爲使用英語的創作家，葉慈面臨的首要問題是題材。這與
十九世紀中葉以來研究和翻譯蓋爾語文學的學者和翻譯家們所面
臨的問題不盡相同。他既必須背離英國文學的傳統，退回到愛爾
蘭的本土風景中去尋找靈感，又必須把所獲納入英語的包裝。1886
年，葉慈結識了芬尼亞運動領導人、愛國志士約翰·歐李瑞。在
他的影響下，葉慈開始接觸愛爾蘭本土詩人的具有民族意識的作
品，他自己的創作也開始從古希臘和印度題材轉向愛爾蘭民俗和
神話題材。1889 年出版的第一本詩集《烏辛漫遊記及其他》就反
映了葉慈早期創作方向的轉變和確定。

　　同年，葉慈結識了狂熱的民族主義者茉德·岡。由於她的美
貌的吸引，年輕的葉慈多少有些身不由己地進一步捲入了爭取愛
爾蘭民族自治的政治運動旋渦之中，就好像他筆下的詩人烏辛被
仙女尼婭芙誘引到魔島上一樣。但他畢竟不是政客，而是詩人。
他不可能採取任何激烈的實際行動，而只是盡詩人的本份：

> 知道吧，我願被視爲
> 一個群體中的眞兄弟，
> 爲減輕愛爾蘭的創痛，
> 大夥把謠曲民歌唱誦；
> 而不願比他們差毫分，
> 　　　　〈致未來歲月裡的愛爾蘭〉

　　葉慈的第二本詩集《女伯爵凱瑟琳及各種傳說和抒情詩》
(1892) 繼續且更集中地以愛爾蘭爲題材，以象徵的手法表現詩人
的民族感情，愛爾蘭被「想像成與人類一同受難」的「玫瑰」。他
幻想通過創造一種建立在凱爾特文化傳統之上的英語文學來達到
統一兩半──天主教和新教徒的──愛爾蘭的目的。他相信，如
果現代詩人把他的故事置於自己的鄉土背景中，他的詩就會像古
代的詩一樣更細密地滲入人們的思想之中。早在 1888 年葉慈就曾
說過，比較偉大的詩人視一切都與民族生活相關聯，並通過民族
生活與宇宙和神聖生活相關聯：詩人只能用戴著「他的民族手套」
的手伸向宇宙。他還認爲，沒有民族就沒有較偉大的詩，猶如沒
有象徵就沒有宗教[1]。在他眼裡，愛爾蘭是一個「大記憶」，貯存著
比英格蘭更爲悠久的歷史，是一個充滿了詩的象徵的倉庫。

　　世紀之交的愛爾蘭雖民族情緒高漲，但社會形勢複雜。在目
睹了政客的背信棄義、黨派的勾心鬥角、不同宗教信仰的民眾的
互相仇恨和愚昧無知等現象後，葉慈意識到自己所崇尚的以十八
世紀愛爾蘭社會爲代表的新教貴族政治理想與現實的發展是背道
而馳的。而茉德・岡等共和黨人所熱衷的暴力行動也令他反感。
因此他不久便對政治產生了幻滅感，而又回到了他的藝術王國：

> 凡事都能誘使我拋開這詩歌藝術：
> 從前是一女人的臉，或更其不如──
> 我那傻瓜治理的國土貌似的需要；
> 　　　〈凡事都能誘使我〉

　　1899 年，詩集《葦叢中的風》問世，獲當年最佳詩集「學院」
獎，確立了葉慈作爲第一流愛爾蘭詩人的地位。有論者認爲這部

詩集標誌著現代主義詩歌的開端，猶如一百年前華茲華斯和柯立芝合著的《抒情歌謠集》標誌著英國浪漫主義詩歌的開端。其實葉慈深受浪漫主義詩人布雷克、雪萊等的影響，是主張「向後看」的：

> 我們是最後的浪漫主義者——曾選取
> 傳統的聖潔和美好、詩人們
> 稱之爲人民之書中所寫的
> 一切、最能祝福人類心靈
> 或提昇一個詩韻的一切作爲主題；
>
> 〈庫勒和峇里鄺，1931〉

在這首詩裡，葉慈把葛列格里夫人(也包括他自己)看作是貴族文化傳統的「一位最後的繼承人」，她(他)們所居住的庫勒莊園和峇里鄺塔堡成了古老文明的象徵。在另一首詩《紀念羅伯特·葛列格里少校》裡，葛列格里夫人的兒子羅伯特則被視爲文藝復興式「完人」的一個現代樣板。在葉慈眼裡，貴族是人類精華知識的保存者和傳承者。與此相對的是保存和傳播口頭的民間知識的乞丐、浪人、農夫、修道者，甚至瘋人們。葉慈有許多詩作就是以這些人物爲角色，或者乾脆是他們所說所唱的轉述。這些構成了葉慈的智慧來源的兩個極端。然而，在現代風雲的衝擊之下，這一切都在漸漸消亡。峇里鄺塔堡前的古橋在內戰期間被毀；庫勒莊園也在葛列格里夫人逝世後被迫出賣，後來被夷平；羅伯特則在第一次世界大戰中陣亡。社會和人們的生活方式都發生了劇變。葉慈不禁哀嘆：

> 浪漫的愛爾蘭已死亡消逝，

與歐李瑞一起在墳墓中。

〈1913年9月〉

但是，1916年復活節抗英起義震驚了對政治和現實失望的詩人。葉慈想不到從他平素看不起的城市平民中產生了他理想中古愛爾蘭的庫胡林式的悲劇英雄，他看到了一種崇高精神的爆發：

一切都變了，徹底變了：

一個可怕的美誕生了。

〈1916年復活節〉

感奮之餘，他及時做出了一位詩人所能做的最好的反應：「我們的事／是低喚一個又一個名姓，／像母親呼喚她的孩子，／當昏沉的睡意終於降臨／在野跑的肢體之上時。」他還在〈十六個死者〉、〈玫瑰樹〉以及晚期的〈歐拉希利族長〉等詩篇中以他特有的語調謳歌了死難的起義者。

此後，他似乎又恢復了對現象世界冷眼旁觀的態度，不輟地在變化中尋求永恆。然而他對社會現實的敏感不但沒有減弱，反而更加深刻了。中晚期的組詩《內戰期間的沉思》和長詩〈一九一九年〉反映了他在內戰的背景前對人類文明和心理的沉思。他更關心的是人類文明的創造，因而譴責任何形式的破壞。

總之，是「她的歷史早已開始／在上帝創造天使的家族之前」的「這盲目苦難的土地」——愛爾蘭——造就了葉慈和他的詩。在他去世前一年所作的〈布爾本山下〉一詩中，他總結了他畢生的信念，並告誡後來的同志：

愛爾蘭詩人，把藝業學好，

歌唱一切優美的創造；

‥‥‥‥‥‥‥‥‥

歌唱田間勞作的農民，

歌唱四野奔波的鄉紳，

歌唱僧侶的虔誠清高，

歌唱酒徒的放蕩歡笑；

也歌唱快樂的公侯命婦──

‥‥‥‥‥‥‥‥‥

把你們的心思拋向往昔，

以使我們在未來歲月裡可能

依然是不可征服的愛爾蘭人。

二

　　葉慈又是個自傳性很強的詩人。他主張寫自己主觀的切身體驗，而非對外界的客觀觀察。他在〈拙作總序〉（1937）一文中開宗明義地說：「一個詩人總是寫他的私生活，在他最精緻的作品中寫生活的悲劇，無論那是什麼，悔恨也好，失戀也好，或者僅僅是孤獨；他從不直話直說，不像與人共進早餐時那樣，而總是有一種幻覺效果」[2]。這決定了他的詩是象徵主義的，而非寫實主義的。他認為，他的一生是一種生活實驗，後人有權利知道。抒情詩人的生活應當被人了解，這樣他的詩就不至於被當做無根之花，而是被當做一個人的話語來理解[3]。他的詩以大量的篇幅和坦誠的筆觸記錄了他個人的經驗和情感，尤其是他對友誼和愛情的珍重。女性在他的生活和藝術中都佔據了顯要地位。在〈朋友們〉一詩中，他寫到了三位對他一生影響重大的女友：「現在我必須讚揚這三位──／三位曾經造就了／我生活中的歡樂的女士：」

其一是奧古斯塔‧葛列格里夫人(1852-1932)。葉慈認爲她使他得以專注於文學。她不僅在精神上給他以理解和支持，而且在物質上爲他提供理想的寫作條件，照顧他的起居。他在她的庫勒莊園度過許多夏天，「在凱爾納諾在那古老的屋頂下找到／一個更嚴厲的良心和一個更友善的家」(〈責任‧跋詩〉)，在那裡寫出了《在那七片樹林裡》、《庫勒的野天鵝》、〈庫勒莊園，1929〉等大量詩作。她還與他一起蒐集民間傳說，從事戲劇活動，在愛爾蘭文學復興運動中起到了骨幹作用。她翻譯的蓋爾語神話傳說被認爲是上乘之作，爲葉慈的詩創作提供了不少素材。她的劇作也深受愛爾蘭觀眾的歡迎。

其二是奧麗薇亞‧莎士比亞(1867-1938)。她是葉慈詩友萊奧內爾‧約翰生的表妹，是一位小說家。1894 年當葉慈正陷於對茉德‧岡的無望戀情的旋渦裡無法自拔時，約翰生把奧麗薇亞介紹給了他。她聰慧而善解人意，與葉慈相處的很融洽。他們曾考慮結婚，只因她丈夫不同意離婚而未果。他們同居了近一年，直到葉慈再遇茉德‧岡時，奧麗薇亞發現他對茉德‧岡仍不能忘情，遂離開了他。「額白髮濃雙手安詳，／我有個美麗的女友，／逐夢想舊日的絕望／終將在愛情中結束：／一天她窺入我心底／見那裡有你的影像；／她哭泣著從此離去。」(〈戀人傷悼失戀〉) 但他們始終保持著友誼；葉慈與她通信比與任何男女朋友都多而詳細。他在詩藝、政治、個人等各種問題上徵求她的意見，而她的評論非常富於才智。葉慈在她去世後曾對人說：「四十多年來她一直是我在倫敦的生活中心，在所有那段時間裡我們從未爭吵過，偶爾有些傷心事，但從未有過分歧。」

其三即茉德‧岡(1866-1953)。「頎長而高貴，胸房和面頰／却像蘋果花一樣色澤淡雅」(〈箭〉)。這是葉慈初見她時的印象。

當時他們都廿三歲。他立即被她的美貌征服了，「我一生的煩惱開始了」。她是一個堅定不移的民族主義者，爲了爭取愛爾蘭獨立不惜代價不擇手段。葉慈追隨她參加了一系列革命活動，一再向她求婚，並爲她寫下了大量詩篇。有論者稱這些作品是現代英語詩歌中最美麗的愛情詩。而她一直保持著距離，終於 1898 年向他透露了她與一位法國政客的同居關係。他們的關係一度降溫，但給葉慈以毀滅性打擊的是 1903 年茉德‧岡與麥克布萊德結婚的消息。此後，加之劇院事務的煩擾，葉慈的心情很壞，詩風也隨之大變。從詩集《在那七片樹林裡》（1904）到《責任》（1914），詩人逐漸拋棄了早期朦朧華美「綴滿剪自古老／神話的花邊刺繡」的「外套」而「赤身行走」了（〈一件外套〉）。

　　後來，葉慈又多次向離婚了的茉德‧岡求婚，又都遭到了拒絕。不得回報的愛昇華成了一篇篇感情複雜、思想深邃、風格高尚的詩，貫穿於葉慈的第二本到最後一本詩集中。在這些詩裡，茉德‧岡成了玫瑰、特洛伊的海倫、胡里漢的凱瑟琳、帕拉斯‧雅典娜、黛爾德等。有論者認爲還不曾有過哪位詩人像葉慈這樣把一個女人讚美到如此程度。葉慈意識到是茉德‧岡對他的不理解成就了他的詩，否則「我也許把蹩腳文字抛却，／心滿意足地去過生活」（〈文字〉）。茉德‧岡也曾對葉慈說，世人會因她沒有嫁給他而感謝她的。

　　葉慈對愛情的看法一如他對宇宙的看法，是二元的。在早期的〈阿娜殊雅與維迦亞〉一詩中他就表達了「一個男人爲兩個女人所愛」的主題。到了晚期的組詩《或許可譜曲的詞》和〈三叢灌木〉及伴隨的幾首歌等，這種靈魂與肉體之愛一而二、二而一的信念更被表現得淋漓盡致。他對茉德‧岡的愛應該說是靈肉兼有的，很可能最初還是出於對其肉體美的愛悅，但青年人耽於理想的氣

質使他的愛在詩創作中向靈魂的境界昇華：「用古老的崇高方式把你熱愛」(〈亞當所受的詛咒〉)；「愛你靈魂的至誠」(〈當你年老時〉)。中年以後，他似乎在較平和的心境裡超然把愛情抽象化，當做哲學觀照的對象了。而到了晚年，他就好像是做夠了夢的佛格斯，洞知了一切，肉體却衰朽了，於是爆發出對生命的強烈慾望：「可是啊，但願我再度年輕，／把她摟在我的懷抱。」(〈政治〉)

葉慈曾說，他年輕的時候，他的繆斯是年老的，而他變老的時候，他的繆斯却變年輕了。意思是說，年輕時他追求智慧，年老時却又羨慕青春。「肉體衰老即智慧；年輕時／我們彼此相愛却懵懂無知。」智慧與青春的不可兼得，亦即靈與肉的對立鬥爭成了葉慈「藝術與詩歌的至高主題」(〈長久沉默之後〉) 之一。

三

有一回，一位學者問晚年的葉慈，他的詩歌的最大特點是什麼。葉慈不假思索地回答說：「智慧」。「哲學是個危險的主題」，葉慈還這樣認為。但他的中晚期詩越來越向哲學靠近了。對於葉慈來說，詩的內容比外形的價值大。他認為詩若不表現高於它自身的東西便毫無價值可言，它首先至少應該是「人可以進入其中漫遊而藉以擺脫生活之煩擾的境地」[4]。這或許可以解釋為什麼葉慈一生執著追求建立超乎詩之上的「信仰」體系，而不像一般現代派詩人那樣熱衷於詩藝技巧的實驗。

1917 年，葉慈與喬吉－海德－李斯結婚。妻子為改善他當時的憂鬱心境 (婚前葉慈曾向茉德‧岡之女伊索德求婚而遭拒)，在蜜月裡投合他對神祕事物的愛好，嘗試起扶乩活動來。據她說，這是「為你的詩提供隱喻」。這果然引起了葉慈的興趣。他運用所閱

讀的新柏拉圖主義及東方神祕主義等哲學對妻子「自動書寫」的
那些下意識的玄祕「作品」的「散碎句子」加以整理、分析、詮
釋，終於 1925 年完成了一部奇書《幻景》。這標誌著葉慈信仰體
系的完成。書的內容涉及用幾何圖形解釋歷史變化的歷史循環
說、用東方月相學解釋人類個性的個性類型說以及靈魂轉世說。
透過想像和邏輯，來自各種文化的神祕象徵得以秩序化，形成了
一個自圓其說的骨架。但由於該書近乎荒誕不經又駁雜晦澀，遂
贏得了「龐雜而古怪的偽哲學」或「粗劣而無價值的自製品」之
譏。葉慈本人則希望該書能夠被看作是一部神話而非歷史或玄
學，稱它是一個「集體無意識」，一個神話學的意象庫。

詩集《庫勒的野天鵝》（1919）就已顯示了葉慈開始從日常生
活主題轉向哲理冥想主題。在隨後的一本詩集《麥克爾·羅巴蒂
斯與舞蹈者》（1921）的前言中，葉慈解釋說：「歌德說過，詩人
需要哲學，但他必須使之保持在他的作品之外。」而葉慈自己却
禁不住要把哲學揉進詩作中去。他也承認這本詩集中的某些作品
很難懂。例如著名的〈再度降臨〉一詩就利用歷史循環說和基督
教神祕主義等概念，預言自耶穌降生以來近兩千年的基督教文明
即將告一段落，世界正臨近一場大破壞。因此，要讀懂這些詩，
必須對葉慈的信仰和哲學有所了解。

葉慈曾經說，沒有宗教他就無法生存下去。然而在他父親的
影響下，達爾文及其他一些英國思想家的懷疑主義阻礙了他接受
正統基督教，而為了反抗他們「對生命的機械簡化」[5]，他必須找到
新的精神支柱。大約在 1884 年，葉慈讀到了一本英國人 A．P．
辛內特撰著的名為《密宗佛教》的書，深受影響。稍後他在都柏
林聽了印度婆羅門摩希尼·莫罕·查特基對印度教義的闡釋，從
此樹立了他對輪迴轉世學說的終生信仰（〈摩希尼·查特基〉）。

1887-1891 年在倫敦居住期間，他又參加了那裡風靡一時的「異教運動」，鑽研起東、西方的各種祕術，冀圖通過實驗尋求永恆世界的證明，與未知世界建立直接聯繫。他認為，來自科學或其他世俗知識的「灰色真理」和基督教的「上帝之道」都無法令人滿意地解釋人類靈魂的奧祕，所以他鄙棄關於物的「客觀真理」而追求關於人的「主觀真理」：「並沒有真理，／除了在你自己的心裡」（〈快樂的牧人之歌〉）。這顯然是來自佛教和印度教的觀念。他的最早的詩作之一〈印度人論上帝〉更以生動的寓言形式表述了他對於主觀真理的理解，是「葉慈最堅定的信念之一——真實在於觀者的眼中——的早期陳述」[6]。

與此同時，葉慈還在與人合編《威廉‧布雷克詩全集》。布雷克的基督教神祕主義影響融入了他的異端思想，使他進一步發展和堅定了宇宙二元論信念：

> 然而，我們能夠以肉體感官接觸和看到的那一部分創造受著撒旦的力量的影響，那魔鬼的名字之一是「曖昧」，而我們能夠以精神感官觸及和看到的另一部分創造——我們稱之為「想像」——才是真正的「上帝之體」和唯一的真實。[7]

他還相信，在各種玄祕法術中，有三條自古相傳的基本教義：1）人的精神可以相互交流，而造就一個大精神；2）人的記憶也同樣是流動的，且是造化的大記憶的一部分；3）此大精神和大記憶可以用象徵招致[8]。後來，他把這些概念與新柏拉圖主義哲學的「世界靈魂」相認同，視之為「一個不再屬於任何個人或鬼魂的形象倉庫」。作為詩人，為「招致」或表達某種隱祕的東西，他不得不更注重作為象徵的形象，「他照他那類人的方式，僅僅找到了／

形象」（〈月相〉）。《幻景》一書可以說就是葉慈象徵主義體系的集成，也是理解葉慈中晚期詩創作的一把鑰匙。它為他的玄學詩提供了豐富的主題和意象，使作品寓義深刻而又免於抽象枯澀。同時他又在埃茲拉・龐德的建議下採用當代的「現實」素材和意象，從而使創作避免了走進概念化的死胡同的危險，在藝術上達到了他所說的「浪漫主義與現實主義性質的結合」。

詩集《塔堡》（1928）和《旋梯及其他》（1933）即以葉慈實際居住的峇里麗古堡及其中盤旋而上的樓梯為象徵，暗示歷史運動的軌跡和靈魂輪迴的歷程。葉慈認為，人類文明一如個人，都是靈魂的體現，其中陰陽兩極力量交互作用，運動形式猶如兩個相對滲透的圓錐體的螺旋轉動，往復循環，周而復始。這種思想和象徵在稍前的〈再度降臨〉和稍後的〈旋錐體〉等許多詩作中都有所表現。而〈麗達與天鵝〉這首具有「可怕的美」的十四行詩則用細緻、感性的描寫再現神話傳說的場景，暗示陽與陰、力與美的衝突和結合，把基督紀元前的古希臘文明的衰亡歸因於性愛和戰爭這兩種人類本能。葉慈這一時期所關心的根本問題還是靈魂如何超脫生死，得以不朽。他對赫拉克里特所謂的「此生彼死，此死彼生」的相對主義觀點加以重新解釋，同時襲用柏拉圖的「精靈」說，認為靈魂不滅，可以不斷轉世再生，逐漸達到完善境界，即成為介乎神人之間的一種存在──「精靈」，而後不朽。他還認為，人死後，靈魂可藉藝術的力量通過「世界靈魂」互相溝通。〈航往拜占庭〉一詩即表達了詩人希冀借助於藝術而達到不朽的願望。姊妹篇〈拜占庭〉則表現靈魂脫離輪迴走向永恆之前被藝術淨化的過程。

四

葉慈曾自稱年輕時有三大興趣，其一在於民族主義，其二在於詩，其三在於哲學。這些興趣在他一生中從未減退，而是互相滲透、融合，最終被「錘鍊統一」，形成體系。象徵的系統性是葉慈詩歌創作的一大特點。而他的全部詩作就是他追求自我完善的一生的象徵。

葉慈最初是通過研讀傳統英詩(史賓塞、布雷克、雪萊等)和從事神祕主義活動而自發地發展出自己的象徵主義的。但他也在批評家阿瑟・賽蒙斯的影響下接受了注重作品本身的法國象徵主義的基本理論。在藝術實踐中，他不斷提出問題，對那些理論重新加以解釋、批判的吸收過來，以改進自己的詩藝。他把詩視爲一種由意象、節奏和聲音構成的複雜的「音樂關係」；這些成分按一定方式結合，產生情感經驗的象徵，而這種象徵非單純用文字所能表現。他認爲，正是建築在主題之上的象徵賦予詩以最終的形式。因此，藝術作品即各種構成因素的形式排列，而引起欣賞者個人感受的是排列的「順序」。這種順序並不提供任何意義，却又具有欣賞者根據自己的感受賦予它的一切可能的「意義」：這就是「象徵」。假如人們承認他們是爲詩的象徵所感動的話，那就不再可能否認形式的重要性[9]。爲了追求更大的形式，葉慈在不同的詩裡反覆使用某些主導意象，這樣就在詩與詩之間造成某種聯繫；在每一本詩集裡，詩作的順序不是按寫作時間先後排列的，而是按照主題的相互關聯重新組合的，這樣，借用葉慈所相信的祕法教義作類比，詩篇與詩篇的象徵融匯交流，從而造就一個大象徵。因此，儘管葉慈多短小篇什，却有論者稱他的作品具有「史詩的性質」。

　　然而，葉慈所注重的形式與先鋒派所追求的形式不同。他幾乎從不做技巧上的實驗創新，不用自由體寫詩（可能只嘗試過一次，即〈美麗高尚的傢伙們〉一詩），而是「強迫自己接受那些與英語語言同時發展起來的傳統格律」。這是爲了避免個人化，而只有非個人的東西才會不朽。「我必須選擇一種傳統的詩節，甚至我所做的改動也必須看起來像是傳統詩節。……我是一群人，我是一個孤獨的人，我什麼也不是。」[10]這就是葉慈，一個在傳統與現代、個人與群體之間來回奔跑的詩人。誠如一位論者所說，他「在現代作家中最具現代感，而無須是現代主義者」。[11]

　　埃茲拉・龐德初遇葉慈時稱他是唯一值得認眞研究的當代詩人，視他爲前期象徵主義和後期象徵主義之間的橋樑。艾略特則稱他是「廿世紀最偉大的英語詩人」。如果說1923年的諾貝爾文學獎含有偶然或非文學的因素的話，那麼這兩位同時代的大師的評語是否會少點兒恭維和溢美呢？

　　不管怎樣，葉慈一生做了他想做的事情，「我絲毫不曾動搖，／而使某種東西達到了完美」（〈那又怎樣〉），以至在臨終時能夠對自己的靈魂驕傲地喊出：「冷眼一瞥／生與死。／騎者，去也！」遵照詩人在〈布爾本山下〉一詩中的遺囑，他的遺體於1948年從法國運回愛爾蘭，歸葬於給他的童年以歡樂、給他的詩歌以靈感的故鄉史萊果，這似乎是他完滿的人生之旅的象徵，而他的靈魂仍駕著飛馬珀伽索斯，超越生死，馳向永恆。

五

　　作爲愛爾蘭最偉大的詩人和世界文學巨匠之一，葉慈對各種語言的現代詩歌（也包括我國的）產生了巨大的影響。在西方，葉慈研究已成了一門學問，有關他的各種學術著作多不勝數。而在

華語地區，至今也有了葉慈作品的多種中譯本。

　　葉慈的創作豐富，思想駁雜，幾乎每個方面都有文章可做。所以，在篇幅如此有限的序文裡要對葉慈做全面而準確的勾畫是不可能的。好在這裡為中文讀者提供了葉慈抒情詩代表作品的中譯及詳細的註釋。至於如何評判和接受，則任憑讀者見仁見智。

　　本書正文主要是根據理查‧J‧芬吶阮編《葉慈詩集新編》（The Poems of W. B. Yeats, ed. Richard J. Finneran, NY: Macmillan, 1983）並參考彼得‧奧爾特與拉塞爾‧K‧奧斯帕赫合編《校刊本葉慈詩集》（The Variorum Edition of the Poems of W. B. Yeats, eds. Peter Allt & Russell K. Alspach, NY: Macmillan, 1957; 5th printing, 1971）選譯的，共計 169 首抒情詩，足以代表詩人各個時期的創作風格。譯文以忠實為務，即盡量做到在內容和風格上貼近原文。註釋除參考以上二書外還參考了其他有關文獻資料，譯者平素的研究心得也在具體註文中有所體現，但力求客觀，不臆解；形式則採取標行註釋的辦法，一則為保持與原文行句對應，二則為譯文整齊美觀。附錄部分編譯自其他書籍，意在為讀者較完整地了解葉慈其人其詩提供一些必要的背景材料。由於譯者能力所限，書中謬誤必定不少，敬待讀者指正。

傅　浩

一九九九年十一月於北京

註釋：

1. Louis MacNeice: *The Poetry of W. B. Yeats*, (N.Y., 1941), p. 72.
2. *Essays and Introductions*, (Macmillan, 1961), p. 509.
3. Jeffares, A. Norman, *W. B. Yeats: A New Biography*, (Hutchinson,

1988), p. 208.

4. Yeats, quoted by Richard Ellmann in *The Man and the Masks*, (N.Y., 1948), p. 39.

5. See James Hall & Matin Steinmann (eds.): *The Permanence of Yeats*, (N.Y., 1950), p. 217.

6. John Unterecker: A *Reader's Guide to W. B. Yeats*, (London, 1969), p. 70.

7. W. B. Yeats: "Introduction to The Poems of William Blake," in *Critics on Blake*, ed. Judith O'Neill, (London, 1970), p. 22.

8. W. B. Yeats: "Magic," in *Selected Criticism*, ed. A. Norman Jeffares, (London: Pan Books Ltd.,1976), p. 80.

9. See W. B. Yeats: "The Symbolism of Poetry," in op. cit., pp. 43-52.

10. W. B. Yeats: "A General Introduction for my Work," in op. cit., p. 266.

11. E. R. Higgins: "Yeats as Irish Poet," in *Scattering Branches*, ed. Stephen Gwynn, (N.Y., 1940), p. 555.

1889
Crossways
選自《十字路口》

The Sad Shepherd

There was a man whom Sorrow named his friend,
And he, of his high comrade Sorrow dreaming,
Went walking with slow steps along the gleaming
And humming sands, where windy surges wend:
And he called loudly to the stars to bend
From their pale thrones and comfort him, but they
Among themselves laugh on and sing alway:
And then the man whom Sorrow named his friend
Cried out, Dim sea, hear my most piteous stay!
The sea swept on and cried her old cry still,   10
Rolling along in dreams from hill to hill.
He fled the persecution of her glory
And, in a far-off, gentle valley stopping,
Cried all his story to the dewdrops glistening.
But naught they heard, for they are always listening,
The dewdrops, for the sound of their own dropping.
And then the man whom Sorrow named his friend
Sought once again the shore, and found a shell,
And thought, I will my heavy stay tell
Till my own words, re-echoing, shall send   20
Their sadness through a hollow, pearly heart;
And my own tale again for me shall sing,
And my own whispering words be comforting,

悲哀的牧人

有一個人被「哀愁」當做了朋友，
他，渴想著「哀愁」，他那高貴的伙伴，
去沿著那微光閃爍、輕聲吟唱的沙灘
慢步行走，那裡狂風挾著巨浪怒吼。
他向著群星大聲呼喚，請求它們
從銀色寶座上俯下身來安慰他，可
它們只顧自己不斷地大笑和唱歌。
於是那被「哀愁」當做朋友的人
哭喊：昏暗的海，請聽我可悲的故事！
大海洶湧，依然喊著她那古老的嘶喊，　　　　　10
帶著睡夢翻滾過一個又一個山巒。
他從她的壯美榮耀的折磨下逃離，
到一處遙遠、溫柔的山谷中駐停，
向晶瑩的露珠把他全部的故事哭訴。
可它們什麼也沒有聽見，因為露珠
永遠在傾聽它們自身滴落的聲音。
於是那被「哀愁」當做朋友的人
又回到海灘搜尋，找到了一隻空螺，
思忖：我要把我沉痛的故事述說，
直到我自己的、再度迴響的話音　　　　　　　20
把悲哀送進一顆空洞的珍珠般的心裡；
直到我自己的故事重新為我謳歌；
直到我自己的低語令人感到慰藉；

And lo! my ancient burden may depart.

Then he sang softly nigh the pearly rim;

But the sad dweller by the sea-ways lone

Changed all he sang to inarticulate moan

Among her wildering whirls, forgetting him.

Anashuya and Vijaya

A little Indian temple in the Golden Age. Around it a garden; around that the forest. Anashuya, the young priestess, kneeling within the temple.

Anashuya. Send peace on all the lands and flickering corn. —

    O, may tranquillity walk by his elbow

    When wandering in the forest, if he love

    No other. — Hear, and may the indolent flocks

    Be plentiful. — And if he love another,

    May panthers end him. — Hear, and load our king

    With wisdom hour by hour. — May we two stand,

    When we are dead, beyond the setting suns,

    A little from the other shades apart,

    With mingling hair, and play upon one lute.   10

Vijaya [entering and throwing a lily at her]. Hail! hail, my

    Anashuya.

那時，看！我古老的重負就可以脫離。

於是他對著溫潤的螺唇輕輕歌唱；

但是那孤寂的大海邊悲傷的居民

在她那迷人的螺旋中把他的歌聲

都變成了含混的呻吟，把他遺忘。

阿娜殊雅與維迦亞

黃金時代的一座印度小廟。廟外花園環繞；園外森林環抱。
年輕的女祭司阿娜殊雅跪在廟內。

阿娜殊雅：請降和平於所有的土地和搖曳的莊稼。──
　　呵，要是他沒愛別的人，但願
　　他在森林裡漫遊時，寧靜陪伴著他。──
　　請垂聽，但願懶散的羊群繁衍。──
　　假如他愛上另一個，
　　但願群豹將他結果。──請垂聽，且時時
　　賜予我王以智慧的重負。──我們死後，
　　願我們倆站在萬千落日之外，
　　遠離別的幽魂，長髮交纏在一起，
　　撫弄著同一隻琵琶。　　　　　　　　　　10
維迦亞（走進寺內，拋向她一朵百合）：萬福！萬福，我的阿
　　娜殊雅。

Anashuya.   No: be still.

    I, priestess of this temple, offer up

    Prayers for the land.

Vijaya.   I will wait here, Amrita.

Anashuya. By mighty Brahma's ever-rustling robe,

    Who is Amrita? Sorrow of all sorrows!

    Another fills your mind.

Vijaya.   My mother's name.

Anashuya [sings, coming out of the temple].

    A sad, sad thought went by me slowly:

    Sigh, O you little stars! O sigh and shake your blue apparel!

    The sad, sad thought has gone from me now wholly:

    Sing, O you little stars! O sing and raise your rapturous carol   20

    To mighty Brahma, he who made you many as the sands,

    And laid you on the gates of evening with his quiet hands.

               [Sits down on the steps of the temple.]

    Vijaya, I have brought my evening rice;

    The sun has laid his chin on the grey wood,

    Weary, with all his poppies gathered round him.

Vijaya. The hour when Kama, full of sleepy laughter,

    Rises, and showers abroad his fragrant arrows,

    Piercing the twilight with their murmuring barbs.

Anashuya. See how the sacred old flamingoes come,

    Painting with shadow all the marble steps: 30

    Aged and wise, they seek their wonted perches

    Within the temple, devious walking, made

阿娜殊雅：　　別，別出聲。

　我，本廟的祭司，

　在為國土祈禱。

維迦亞：　　　　我願在此恭候，阿沐麗塔。

阿娜殊雅：以偉大梵天永遠飄拂的聖袍的名義，

　阿沐麗塔是誰？無比的悲傷啊！

　另一個人佔據了你的心。

維迦亞：　　　　　　那是我母親的名字。

阿娜殊雅（走出廟外，唱）：

　一縷悲哀、悲哀的思緒緩緩從我身邊流過：

　嘆息吧，啊，小星星！嘆息並抖動你們藍色的衣裙！

　那悲哀、悲哀的思緒此刻已從我這裡全然消逝：　　19

　歌唱吧，啊，小星星！歌唱且揚起你們歡快的讚頌！

　讚美偉大的梵天，他造就了你們，多如沙礫，

　且用平靜的雙手把你們安置在黃昏的門楣上。

　　　　　　　　　　　　　（在寺前台階上坐下。）

　維迦亞，我帶了我的晚飯來；

　太陽已經把他的下頜擱在灰暗的林梢上，

　困倦了，他周圍環繞著朵朵罌粟花。

維迦亞：這正是欲天起身的時辰：他

　帶著睡意大笑著，把芬芳的花箭射出；

　低鳴的矢鏃把蒼茫的暮色穿透。

阿娜殊雅：看，那些神聖的老火烈鳥來了，

　在所有的石階上塗滿了陰影：　　　　　30

　它們年老睿智，在廟裡尋找

　它們慣常的棲處，供它們憂鬱的心緒

To wander by their melancholy minds.

Yon tall one eyes my supper; chase him away,

Far, far away. I named him after you.

He is a famous fisher; hour by hour

He ruffles with his bill the minnowed streams.

Ah! there he snaps my rice. I told you so.

Now cuff him off. He's off! A kiss for you,

Because you saved my rice. Have you no thanks?   40

Vijaya [sings]. *Sing you of her, O first few stars,*

Whom Brahma, touching with his finger, praises, for you hold

The van of wandering quiet; ere you be too calm and old,

Sing, turning in your cars,

Sing, till you raise your hands and sigh, and from your car-heads peer,

With all your whirling hair, and drop many an azure tear.

Anashuya. What know the pilots of the stars of tears?

Vijaya. Their faces are all worn, and in their eyes

Flashes the fire of sadness, for they see

The icicles that famish all the North,   50

Where men lie frozen in the glimmering snow;

And in the flaming forests cower the lion

And lioness, with all their whimpering cubs;

And, ever pacing on the verge of things,

The phantom, Beauty, in a mist of tears;

While we alone have round us woven woods,

And feel the softness of each other's hand, Amrita, while —

Anashuya [going away from him].

徘徊漫遊的迂曲的路徑。

瞧，那高個兒在那兒盯上了我的晚飯；

把它轟走，轟得遠遠的。我用你的名字叫它。

它是個捕魚的好手；時不時地，

它的長嘴巴從水裡叼起小魚兒來。

啊！它在那兒偷吃我的飯。我跟你說過。

快趕它走。它走了！你救了我的米飯，

賞你一個吻；你就不謝謝？　　　　　　　　　　40

維迦亞　（唱）：初現的疏星，你們歌頌她吧，

那受梵天摩頂讚美的人兒！因為

你們前導著漫遊的寂靜；趁著身心未老，

歌唱吧，在你們的車廂中翻騰！

歌唱吧，直到你們舉手嘆息，向車外窺望，

長髮旋舞，灑下許多幽藍的淚珠。

阿娜殊雅：這些淚星的前導知道些什麼？

維迦亞：它們面容憔悴，它們眼中

閃爍著悲哀之火，因為它們目睹

遍野的冰柱使北國陷入飢饉，　　　　　　　50

那裡的人們僵臥在耀眼的雪地裡；

在燃燒的森林裡群獅在顫抖，

它們的幼崽嗚嗚哀嚎；還有，

那永遠遊蕩在萬物邊緣的幽靈——

美，籠罩在一片眼淚的霧靄中；

而唯獨我們身處密織的林蔭裡，

感受著彼此的手掌的溫軟，

阿沐麗塔，而——

Ah me! you love another,

[Bursting into tears.]

And may some sudden dreadful ill befall her!

Vijaya. I loved another; now I love no other.　　　　　60

　　Among the mouldering of ancient woods

　　You live, and on the village border she,

　　With her old father the blind wood-cutter;

　　I saw her standing in her door but now.

Anashuya. Vijaya, swear to love her never more.

Vijaya. Ay, ay.

Anashuya. 　　Swear by the parents of the gods,

　　Dread oath, who dwell on sacred Himalay,

　　On the far Golden Peak; enormous shapes,

　　Who still were old when the great sea was young;

　　On their vast faces mystery and dreams;　　　　70

　　Their hair along the mountains rolled and filled

　　From year to year by the unnumbered nests

　　Of aweless birds, and round their stirless feet

　　The joyous flocks of deer and antelope,

　　Who never hear the unforgiving hound.

　　Swear!

Vijaya. By the parents of the gods, I swear.

Anashuya [sings]. *I have forgiven, O new star!*

　　Maybe you have not heard of us, you have come forth so newly,

　　You hunter of the fields afar!

　　Ah, you will know my loved one by his hunter's arrows truly,　　80

阿娜殊雅（從他身邊跑開）：唉呀，你愛另一個人！

（突然痛哭。）

　　但願可怕的災病降臨在她身上！

維迦亞：我是曾愛過另一個人；如今我只愛你一個。　　60

　　在這森林古木的枯枝敗葉間

　　住著你；在那邊村頭上住著她，

　　守著她年老的父親，那盲目的伐木人。

　　就在剛才我還望見她站在家門裡。

阿娜殊雅：維迦亞，發誓不要再愛她吧！

維迦亞：是，是。

阿娜殊雅：　　　　憑著萬神始祖的名義，

　　發個重誓！在神聖的喜馬拉雅山上，

　　在那遙遠的金峰頂，居住著萬神的始祖，

　　碩大的身形；當大海年輕時，他們久已蒼老；

　　他們寬廣的面龐帶著神祕和夢幻；　　　　70

　　他們滾滾的髮浪奔瀉在群山之間，

　　無畏的鳥雀一年年在其中修築起

　　無數窠巢；他們凝立的腳畔

　　環聚著一群群歡快的鹿和羊，

　　它們從未聽見過無情的犬吠。

　　起誓吧！

維迦亞：　　以萬神的始祖的名義，我發誓。

阿娜殊雅（唱）：我已經寬恕了，呵，新星！

　　你剛剛來臨，也許還不曾聽說過我們。

　　你這遙遠的曠野上的獵人！

　　啊，憑藉他射獵的飛矢，你會認出我的愛人；　　80

Shoot on him shafts of quietness, that he may ever keep
A lonely laughter, and may kiss his hands to me in sleep.

Farewell, Vijaya. Nay, no word, no word;
I, priestess of this temple, offer up
Prayers for the land.

[Vijaya goes.]

     O Brahma, guard in sleep
The merry lambs and the complacent kine,
The flies below the leaves, and the young mice
In the tree roots, and all the sacred flocks
Of red flamingoes; and my love, Vijaya;
And may no restless fay with fidget finger   90
Trouble his sleeping: give him dreams of me.

The Indian upon God

I passed along the water's edge below the humid trees,
My spirit rocked in evening light, the rushes round my knees,
My spirit rocked in sleep and sighs; and saw the moorfowl pace
All dripping on a grassy slope, and saw them cease to chase
Each other round in circles, and heard the eldest speak:
Who holds the world between His bill and made us strong or weak

請把寧靜的長箭射向他，好讓他永遠保存
一聲孤寂的大笑，且在睡夢裡向我飛吻。

再見，維迦亞。不，別說話，別說話；
我，本廟的祭司，
在為國土祈禱。

（維迦亞離去。）

　　　　大梵天啊，請庇護
酣睡中快樂的羊群，愜意的牛群，
樹葉底下的飛蟲，樹根深處的田鼠，
所有的神聖的紅色火烈鳥；
還有我的愛，維迦亞；
但願沒有好動的小精靈用活潑的手指　　　　90
攪擾他的睡眠：讓他夢見我。

印度人論上帝

我在潮濕的樹木下面沿著湖岸漫步閒行，
我的魂魄搖盪在暮靄裡，雙膝深陷在水草叢中，
我的魂魄搖盪在睡眠和嘆息中；看見一群水雞
濕淋淋地在草坡上踱步，又見他們停止
彼此繞圈嬉逐，聽那最年老的開口演說：
把這世界銜在喙間並把我單造就得或弱或強者，

Is an undying moorfowl, and He lives beyond the sky.

The rains are from His dripping wing, the moonbeams from His eye.

I passed a little further on and heard a lotus talk:

Who made the world and ruleth it, He hangeth on a stalk,　　　10

For I am in His image made, and all this tinkling tide

Is but a sliding drop of rain between His petals wide.

A little way within the gloom a roebuck raised his eyes

Brimful of starlight, and he said: *The Stamper of the Skies,*

He is a gentle roebuck; for how else, I pray, could He

Conceive a thing so sad and soft, a gentle thing like me?

I passed a little further on and heard a peacock say:

Who made the grass and made the worms and made my feathers gay,

He is a monstrous peacock, and He waveth all the night

His languid tail above us, lit with myriad spots of light.　　　20

The Indian to his Love

The island dreams under the dawn

And great boughs drop tranquillity;

The peahens dance on a smooth lawn,

A parrot sways upon a tree,

Raging at his own image in the enamelled sea.

是一隻不死的水雞，他居住在九天之上；
月光灑自他的眼睛，雨水降自他的翅膀。
我繼續向前走不遠，聽見一朵荷花在闊論高談：
世界的創造和統治者他懸掛在一根莖端，　　　　　　10
因爲我就是依他的形象塑造的，這叮咚的潮水
不過是他寬闊的花瓣間一顆滾動的雨滴。
不遠處的黑暗裡，一隻雄獐抬起滿含著
星光的眼睛，他說：重重天穹的鑄造者
是一隻高雅的獐鹿；否則的話，請問，他怎能
構想出如此多愁善感，像我這樣的高雅的生靈？
我又繼續向前走不遠，聽見一隻孔雀說：
那創造百草、千蟲和我的悅目的羽毛者
是一隻巨大的孔雀，他整夜在我們的頭頂上面
揮動著疲倦的尾羽，上面亮著成千上萬個光斑。　　　20

印度人致所愛

海島在晨光下做夢，
粗大的樹枝滴瀝著靜謐；
孔雀群舞在柔滑的草坪，
一隻鸚鵡在樹梢搖擺，
朝如鏡的海面上自己的身影怒啼。

Here we will moor our lonely ship

And wander ever with woven hands,

Murmuring softly lip to lip,

Along the grass, along the sands,

Murmuring how far away are the unquiet lands: 10

How we alone of mortals are

Hid under quiet boughs apart,

While our love grows an Indian star,

A meteor of the burning heart,

One with the tide that gleams, the wings that gleam and dart,

The heavy boughs, the burnished dove

That moans and sighs a hundred days:

How when we die our shades will rove,

When eve has hushed the feathered ways,

With vapoury footsole by the water's drowsy blaze.   20

The Falling of the Leaves

Autumn is over the long leaves that love us,

And over the mice in the barley sheaves;

Yellow the leaves of the rowan above us,

And yellow the wet wild-strawberry leaves.

在這裡我們要繫泊孤寂的船，
手挽著手永遠地漫遊，
唇對著唇細語喃喃，
沿著草叢，沿著沙丘，
訴說那不平靜的國土有多麼遙遠：　　　　　　　　　10

訴說世俗中唯獨我們兩人
是怎樣遠遠在寧靜的樹下藏躲，
而我們的愛情長成一顆印度星辰，
一顆燃燒的心的流火，
帶有那粼粼的海潮、那疾閃的羽翮、

那沉重的枝柯、那嘆息嗚咽
長達百日的銀光閃閃的鴿子：
訴說我們死後，魂魄將怎樣漂泊，
當黃昏的寂靜籠罩鋪滿羽毛的道路之時，
在那海水困倦的磷光邊留下模糊的足跡。　　　　　20

葉落

秋色降臨在喜愛我們的長長樹葉，
也降臨在麥捆裡小小田鼠的身上；
我們頭頂上的山梨樹葉已變成黃色，
露水浸濕的野草莓葉也變得焦黃。

The hour of the waning of love has beset us,
And weary and worn are our sad souls now;
Let us part, ere the season of passion forget us,
With a kiss and a tear on thy drooping brow.

Ephemera

'Your eyes that once were never weary of mine
Are bowed in sorrow under pendulous lids,
Because our love is waning.'
                         And then she:
'Although our love is waning, let us stand
By the lone border of the lake once more,
Together in that hour of gentleness
When the poor tired child, Passion, falls asleep:
How far away the stars seem, and how far
Is our first kiss, and ah, how old my heart!'

Pensive they paced along the faded leaves,   10
While slowly he whose hand held hers replied:
'Passion has often worn our wandering hearts.'

The woods were round them, and the yellow leaves
Fell like faint meteors in the gloom, and once

我們已經困處於愛情凋萎的時刻，
如今我們憂傷的靈魂厭倦而消沉；
分手吧，趁情熱季節未把我們忘却，
在你低垂的額頭留一個含淚的吻。

蜉蝣

「從前你的雙眼從不厭看我的雙眼，
如今却低垂在哀愁的眼簾下面，
因爲我們的愛情正在枯萎。」

接著她說：

「儘管我們的愛情正在枯萎，讓你我
再一次在那孤寂的湖畔佇立，
共度那溫柔的時刻——
當那可憐的孩子，疲倦的情熱，睡去。
群星看上去是多麼遙遠；多麼遙遠呵，
我們的初吻；啊，我的心多麼衰老！」

他們憂鬱地踏過褪色的落葉；
手握著她的手，他慢慢地回答：
「情熱常常消損我們漂泊的心。」

樹林環繞著他們；枯黃的秋葉隕落，
就像夜空中暗淡的流星；從前，

10

A rabbit old and lame limped down the path;
Autumn was over him: and now they stood
On the lone border of the lake once more:
Turning, he saw that she had thrust dead leaves
Gathered in silence, dewy as her eyes,
In bosom and hair.   20
                    'Ah, do not mourn,' he said,
'That we are tired, for other loves await us;
Hate on and love through unrepining hours.
Before us lies eternity; our souls
Are love, and a continual farewell.'

The Stolen Child

Where dips the rocky highland
Of Sleuth Wood in the lake,
There lies a leafy island
Where flapping herons wake
The drowsy water-rats;
There we've hid our faery vats,
Full of berries
And of reddest stolen cherries.
Come away, O human child!

一隻老兔一瘸一拐在這路上走，
身上披滿了秋色：如今他們兩人
又一次站在了這孤寂的湖畔：
驀回頭，他看見她淚眼晶瑩，
把默默掇拾的死葉，狠狠地
塞進胸襟和頭髮裡。   20

          「啊，別傷心，」他說，
「別說我們已倦怠，因爲還有別的愛等著我們；
在無怨無艾的時刻裡去恨去愛吧！
我們的面前是永恆；我們的靈魂
就是愛，是一聲連綿無盡的道別。」

被拐走的孩子

斯利什森林所在的陡峭
高地浸入湖水之處，
有一個蓊鬱的小島，
那裡有振翅的白鷺
把瞌睡的水鼠驚擾；
在那裡我們已藏好
盛滿著漿果的魔桶，
還有偷來的櫻桃紅通通。
來呀，人類的孩子！

To the waters and the wild 10

With a faery, hand in hand,

For the world's more full of weeping than you can understand.

Where the wave of moonlight glosses

The dim grey sands with light,

Far off by furthest Rosses

We foot it all the night,

Weaving olden dances,

Mingling hands and mingling glances

Till the moon has taken flight;

To and fro we leap 20

And chase the frothy bubbles,

While the world is full of troubles

And is anxious in its sleep.

Come away, O human child!

To the waters and the wild

With a faery, hand in hand,

For the world's more full of weeping than you can understand.

Where the wandering water gushes

From the hills above Glen-Car,

In pools among the rushes 30

That scarce could bathe a star,

We seek for slumbering trout

And whispering in their ears

Give them unquiet dreams;

到那湖水和荒野裡，　　　　　　　　　　　10
跟一個仙女，手拉著手，
因爲人世充溢著你無法明白的悲愁。

在極遠的羅西斯角岸邊，
那月光的浪潮
沖洗著朦朧的銀色沙灘；
在那裡我們徹夜踏著腳，
把古老的舞步編織；
交流著眼神，交纏著手臂，
直到月亮飛逃；
我們往來跳躍，　　　　　　　　　　　　20
追逐著飛濺的水泡，
而人世却充滿煩惱，
正在睡夢裡焦灼。
來呀，人類的孩子！
到那湖水和荒野裡，
跟一個仙女，手拉著手，
因爲人世充溢著你無法明白的悲愁。

格倫卡湖上的山坳裡
奔湧的泉水四處流淌；
水草叢生的深潭淺池　　　　　　　　　　30
難得能沐浴一絲星光；
在那裡我們尋找沉睡的鱒魚；
在它們耳邊輕輕地低語，
給它們以不平靜的夢想；

Leaning softly out
From ferns that drop their tears
Over the young streams.
Come away, O human child!
To the waters and the wild
With a faery, hand in hand,   40
For the world's more full of weeping than you can understand.

Away with us he's going,
The solemn-eyed:
He'll hear no more the lowing
Of the calves on the warm hillside
Or the kettle on the hob
Sing peace into his breast,
Or see the brown mice bob
Round and round the oatmeal-chest.
For he comes, the human child,   50
To the waters and the wild
With a faery, hand in hand,
From a world more full of weeping than he can understand.

Down by the Salley Gardens

Down by the salley gardens my love and I did meet;

從滴灑著淚珠的草叢深處
緩緩地把頭探出，
在那年輕的溪水之上。
來呀，人類的孩子！
到那湖水和荒野裡，
跟一個仙女，手拉著手，   40
因爲人世充溢著你無法明白的悲愁。

那眼神憂鬱的孩子，
他就要跟我們離去：
他將不再聽見群群的牛崽
在那暖暖的山坡上低吼；
將不再聽見火爐上的水壺
使他心中充滿寧靜的歌吟；
也不再會看見棕色的家鼠
圍著食櫃前前後後地逡巡。
因爲他來了，那人類的孩子，   50
到這湖水和荒野裡，
跟一個仙女，手拉著手，
從一個充溢著他無法明白的悲愁的世界。

經柳園而下

我的愛人和我確曾相會在柳園下邊；

She passed the salley gardens with little snow-white feet.

She bid me take love easy, as the leaves grow on the tree;

But I, being young and foolish, with her would not agree.

In a field by the river my love and I did stand,

And on my leaning shoulder she laid her snow-white hand.

She bid me take life easy, as the grass grows on the weirs;

But I was young and foolish, and now am full of tears.

The Meditation of the Old Fisherman

You waves, though you dance by my feet like children at play,

Though you glow and you glance, though you purr and you dart;

In the Junes that were warmer than these are, the waves were more gay,

When I was a boy with never a crack in my heart.

The herring are not in the tides as they were of old;

My sorrow! for many a creak gave the creel in the cart

That carried the take to Sligo town to be sold,

When I was a boy with never a crack in my heart.

And ah, you proud maiden, you are not so fair when his oar

Is heard on the water, as they were, the proud and apart,   10

Who paced in the eve by the nets on the pebbly shore,

When I was a boy with never a crack in my heart.

她那一雙雪白的小腳款款走過柳園。
她讓我從容看待愛情，如樹頭生綠葉，
可我，年少無知，不願聽從她的勸誡。

我的愛人和我確曾佇立在河畔田間；
她那只雪白的小手搭著我斜倚的肩。
她讓我從容看待人生，如堰上長青草，
可我，那時年少無知，如今悔淚滔滔。

老漁夫的幽思

海浪，雖然你們像玩耍的孩子在我腳邊跳舞，
雖然你們眼發亮，臉放光，你們叫聲歡，腳步輕，
但是在從前比現在更暖和的六月，那海浪更歡娛，
那時候我還是個小伙子，心裡沒有一絲裂痕。

大潮裡再也不像往日那樣游動著群群的鯡魚；
真令人悲傷！因為當年那大車上的藤筐響個不停，
滿載著剛捕來便要出賣的鮮魚到史萊果縣城裡去，
那時候我還是個小伙子，心裡沒有一絲裂痕。

啊，驕傲的女孩，聽他的槳聲在水面上盪響，
你並不比她們漂亮，那些驕傲而與眾不同的美人，
她們曾經在黃昏時散步，在卵石灘上的魚網近旁，
那時候我還是個小伙子，心裡沒有一絲裂痕。

10

1893
The Rose

選自《玫瑰》

Fergus and the Druid

Fergus. This whole day have I followed in the rocks,

And you have changed and flowed from shape to shape,

First as a raven on whose ancient wings

Scarcely a feather lingered, then you seemed

A weasel moving on from stone to stone,

And now at last you wear a human shape,

A thin grey man half lost in gathering night.

Druid. What would you, king of the proud Red Branch kings?

Fergus. This would I say, most wise of living souls:

Young subtle Conchubar sat close by me   10

When I gave judgment, and his words were wise,

And what to me was burden without end,

To him seemed easy, so I laid the crown

Upon his head to cast away my sorrow.

Druid. What would you, king of the proud Red Branch kings?

Fergus. A king and proud! and that is my despair.

I feast amid my people on the hill,

And pace the woods, and drive my chariot-wheels

In the white border of the murmuring sea;

And still I feel the crown upon my head.   20

Druid. What would you, Fergus?

Fergus.   Be no more a king

But learn the dreaming wisdom that is yours.

佛格斯與祭司

佛格斯：這一整日我都在山岩間追尋，

你却頻頻地流動，變化身形，

先是一隻渡鴉，蒼老的雙翅

幾乎片羽不留，然後你好似

一隻黃鼬穿行在塊塊亂石間，

如今你終於披上了人的外形，

骨瘦鬢斑半隱在漸濃夜色中。

祭　司：你有何心願，驕傲的紅枝眾王之王？

佛格斯：生靈中的最智者，我想要說的是：

在我斷事決疑之時，年輕機靈的　　　　　　　　10

康納哈坐在我身邊，他言語聰慧，

在我看起來像是無盡負擔的事務

對他却似很容易，因此我將王冠

戴在他的頭上，以拋却我的憂愁。

祭　司：你有何心願，驕傲的紅枝眾王之王？

佛格斯：稱王且驕傲！就是這令我絕望。

我如今與我的臣民歡宴在山巔，

漫步在深林，駕馭著戰車奔馳

在喃喃低語的大海白色的邊緣；

但我依然覺得王冠在我頭頂上。　　　　　　　　20

祭　司：你有何心願，佛格斯？

佛格斯：　　　　　　　　　　　不再為王，

而學習你那夢幻的智慧。

Druid. Look on my thin grey hair and hollow cheeks

And on these hands that may not lift the sword,

This body trembling like a wind-blown reed.

No woman's loved me, no man sought my help.

Fergus. A king is but a foolish labourer

Who wastes his blood to be another's dream.

Druid. Take, if you must, this little bag of dreams;

Unloose the cord, and they will wrap you round.   30

Fergus. I see my life go drifting like a river

From change to change; I have been many things —

A green drop in the surge, a gleam of light

Upon a sword, a fir-tree on a hill,

An old slave grinding at a heavy quern,

A king sitting upon a chair of gold —

And all these things were wonderful and great;

But now I have grown nothing, knowing all.

Ah! Druid, Druid, how great webs of sorrow

Lay hidden in the small slate-coloured thing!   40

The Rose of Peace

If Michael, leader of God's host

When Heaven and Hell are met,

祭　司：看我灰髮稀疏，雙頰深陷，

　　　　看這雙手也許拿不動刀劍，

　　　　這身體抖瑟瑟似風中蘆葦。

　　　　沒有女人愛過我，沒有男人求過我。

佛格斯：一個國王不過是個愚蠢的苦力，

　　　　他浪費他的血以成為別人的夢。

祭　司：喏，你一定要，就拿去這小袋夢；

　　　　解開那繩索，夢幻就會把你圍裹。　　　　　　　30

佛格斯：我眼看我的生命漂流像條河，

　　　　變化不輟；我曾是許多東西——

　　　　波浪中一滴碧沫，一柄劍上

　　　　寒光一抹，山丘上冷杉一棵，

　　　　一個推著沉重的石磨的老奴，

　　　　一位坐在黃金寶座上的國王——

　　　　所有這些都曾經美妙而偉大；

　　　　如今我身成無物，心知一切。

　　　　啊！祭司，巨大的憂愁之網

　　　　怎藏匿在這小小灰色物件裡！　　　　　　　40

和平的玫瑰

　　假如在天堂和地獄相遇之時，

　　上帝的天兵之帥米迦勒

Looked down on you from Heaven's door-post
He would his deeds forget.

Brooding no more upon God's wars
In his divine homestead,
He would go weave out of the stars
A chaplet for your head.

And all folk seeing him bow down,
And white stars tell your praise,   10
Would come at last to God's great town,
Led on by gentle ways;

And God would bid His warfare cease,
Saying all things were well;
And softly make a rosy peace,
A peace of Heaven with Hell.

A Faery Song

Sung by the people of Faery over Diarmuid and Grania,
in their bridal sleep under a Cromlech.

We who are old, old and gay,
O so old!

從天國的門柱旁俯身凝視你，
那他就會忘記他的功業。

不再在他神聖的住宅裡
爲上帝謀劃戰爭，
他將會去用群星爲你
編織珠冠一頂。

看見他俯首鞠躬，
瑩白的星星把你讚美，　　　　　　　　　10
世人終會被溫和的道路引領，
來到上帝的偉大城市；

上帝將會下令停止他的戰爭，
說，一切都是好的，
且輕柔地造出一個玫瑰色的和平，
一個天堂與地獄的媾和。

仙謠

在一石柵欄下面，狄阿米德和格拉妮婭新婚同眠時，
環繞他倆的群仙所唱。

我們，老而又老又快活，
啊，這麼老！

Thousands of years, thousands of years,
If all were told:

Give to these children, new from the world,
Silence and love;
And the long dew-dropping hours of the night,
And the stars above:

Give to these children, new from the world,
Rest far from men.   10
Is anything better, anything better?
Tell us it then:

Us who are old, old and gay,
O so old!
Thousands of years, thousands of years,
If all were told.

The Lake Isle of Innisfree

I will arise and go now, and go to Innisfree,
And a small cabin build there, of clay and wattles made:
Nine bean-rows will I have there, a hive for the honey-bee,
And live alone in the bee-loud glade.

成千上萬歲，成千上萬歲，
如果全都算到：

給這些從塵世新來的孩子
寧靜和愛情；
還有叮咚滴露的長夜良辰
和頭上的星星：

給這些從塵世新來的孩子
遠離人群的安歇。　　　　　　　　　　10
可有更好的事，更好的事？
那就給我們說說：

我們，老而又老又快活，
啊，這麼老！
成千上萬歲，成千上萬歲，
如果全都算到。

湖島因尼斯弗里

現在我要起身離去，前去因尼斯弗里，
用樹枝和泥土，在那裡築起小屋：
我要種九壟菜豆，養一箱蜜蜂在那裡，
在蜂吟嗡嗡的林間空地幽居獨處。

And I shall have some peace there, for peace comes dropping slow,
Dropping from the veils of the morning to where the cricket sings;
There midnight's all a glimmer, and noon a purple glow,
And evening full of the linnet's wings.

I will arise and go now, for always night and day
I hear lake water lapping with low sounds by the shore;   10
While I stand on the roadway, or on the pavements grey,
I hear it in the deep heart's core.

A Cradle Song

The angels are stooping
Above your bed;
They weary of trooping
With the whimpering dead.

God's laughing in Heaven
To see you so good;
The Sailing Seven
Are gay with His mood.

I sigh that kiss you,
For I must own   10

我將享有些寧靜，那裡寧靜緩緩滴零
從清晨的薄霧到蟋蟀鳴唱的地方；
在那裡半夜清輝粼粼，正午紫光耀映，
黃昏的天空中佈滿著紅雀的翅膀。

現在我要起身離去，因為在每夜每日
我總是聽見湖水輕舐湖岸的響聲；　　　　　　10
佇立在馬路上，或灰色的人行道上時，
我都在內心深處聽見那悠悠水聲。

搖籃曲

天使們正俯身
在你的臥床前；
它們已感倦困
與死魂靈相伴。

上帝在天大笑
看你這般健美；
那巡行的七曜
也因之而欣慰。

我吻你又嘆息，
因我必須承認　　　　　　　　　　　　　　10

That I shall miss you
When you have grown.

The Sorrow of Love

The brawling of a sparrow in the eaves,
The brilliant moon and all the milky sky,
And all that famous harmony of leaves,
Had blotted out man's image and his cry.

A girl arose that had red mournful lips
And seemed the greatness of the world in tears,
Doomed like Odysseus and the labouring ships
And proud as Priam murdered with his peers;

Arose, and on the instant clamorous eaves,
A climbing moon upon an empty sky,   10
And all that lamentation of the leaves,
Could but compose man's image and his cry.

我將會失去你，
當你長大成人。

愛的悲傷

屋簷下的一隻麻雀的聒噪，
皎潔的明月和如水的夜空，
還有樹葉精彩和諧的歌調，
遮掩了人類的影像和哭聲。

一個紅唇悽然的少女浮現，
世界的偉大彷彿浸滿淚水，
像奧德修斯船隊歷盡艱難，
像普里阿摩率部傲然戰死。

浮現，在這喧鬧的簷角上，
空曠的天穹裡上升的月輪，
還有樹葉的一切哀悼悲傷，
只能構成人的影像和哭聲。

10

When You are Old

When you are old and grey and full of sleep,
And nodding by the fire, take down this book,
And slowly read, and dream of the soft look
Your eyes had once, and of their shadows deep;

How many loved your moments of glad grace,
And loved your beauty with love false or true,
But one man loved the pilgrim soul in you,
And loved the sorrows of your changing face;

And bending down beside the glowing bars,
Murmur, a little sadly, how Love fled   10
And paced upon the mountains overhead
And hid his face amid a crowd of stars.

The White Birds

I would that we were, my beloved, white birds on the foam of the sea!
We tire of the flame of the meteor, before it can fade and flee;
And the flame of the blue star of twilight, hung low on the rim of the sky,
Has awaked in our hearts, my beloved, a sadness that may not die.

當你年老時

當你年老，鬢斑，睡意昏沉，
在爐旁打盹時，取下這本書，
慢慢誦讀，夢憶從前你雙眸
神色柔和，眼波中倒影深深；

多少人愛你風韻嫵媚的時光，
愛你的美麗出自假意或真情，
但唯有一人愛你靈魂的至誠，
愛你漸衰的臉上愁苦的風霜；

彎下身子，在熾紅的壁爐邊，
憂傷地低訴，愛神如何逃走，　　　　　10
在頭頂上的群山巔漫步閒遊，
把他的面孔隱沒在繁星中間。

白鳥

我但願我們是，親愛的，浪尖上的一雙白鳥！
流星尚未來得及隕逝，我們已厭倦它的閃耀；
低懸在天邊之上，暮色裡的那顆藍星的幽光
喚醒了你我心中，親愛的，一縷不死的憂傷。

A weariness comes from those dreamers, dew-dabbled, the lily and rose;

Ah, dream not of them, my beloved, the flame of the meteor that goes,

Or the flame of the blue star that lingers hung low in the fall of the dew:

For I would we were changed to white birds on the wandering foam: I

    and you!

I am haunted by numberless islands, and many a Danaan shore,   9

Where Time would surely forget us, and Sorrow come near us no more;

Soon far from the rose and the lily and fret of the flames would we be,

Were we only white birds, my beloved, buoyed out on the foam of the sea!

A Dream of Death

I dreamed that one had died in a strange place

Near no accustomed hand;

And they had nailed the boards above her face,

The peasants of that land,

Wondering to lay her in that solitude,

And raised above her mound

A cross they had made out of two bits of wood,

And planted cypress round;

And left her to the indifferent stars above

Until I carved these words: 10

一絲倦意來自那些露濕的夢者：玫瑰和百合；
啊，別夢想，親愛的，那飛逝的流星的閃爍，
或者那低懸在露滴中滯留不去的藍星的耀熠：
因為我但願我們化作浪尖上的白鳥：我和你！

我心頭縈繞著無數島嶼，和許多姐娜的海濱，
在那裡時光肯定會遺忘我們，悲傷不再來臨；　　　　　10
很快我們就會遠離玫瑰、百合和星光的侵蝕，
只要我們是雙白鳥，親愛的，出沒在浪花裡！

夢死

我夢見有一人死在一個陌生地方，
身邊無故又無親；
他們釘起幾塊木板遮蓋她的面龐，
那些當地的農民
好奇地把她安置在那荒郊野地裡，
又在她的墳頂上
把一具兩根木頭做的十字架豎起，
四周種柏樹成行；
從此把她留給頭頂上冷漠的星輝
直到我刻下此話：　　　　　10

She was more beautiful than thy first love,
But now lies under boards.

The Countess Cathleen in Paradise

All the heavy days are over;
Leave the body's coloured pride
Underneath the grass and clover,
With the feet laid side by side.

Bathed in flaming founts of duty
She'll not ask a haughty dress;
Carry all that mournful beauty
To the scented oaken press.

Did the kiss of Mother Mary
Put that music in her face?   10
Yet she goes with footstep wary,
Full of earth's old timid grace.

'Mong the feet of angels seven
What a dancer, glimmering!
All the heavens bow down to Heaven,
Flame to flame and wing to wing.

她從前比你初戀的愛人還要美麗，
如今卻睡在地下。

女伯爵凱瑟琳在天堂

所有沉重的日子都已過完；
留下那軀體的斑斕裝飾
在那雜蕪叢生的蒿草下面，
還有那雙腳並放在一起。

浸浴在熾燃的責任之泉裡，
她並不要求高貴的服裝；
搬走那一切慘淒淒的美麗
塞進那馥郁的橡木衣箱。

聖母馬利亞的親吻可曾否
使她的臉上盪漾起音樂？
但她依然小心地款款移步，
優雅中透著塵世的羞怯。

在那七大天使的腳步中間，
一位舞者何等飄忽閃爍！
諸天的眾神齊向上帝禮讚，
光焰交射，羽翼相銜接。

10

Who goes with Fergus?

Who will go drive with Fergus now,
And pierce the deep wood's woven shade,
And dance upon the level shore?
Young man, lift up your russet brow,
And lift your tender eyelids, maid,
And brood on hopes and fear no more.

And no more turn aside and brood
Upon love's bitter mystery;
For Fergus rules the brazen cars,
And rules the shadows of the wood,   10
And the white breast of the dim sea
And all dishevelled wandering stars.

The Man who dreamed of Faeryland

He stood among a crowd at Drumahair;
His heart hung all upon a silken dress,
And he had known at last some tenderness,
Before earth took him to her stony care;

誰跟佛格斯同去？

現在誰願跟佛格斯乘車同走，
穿透那幽深樹林密織的網，
在平坦的海岸上跳舞？
小伙子，揚起你棕紅的眉頭，
抬起你柔和的眼皮，姑娘，
別再尋思希望和恐懼。

別再轉向一邊思尋
愛情的苦澀的神祕；
因爲佛格斯駕馭著黃銅戰車，
統治著那森林的濃蔭，
那茫茫大海的雪白胸臆，
和亂髮紛披的流浪星火。

10

夢想仙境的人

他佇立在竺瑪海爾的一群人中；
他曾全心繫掛著一件絲綢裙衫，
在大地給予他石硬的關懷之前，
他終於懂得了些許的蜜意柔情；

But when a man poured fish into a pile,
It seemed they raised their little silver heads,
And sang what gold morning or evening sheds
Upon a woven world-forgotten isle
Where people love beside the ravelled seas;
That Time can never mar a lover's vows   10
Under that woven changeless roof of boughs:
The singing shook him out of his new ease.

He wandered by the sands of Lissadell;
His mind ran all on money cares and fears,
And he had known at last some prudent years
Before they heaped his grave under the hill;
But while he passed before a plashy place,
A lug-worm with its grey and muddy mouth
Sang that somewhere to north or west or south
There dwelt a gay, exulting, gentle race   20
Under the golden or the silver skies;
That if a dancer stayed his hungry foot
It seemed the sun and moon were in the fruit:
And at that singing he was no more wise.

He mused beside the well of Scanavin,
He mused upon his mockers: without fail
His sudden vengeance were a country tale,
When earthy night had drunk his body in;
But one small knot-grass growing by the pool

但是當一人把魚兒倒成一堆時，
彷彿魚兒都抬起銀色的小腦袋，
歌唱金色的清晨或黃昏灑落在
一座編織的世外海島上的東西，
在那裡人們相愛在紛亂的海邊；
在那樹枝編結的不變的屋頂下　　　　　　　　　　10
時光永遠無法毀壞戀人的誓約：
這歌唱很快把他重又撼入不安。

他在利薩代爾莊園的湖濱漫遊；
他曾一心患得患失地想著金錢，
在歲月在山腳給他堆成墳墓前，
他終於懂得了一些節儉的年頭；
但是當他走過一處濕地的時候，
一隻沙蝎張著灰色的沾泥的嘴
歌唱北方或西方或南方的某地
有著一個快樂狂放溫和的民族　　　　　　　　　　20
居住在金色或銀色的天空之下；
假如一個舞者停下飢餓的步子，
就彷彿太陽和月亮都結了果實：
聽著那歌唱他變得愚蠢又呆傻。

他在斯卡納文的水井旁邊沉思，
思想譏笑他的人們；毫無疑問
他的突然復仇成了鄉間的傳聞，
當塵世之夜把他的身體吞噬時；
但是池塘邊生長的一株兩耳草

Sang where — unnecessary cruel voice—   30
Old silence bids its chosen race rejoice,
Whatever ravelled waters rise and fall
Or stormy silver fret the gold of day,
And midnight there enfold them like a fleece
And lover there by lover be at peace.
The tale drove his fine angry mood away.

He slept under the hill of Lugnagall;
And might have known at last unhaunted sleep
Under that cold and vapour-turbaned steep,
Now that the earth had taken man and all: 40
Did not the worms that spired about his bones
Proclaim with that unwearied, reedy cry
That God has laid His fingers on the sky,
That from those fingers glittering summer runs
Upon the dancer by the dreamless wave.
Why should those lovers that no lovers miss
Dream, until God burn Nature with a kiss?
The man has found no comfort in the grave.

用不必要的殘忍聲音歌唱那裡——　　　　　　30
古老的靜寂命令它的選民歡喜，
無論漲起和落下什麼樣的浪潮，
風暴的白銀怎樣侵蝕白晝黃金；
那裡深夜將像羊毛把他們圍裹，
那裡戀人偎著戀人將共享安樂。
這傳說驅散了他的稀薄的怨忿。

他長眠在盧格納郭爾山丘之下；
既然大地已接受了萬物和人類，
他或許終於懂得了無擾的沉睡
在那寒冷的霧氣籠罩的山坡下：　　　　　　40
難道蠕動在他屍骨周圍的蛆蟲
不曾以那不倦的尖厲嘶叫宣稱
上帝已將他的手指按在了天穹，
朦朧閃爍的夏季流溢出那指縫
把那無夢的海浪邊的舞者淹沒。
那些無戀人思念的戀人為何要
夢，直到上帝以一吻焚燬創造？
那人在墓中不曾找到一絲慰藉。

The Lamentation of the Old Pensioner

Although I shelter from the rain
Under a broken tree,
My chair was nearest to the fire
In every company
That talked of love or politics,
Ere Time transfigured me.

Though lads are making pikes again
For some conspiracy,
And crazy rascals rage their fill
At human tyranny;   10
My contemplations are of Time
That has transfigured me.

There's not a woman turns her face
Upon a broken tree,
And yet the beauties that I loved
Are in my memory;
I spit into the face of Time
That has transfigured me.

退休老人的哀傷

雖然我現在躲避雨淋
在一棵斷樹下面，
但我的座椅也曾緊靠爐火
在每一群高談
愛情或政治的人們之中，
在時光把我變老之前。

雖然少年人又在製造槍矛，
準備舉行反叛，
瘋狂的流氓們向人間暴政
發洩滿腔怒焰；
但我的沉思却專注在
那改變了我的時光上面。

沒有一個女人轉過臉
回顧一棵斷樹幹，
但我曾經愛過的美人兒們
依然在我記憶裡邊；
我啐唾在時光的臉上——
它已把我改變。

10

The Two Trees

Beloved, gaze in thine own heart,
The holy tree is growing there;
From joy the holy branches start,
And all the trembling flowers they bear.
The changing colours of its fruit
Have dowered the stars with merry light;
The surety of its hidden root
Has planted quiet in the night;
The shaking of its leafy head
Has given the waves their melody,   10
And made my lips and music wed,
Murmuring a wizard song for thee.
There the Loves a circle go,
The flaming circle of our days,
Gyring, spiring to and fro
In those great ignorant leafy ways;
Remembering all that shaken hair
And how the winged sandals dart,
Thine eyes grow full of tender care:
Beloved, gaze in thine own heart.   20

Gaze no more in the bitter glass
The demons, with their subtle guile,

兩棵樹

親愛的，凝視你自己的心裡，
那神聖的樹就在那裡生長；
從歡樂中生發出神聖的繁枝，
顫巍巍的花朵綴滿枝頭上。
它那果實變幻的斑斕的色彩
用悅目的光給群星作嫁資；
它那隱蔽著的根須實實在在
已經把寂靜栽種在黑夜裡；
它那滿頭的繁葉頻頻的搖曳
賦予了海浪以澎湃的旋律，　　　　　　　　10
也使我的雙唇得與音樂結合，
為你低唱一支迷幻的歌曲。
在那裡愛神們繞圈翩翩起舞，
把我們的如火的青春環繞，
旋轉著，纏繞著，反反覆覆，
沿著樹葉覆蓋的無知大道；
憶想起那一簇長髮簌簌抖開
和那有翅的草鞋如何急馳，
你的雙眼就充滿溫柔的關懷：
親愛的，凝視你自己心裡。　　　　　　　　20

別再凝視那苦澀慘凄的鏡面，
魔鬼們心懷著狡詐的詭計，

Lift up before us when they pass,

Or only gaze a little while;

For there a fatal image grows

That the stormy night receives,

Roots half hidden under snows,

Broken boughs and blackened leaves.

For all things turn to barrenness

In the dim glass the demons hold,   30

The glass of outer weariness,

Made when God slept in times of old.

There, through the broken branches, go

The ravens of unresting thought;

Flying, crying, to and fro,

Cruel claw and hungry throat,

Or else they stand and sniff the wind,

And shake their ragged wings; alas!

Thy tender eyes grow all unkind:

Gaze no more in the bitter glass.   40

高高舉起它走過我們的面前，
要麼僅僅凝視它片刻一時；
因爲那裡長著一個致命影像，
它享受著風暴之夜的款待，
根須在積雪下半顯露半埋藏，
枝幹都斷折，葉子已焦黑。
因爲萬物都變得不育而貧瘠
在那群魔高擎的昏暗鏡中，　　　　　　　　　30
那屬於外部世界煩惱的鏡子
是在遠古上帝沉睡時造成。
那裡，在那斷殘的枝椏中間
穿行著不安思緒的黑烏鴉；
飛翔著，啼叫著，往往返返，
飢餓的喉嚨，兇殘的腳爪，
要麼它們就抖動蓬亂的羽翼，
兀立著嗤笑那狂風；老天！
你溫柔的眼睛變得冷酷無比：
別再凝視苦澀悽慘的鏡面。　　　　　　　　　40

To Some I have Talked with by the Fire

While I wrought out these fitful Danaan rhymes,

My heart would brim with dreams about the times

When we bent down above the fading coals

And talked of the dark folk who live in souls

Of passionate men, like bats in the dead trees;

And of the wayward twilight companies

Who sigh with mingled sorrow and content,

Because their blossoming dreams have never bent

Under the fruit of evil and of good:

And of the embattled flaming multitude   10

Who rise, wing above wing, flame above flame,

And, like a storm, cry the Ineffable Name,

And with the clashing of their sword-blades make

A rapturous music, till the morning break

And the white hush end all but the loud beat

Of their long wings, the flash of their white feet.

致曾與我擁火而談的人

在我製作出這些斷續的妲娜詩句時，
我的心就會洋溢著對往昔的夢憶，
那時我們俯身圍擁著那將熄的碳火，
談論那些像枯樹中的蝙蝠，生活
在熱情的人們的靈魂裡的蒙昧人民；
談論那些固執倔強的遠古的族群，
他們的嘆息之中混合著滿足和悲哀，
因爲他們像繁花般盛開的夢從來
不曾在那善與惡的果實下折腰屈躬：
談論那列陣備戰光輝耀眼的大眾，
他們齊飛舉，羽翼交疊，光焰萬道，
聲如雷鳴，高呼那不可道的名號，
用他們的刀劍的鏗鏘撞擊聲合奏出
一曲狂喜的樂章，直到晨光綻露，
白色的寂靜終止一切，除了他們那
長翼的轟鳴，他們那素足的光華。

10

1899
The Wind Among the Reeds
選自《葦叢中的風》

The Everlasting Voices

O sweet everlasting Voices, be still;
Go to the guards of the heavenly fold
And bid them wander obeying your will,
Flame under flame, till Time be no more;
Have you not heard that our hearts are old,
That you call in birds, in wind on the hill,
In shaken boughs, in tide on the shore?
O sweet everlasting Voices, be still.

The Lover tells of the Rose in his Heart

All things uncomely and broken, all things worn out and old,
The cry of a child by the roadway, the creak of a lumbering cart,
The heavy steps of the ploughman, splashing the wintry mould,
Are wronging your image that blossoms a rose in the deeps of my heart.

The wrong of unshapely things is a wrong too great to be told;
I hunger to build them anew and sit on a green knoll apart,
With the earth and the sky and the water, re-made, like a casket of gold
For my dreams of your image that blossoms a rose in the deeps of my heart.

不絕的話音

呵，甜美的不絕的話音，靜一靜；
去找那些護衛天國的羊欄的看守，
命令他們遵從你的意願漫遊巡行，
光焰疊光焰，直到時間不再存在；
難道你不曾聽說你在搖顫的枝頭，
在群鳥之中，在岸上的潮水之中，
在山風中召喚的我們的心已老邁？
呵，甜美的不絕的話音，靜一靜。

戀人述說他心中的玫瑰

醜陋殘缺的萬物，破損陳舊的萬物，
路邊孩童的啼哭，笨重大車的尖響，
拋撒著冬季肥土的耕夫的沉重腳步，
都在傷害著你的影像：一朵玫瑰在我心底開放。

那些醜惡的東西犯下了彌天的大過；
我渴望重造它們，然後遠坐綠坡上，
守著新鑄的天地海洋，像一隻金盒
盛著我夢中你的影像：一朵玫瑰在我心底開放。

The Fish

Although you hide in the ebb and flow
Of the pale tide when the moon has set,
The people of coming days will know
About the casting out of my net,
And how you have leaped times out of mind
Over the little silver cords,
And think that you were hard and unkind,
And blame you with many bitter words.

Into the Twilight

Out-worn heart, in a time out-worn,
Come clear of the nets of wrong and right;
Laugh, heart, again in the grey twilight,
Sigh, heart, again in the dew of the morn.

Your mother Eire is always young,
Dew ever shining and twilight grey;
Though hope fall from you and love decay,
Burning in fires of a slanderous tongue.

魚

儘管曉月西沉後你隱匿
在那灰白的落潮深處，
來日裡的人們也將知悉
我是怎樣把魚網拋出，
而你又是怎樣無數次地
躍過那些細細的銀索，
他們會認為你薄情寡義，
並且狠狠地把你斥責。

到曙光裡來

衰殘的心，在一個衰殘的時代，
來呀，擺脫那是是非非的羅網；
大笑吧，心，又見灰白的曙光，
嘆息吧，心，又見清晨的露滴。

你的母親愛爾她永遠年輕不老，
露滴永遠晶瑩，曙光永遠灰白；
雖然希望離你而去，愛情衰敗，
在一條毀謗之舌的毒焰中焚燒。

Come, heart, where hill is heaped upon hill:

For there the mystical brotherhood   10

Of sun and moon and hollow and wood

And river and stream work out their will;

And God stands winding His lonely horn,

And time and the world are ever in flight;

And love is less kind than the grey twilight,

And hope is less dear than the dew of the morn.

The Song of Wandering Aengus

I went out to the hazel wood,

Because a fire was in my head,

And cut and peeled a hazel wand,

And hooked a berry to a thread;

And when white moths were on the wing,

And moth-like stars were flickering out,

I dropped the berry in a stream

And caught a little silver trout.

When I had laid it on the floor

I went to blow the fire aflame,   10

But something rustled on the floor,

來吧，心，到這層巒疊嶂之地：
因為太陽和月亮，山谷和森林，　　　　　　　　　　10
大川和小溪的神祕的兄弟親情
在這裡將努力實現它們的意志；

上帝佇立著吹響他孤獨的號角，
時光和世界永遠都在匆匆飛逝；
愛情不比灰白的曙光那樣仁慈，
希望不比清晨的露滴那樣親切。

漫遊的安格斯之歌

我出門來到榛樹林裡，
因為頭中燃著一團火，
砍下一段榛枝削成桿，
在一根線端鉤掛漿果；
在粉白蛾子展翅飛舞，
粉蛾似的星星閃現時，
我把漿果投到溪水裡，
釣起一條小小的銀魚。

我把它放在了地面上，
然後去把火苗兒吹起，　　　　　　　　　　　10
可是地面上沙沙作響，

And some one called me by my name:
It had become a glimmering girl
With apple blossom in her hair
Who called me by my name and ran
And faded through the brightening air.

Though I am old with wandering
Through hollow lands and hilly lands,
I will find out where she has gone,
And kiss her lips and take her hands;   20
And walk among long dappled grass,
And pluck till time and times are done
The silver apples of the moon,
The golden apples of the sun.

The Song of the Old Mother

I rise in the dawn, and I kneel and blow
Till the seed of the fire flicker and glow;
And then I must scrub and bake and sweep
Till stars are beginning to blink and peep;
And the young lie long and dream in their bed
Of the matching of ribbons for bosom and head,

有誰在呼喚我的名字；
它變成一個晶瑩少女，
鬢邊簪插著蘋果花兒；
她叫我名字然後跑開，
消失在漸亮的空氣裡。

雖然走遍了深谷高山，
我已經變得衰弱老朽，
但是我仍然要找到她，
吻她的嘴唇牽她的手；　　　　　　　　　　20
走在斑駁的深草叢中，
採擷太陽的金色蘋果，
採擷月亮的銀色蘋果，
直到時光都不再流過。

老母之歌

我黎明即起，跪地吹火
直到爐中火種熠熠閃爍；
然後做飯擦地清掃房間
直到晚星開始眨眼偷看；
年輕人在床上久睡夢想
胸飾和頭飾是否正相當，

And their day goes over in idleness,

And they sigh if the wind but lift a tress:

While I must work because I am old,

And the seed of the fire gets feeble and cold.　　　　　10

The Heart of the Woman

O what to me the little room

That was brimmed up with prayer and rest;

He bade me out into the gloom,

And my breast lies upon his breast.

O what to me my mother's care,

The house where I was safe and warm;

The shadowy blossom of my hair

Will hide us from the bitter storm.

O hiding hair and dewy eyes,

I am no more with life and death,　　　　　　　　　　10

My heart upon his warm heart lies,

My breath is mixed into his breath.

她們的日子消遙又安逸，
風吹髮絲她們也要嘆息：
而我得勞作因爲我老了，
火種已變得微弱冰涼了。　　　　　　10

女人的心

呵，何用那小小房間
洋溢著祈禱和安寧；
他叫我出門潛入夜暗，
我的胸緊貼他的胸。

呵，何用母親的關懷
和安全溫暖的家居；
我濃密的頭髮如花開，
將蔽護我們躲風雨。

呵，頭髮濃密眼晶瑩，
從此不再顧慮死生，　　　　　　　　10
我的心緊貼著他的心，
我的氣息與他相通。

The Lover mourns for the Loss of Love

Pale brows, still hands and dim hair,
I had a beautiful friend
And dreamed that the old despair
Would end in love in the end:
She looked in my heart one day
And saw your image was there;
She has gone weeping away.

He mourns for the Change that has come upon Him and his Beloved, and longs for the End of the World

Do you not hear me calling, white deer with no horns?
I have been changed to a hound with one red ear;
I have been in the Path of Stones and the Wood of Thorns,
For somebody hid hatred and hope and desire and fear
Under my feet that they follow you night and day.
A man with a hazel wand came without sound;
He changed me suddenly; I was looking another way;
And now my calling is but the calling of a hound;

戀人傷悼失戀

額白髮濃雙手安詳，
我有個美麗的女友，
遂夢想舊日的絕望
終將在愛情中結束：
一天她窺入我心底
見那裡有你的影像；
她哭泣著從此離去。

他傷嘆他和愛人所遭遇的變故
並渴望世界末日的來臨

難道你沒有聽見我在呼喚，無角的白鹿？
我已被變成一條獵犬，長著一隻紅耳朵；
我已處身於那荊棘的叢林和石頭的小路，
因爲曾有人把仇恨、希冀、慾望和畏怯
藏在了我腳下，好讓它們日夜把你追逐。
一個手持榛木杖的人曾悄無聲息地前來；
他突然把我變了形；我正扭頭看著別處；
現在我的呼喚只不過是一條獵犬的狂吠；

And Time and Birth and Change are hurrying by.

I would that the Boar without bristles had come from the West   10

And had rooted the sun and moon and stars out of the sky

And lay in the darkness, grunting, and turning to his rest.

He bids his Beloved be at Peace

I hear the Shadowy Horses, their long manes a-shake,

Their hoofs heavy with tumult, their eyes glimmering white;

The North unfolds above them clinging, creeping night,

The East her hidden joy before the morning break,

The West weeps in pale dew and sighs passing away,

The South is pouring down roses of crimson fire:

O vanity of Sleep, Hope, Dream, endless Desire,

The Horses of Disaster plunge in the heavy clay:

Beloved, let your eyes half close, and your heart beat

Over my heart, and your hair fall over my breast,   10

Drowning love's lonely hour in deep twilight of rest,

And hiding their tossing manes and their tumultuous feet.

而時光和誕生和變化正在匆匆地流過去。
我但願，那無鬃的野豬已經從西方來到，　　　　　　10
把太陽和月亮和星星都連根拱到天外去，
然後躺倒在黑暗裡，哼哼著，翻身睡覺。

他讓愛人平靜下來

我聽見那幻影的群馬，它們的長鬃抖顫，
它們的鐵蹄沉重雜沓，它們的眼睛白光閃爍；
北方在它們頭頂上展開匍匐緊貼的夜色，
東方則把她在晨光破曉前的隱匿的歡樂鋪展，
西方飲泣在蒼白的露水中，嘆息著飄逝，
南方紛紛揚揚傾撒著暗紅的火焰的玫瑰花瓣：
呵，睡眠、希冀、夢想、無盡慾望的虛幻，
那災難的群馬都投身進入那沉重的凡胎肉體：
親愛的，讓你的雙眼半閉起，讓你的心
在我的心上跳蕩，讓你的柔髮在我胸上瀉落，　　10
把愛的孤寂時刻淹沒於休憩的深沉暮色，
把它們飛揚的長鬃和它們雜沓的蹄聲都蔽隱。

He reproves the Curlew

O curlew, cry no more in the air,
Or only to the water in the West;
Because your crying brings to my mind
Passion-dimmed eyes and long heavy hair
That was shaken out over my breast:
There is enough evil in the crying of wind.

A Poet to his Beloved

I bring you with reverent hands
The books of my numberless dreams,
White woman that passion has worn
As the tide wears the dove-grey sands,
And with heart more old than the horn
That is brimmed from the pale fire of time:
White woman with numberless dreams,
I bring you my passionate rhyme.

他怨責麻鷸

麻鷸呵，別在空中叫啦，
要麼去向西方大海啼喚；
因爲你的叫聲使我憶起
朦朧秋波和沉重的長髮
曾在我胸上顫抖著披散：
風聲裡已有足夠的惡意。

詩人致所愛

猶如潮水銷蝕鴿灰的沙灘，
那被情熱銷蝕的白晳女人，
我帶給你我無數夢的結集——
以虔誠恭敬的雙手和比起
那由於時光的蒼白的火焰
而飽滿的彎月更古老的心：
擁有無數的夢的白晳女人，
我帶給你我的熱情的詩韻。

He gives his Beloved certain Rhymes

Fasten your hair with a golden pin,
And bind up every wandering tress;
I bade my heart build these poor rhymes:
It worked at them, day out, day in,
Building a sorrowful loveliness
Out of the battles of old times.

You need but lift a pearl-pale hand,
And bind up your long hair and sigh;
And all men's hearts must burn and beat;
And candle-like foam on the dim sand,   10
And stars climbing the dew-dropping sky,
Live but to light your passing feet.

To his Heart, bidding it have no Fear

Be you still, be you still, trembling heart;
Remember the wisdom out of the old days:
Him who trembles before the flame and the flood,
And the winds that blow through the starry ways,

他贈給愛人一些詩句

用金卡別緊你的頭髮，
束起每一綹鬆散髮卷；
我命我心把拙詩製作：
日復一日，夜復一夜，
它從古代的戰爭裡面
造就一曲美麗的哀歌。

你只需舉起一隻玉手，
攏起長髮，嘆息一聲；
人人的心必燃燒狂跳；
朦朧沙灘上白浪似燭，
滴露天空中群星高昇，
只為照亮你過路的腳。

10

致他的心，讓它不要懼怕

安靜，安靜，悸顫的心；
記住那古代的至理名言：
誰要是面對大火和洪水，
面對吹過星空的風抖顫，

Let the starry winds and the flame and the flood
Cover over and hide, for he has no part
With the lonely, majestical multitude.

The Cap and Bells

The jester walked in the garden:
The garden had fallen still;
He bade his soul rise upward
And stand on her window-sill.

It rose in a straight blue garment,
When owls began to call:
It had grown wise-tongued by thinking
Of a quiet and light footfall;

But the young queen would not listen;
She rose in her pale night-gown;   10
She drew in the heavy casement
And pushed the latches down.

He bade his heart go to her,
When the owls called out no more;
In a red and quivering garment

就讓長風、大火和洪水
把他埋葬，因為他不能
屬於那孤獨雄偉的一群。

飾鈴帽

弄臣在花園裡徘徊：
花園裡暮色深寂；
他命靈魂出竅高飛
到她窗台上站立。

在鴟鴞初啼的時分，
它藍衣筆挺飛起：
想著一聲輕悄足音，
它口齒頓變伶俐；

年輕王后卻不願聽，
披著白睡衣起身，
伸手關閉沉重窗櫺，
把道道窗閂插緊。

10

在鴟鴞不再啼之時，
他命心向她飛去；
它身穿抖顫的紅衣，

It sang to her through the door.

It had grown sweet-tongued by dreaming
Of a flutter of flower-like hair;
But she took up her fan from the table
And waved it off on the air.   20

'I have cap and bells,' he pondered,
'I will send them to her and die';
And when the morning whitened
He left them where she went by.

She laid them upon her bosom,
Under a cloud of her hair,
And her red lips sang them a love-song
Till stars grew out of the air.
She opened her door and her window,
And the heart and the soul came through,   30
To her right hand came the red one,
To her left hand came the blue.

They set up a noise like crickets,
A chattering wise and sweet,
And her hair was a folded flower
And the quiet of love in her feet.

隔著門對她唱曲。

夢著一綹如花髮卷，
它歌喉頓變甜蜜；
但她從桌上拿起扇，
把它拂到半空裡。　　　　　　　　　　　　20

「我有飾鈴帽，」他想，
「送給她我就去死」；
留在她經過的地方，
在晨光大白之時。

她把鈴帽貼在胸上，
用如雲濃髮遮蓋，
紅唇對它把情歌唱
直到群星飛天外。

她打開前門和後窗，
那心和靈魂飛進；　　　　　　　　　　　　30
紅的降在她右手上，
藍的落入左手心。

它們閒聊聰穎甜蜜，
似蟋蟀唧唧和鳴；
她頭髮如花瓣合起，
腳下是愛的寧靜。

He tells of a Valley full of Lovers

I dreamed that I stood in a valley, and amid sighs,
For happy lovers passed two by two where I stood;
And I dreamed my lost love came stealthily out of the wood
With her cloud-pale eyelids falling on dream-dimmed eyes:
I cried in my dream, O *women, bid the young men lay*
Their heads on your knees, and drown their eyes with your hair,
Or remembering hers they will find no other face fair
Till all the valleys of the world have been withered away.

He tells of the Perfect Beauty

O cloud-pale eyelids, dream-dimmed eyes,
The poets labouring all their days
To build a perfect beauty in rhyme
Are overthrown by a woman's gaze
And by the unlabouring brood of the skies:
And therefore my heart will bow, when dew
Is dropping sleep, until God burn time,
Before the unlabouring stars and you.

他描述一個滿是戀人的山谷

我夢見我站在一個山谷中，在一片嘆息聲裡，
因為一對對幸福的戀人聯翩走過我站立之處；
我夢見我失去的愛人從那樹林裡悄悄地溜出，
她朦朧似夢的眼眸上低垂著潔白如雲的眼皮：
我在夢中高喊：啊，女人，讓小伙子們把頭
枕在你們膝上，用你們的長髮淹沒他們的眼，
否則憶起她的臉，他們會覺得別無美好容顏，
直到這世上所有的山谷都漸漸消失不復存留。

他談論絕色美人

呵，潔白如雲的眼皮，朦朧似夢的眼眸，
詩人們終日辛苦勞作，想要
用詩韻塑造一個絕色的美人，
却被一個女人的凝睇擊倒，
被天國的悠閒的群雛征服：
因此，在露水滴瀝著睡意的時辰，
我的心將磬折，在那悠閒的群星
和你面前，直到上帝把時間耗盡。

The Travail of Passion

When the flaming lute-thronged angelic door is wide;
When an immortal passion breathes in mortal clay;
Our hearts endure the scourge, the plaited thorns, the way
Crowded with bitter faces, the wounds in palm and side,
The vinegar-heavy sponge, the flowers by Kedron stream;
We will bend down and loosen our hair over you,
That it may drop faint perfume, and be heavy with dew,
Lilies of death-pale hope, roses of passionate dream.

The Poet pleads with the Elemental Powers

The Powers whose name and shape no living creature knows
Have pulled the Immortal Rose;
And though the Seven Lights bowed in their dance and wept,
The Polar Dragon slept,
His heavy rings uncoiled from glimmering deep to deep:
When will he wake from sleep?

Great Powers of falling wave and wind and windy fire,
With your harmonious choir

受難之苦

當那光焰四射琴瑟齊鳴的天使之門開敞；
一股不朽的激情呼吸在必朽的泥土裡面；
我們的心忍受著鞭笞、荊棘冠冕、擠滿
愁苦面孔的道路、手掌和腰脅處的創傷、
浸滿醋液的海綿、基仲溪畔的野花之時，
我們將躬身俯首，披散開長髮把你遮護，
讓髮絲滴瀝淡淡幽香，沉甸甸沾滿甘露，
死白的希望之百合，激情的夢想之玫瑰。

詩人祈求四大之力

沒有生靈知道其名稱和形狀的威力
摧折了那不朽的玫瑰；
儘管那七星在舞蹈間曾躬身而哭泣，
那天軸之龍照舊沉睡，
它沉重的環節綿延在波光粼粼的海洋中：
何時它會從酣眠中覺醒？

巨浪、狂風和大火的偉大力量，
用你們和諧的合唱

Encircle her I love and sing her into peace,
That my old care may cease;   10
Unfold your flaming wings and cover out of sight
The nets of day and night.

Dim Powers of drowsy thought, let her no longer be
Like the pale cup of the sea,
When winds have gathered and sun and moon burned dim
Above its cloudy rim;
But let a gentle silence wrought with music flow
Whither her footsteps go.

He wishes his Beloved were Dead

Were you but lying cold and dead,
And lights were paling out of the West,
You would come hither, and bend your head,
And I would lay my head on your breast;
And you would murmur tender words,
Forgiving me, because you were dead:
Nor would you rise and hasten away,
Though you have the will of the wild birds,
But know your hair was bound and wound

環繞我所愛的她，把她哄入安寧，

以使我衰老的憂慮消停；　　　　　　　　　10

展開你們閃耀的翅膀，把晝夜的羅網

嚴嚴實實的覆蓋遮擋。

昏沉思緒的微弱力量，讓她別再

像那大海的白色酒杯，

當八風匯聚，日、月暗淡地燃燒在

它那雲霧蒸騰的邊沿時；

而讓一片用音樂織成的柔和寂靜流往

她的腳步走去的方向。

他願所愛已死

假如你只是躺著，冰冷死透，

三光正朝著西天外暗淡消亡，

你就會來這裡，低下你的頭，

我就會把我的頭枕在你胸上；

你就會喃喃低語溫柔的話語，

把我寬恕，因為你已經死去：

縱然你有著野雀一般的心志，

你也就不會起身，匆匆離去，

而是會明白你的長髮被縛繫

About the stars and moon and sun: 10
O would, beloved, that you lay
Under the dock-leaves in the ground,
While lights were paling one by one.

He wishes for the Cloths of Heaven

Had I the heavens' embroidered cloths,
Enwrought with golden and silver light,
The blue and the dim and the dark cloths
Of night and light and the half-light,
I would spread the cloths under your feet:
But I, being poor, have only my dreams;
I have spread my dreams under your feet;
Tread softly because you tread on my dreams.

纏繞在星星月亮和太陽上頭：   10
呵，親愛的人，但願你躺在
那羊蹄草葉覆蓋下的土地裡，
當三光一一暗淡消逝的時候。

他冀求天國的錦緞

假如我有天國的錦繡綢緞，
那用金色銀色的光線織就，
黑夜、白天、黎明和傍晚，
湛藍、灰暗和漆黑的錦繡，
我就把那錦緞舖在你腳下：
可我，一貧如洗，只有夢；
我把我的夢舖在了你腳下；
輕點，因為你踏著我的夢。

The Fiddler of Dooney

When I play on my fiddle in Dooney,
Folk dance like a wave of the sea;
My cousin is priest in Kilvarnet,
My brother in Mocharabuiee.

I passed my brother and cousin:
They read in their books of prayer;
I read in my book of songs
I bought at the Sligo fair.

When we come at the end of time
To Peter sitting in state,   10
He will smile on the three old spirits,
But call me first through the gate;

For the good are always the merry,
Save by an evil chance,
And the merry love the fiddle,
And the merry love to dance:

And when the folk there spy me,
They will all come up to me,
With 'Here is the fiddler of Dooney!'
And dance like a wave of the sea.   20

都尼的提琴手

在都尼當我把琴弦一拉響，
鄉親們便起舞像海浪；
我表兄在基爾瓦內當牧師，
在莫卡拉比是我兄長。

我順路拜訪我的兩位老兄：
他們埋頭念誦祈禱書；
我捧著我從史萊果市場上
買來的歌本潛心攻讀。

如果在世界末日我們來到
使徒彼得的座位跟前，   10
他會對三個老鬼魂微微笑，
却最先叫我跨進門檻；

因為好人們總是快快樂樂，
除非碰上意外的煩惱，
快樂的人們喜歡琴聲悠揚，
快樂的人們喜歡舞蹈：

在那裡的人們一旦看見我，
他們都會來到我身旁，
歡呼「都尼的提琴手來了！」
一同跳起舞來像海浪。   20

1904
In the Seven Woods
選自《在那七片樹林裡》

The Arrow

I thought of your beauty, and this arrow,
Made out of a wild thought, is in my marrow.
There's no man may look upon her, no man,
As when newly grown to be a woman,
Tall and noble but with face and bosom
Delicate in colour as apple blossom.
This beauty's kinder, yet for a reason
I could weep that the old is out of season.

Never give all the Heart

Never give all the heart, for love
Will hardly seem worth thinking of
To passionate women if it seem
Certain, and they never dream
That it fades out from kiss to kiss;
For everything that's lovely is
But a brief, dreamy, kind delight.
O never give the heart outright,
For they, for all smooth lips can say,

箭

過去我一想起你的美麗，這枚箭鏃——
一個狂亂的念頭鑄就——就釘入我髓骨。
如今再沒有一個男人會殷勤注目，沒有，
不像她青春少女初長成的時候，
頎長而高貴，胸房和面頰
却像蘋果花一樣色澤淡雅。
這一位美人更柔媚，然而爲了一個緣故，
我不禁想要痛哭，那舊日的美人已遲暮。

切勿把心全交出

切勿把心全交出，因爲愛情
只要似乎確定，它對於熱情
如火的女人們便似乎用不著
一想，她們永遠也夢想不到
它從一次次親吻間漸漸消逝；
因爲美好可愛的一切不過是
一種短暫、虛幻如夢的愉快。
呵，切勿把心徹底地交出來，
因爲所有滑膩的嘴唇都會說，

Have given their hearts up to the play.   10
And who could play it well enough
If deaf and dumb and blind with love?
He that made this knows all the cost,
For he gave all his heart and lost.

The Withering of the Boughs

I cried when the moon was murmuring to the birds:
'Let peewit call and curlew cry where they will,
I long for your merry and tender and pitiful words,
For the roads are unending, and there is no place to my mind.'
The honey-pale moon lay low on the sleepy hill,
And I fell asleep upon lonely Echtge of streams.
No boughs have withered because of the wintry wind;
The boughs have withered because I have told them my dreams.

I know of the leafy paths that the witches take
Who come with their crowns of pearl and their spindles of wool,   10
And their secret smile, out of the depths of the lake;
I know where a dim moon drifts, where the Danaan kind
Wind and unwind dancing when the light grows cool
On the island lawns, their feet where the pale foam gleams.

她們把心都已交給了那遊戲。　　　　　　　　　10
如果愛到聵聾、喑啞、盲目，
有誰又能做到玩得恰到好處？
作此詩的人他知道全部代價，
因為他曾把心全交又失去啦。

樹枝的枯萎

當月亮對群鳥喃喃低語的時候我大叫：
「讓田鳧啼喚麻鷸鳴叫在它們願意的地方，
我渴望你的愉快、溫和、悲憫的語調，
因為道路無窮，沒有給我心靈的位置。」
蜂蜜般瑩白的月亮低懸在瞌睡的山丘上，
我在溪流縱橫的寂寞的埃赫蒂山上入夢。
沒有一根枝條由於嚴冬的寒風而枯萎；
枝條枯萎是因為我對它們講述了我的夢。

我知道女巫們走的那些樹葉覆蓋的小路，
她們帶著她們的珠冠和紡羊毛的紡錘，　　　10
和她們神祕的微笑，來自湖底的深處；
我知道朦朧的月亮在何處漂浮，姐奴之輩
在何處交纏分解她們的腳步，舞蹈在
白浪閃耀之處，當月光在海島空地上變冷。

No boughs have withered because of the wintry wind;
The boughs have withered because I have told them my dreams.

I know of the sleepy country, where swans fly round
Coupled with golden chains, and sing as they fly.
A king and a queen are wandering there, and the sound
Has made them so happy and hopeless, so deaf and so blind   20
With wisdom, they wander till all the years have gone by;
I know, and the curlew and peewit on Echtge of streams.
No boughs have withered because of the wintry wind;
The boughs have withered because I have told them my dreams.

Adam's Curse

We sat together at one summer's end,
That beautiful mild woman, your close friend,
And you and I, and talked of poetry.
I said, 'A line will take us hours maybe;
Yet if it does not seem a moment's thought,
Our stitching and unstitching has been naught.
Better go down upon your marrow-bones
And scrub a kitchen pavement, or break stones
Like an old pauper, in all kinds of weather;

沒有一根枝條由於嚴冬的寒風而枯萎；
枝條枯萎是因為我對它們講述了我的夢。

我知道那寂靜的國度，那裡天鵝盤旋，
它們且飛且歌，被金色鏈條拴在一起。
一位國王和王后在那裡漫遊，那歌聲
使他們如此快樂而絕望，盲瞽而聾聵，　　　　　20
沒了智慧，竟至於漫遊到歲月全都流逝；
我知道，埃赫蒂山上的麻鷸和田凫也知情。
沒有一根枝條由於嚴冬的寒風而枯萎；
枝條枯萎是因為我對它們講述了我的夢。

亞當所受的詛咒

有一年夏末我們聚坐在一起，
你的密友，那美麗溫柔的女子，
還有你和我，共把詩藝談論。
我說：「一行詩須花幾個時辰，
而假如不像是瞬間的靈感，
我們綴了又拆也都屬枉然。
那你還不如屈膝跪地，
把廚房地板擦洗；或像個老丐
去敲砸石塊，無論天氣好壞；

For to articulate sweet sounds together   10
Is to work harder than all these, and yet
Be thought an idler by the noisy set
Of bankers, schoolmasters, and clergymen
The martyrs call the world.'

                  And thereupon
That beautiful mild woman for whose sake
There's many a one shall find out all heartache
On Finding that her voice is sweet and low
Replied, 'To be born woman is to know —
Although they do not talk of it at school —
That we must labour to be beautiful.'   20

I said, 'It's certain there is no fine thing
Since Adam's fall but needs much labouring.
There have been lovers who thought love should be
So much compounded of high courtesy
That they would sigh and quote with learned looks
Precedents out of beautiful old books;
Yet now it seems an idle trade enough.'

We sat grown quiet at the name of love;
We saw the last embers of daylight die,
And in the trembling blue-green of the sky   30
A moon, worn as if it had been a shell
Washed by time's waters as they rose and fell

因為連綴妙音絕響的工作要比　　　　　　　　10
這些都困難，却還要被
聒噪的錢商、教員和牧師之輩——
殉道者所謂的世俗之人——
認作是游手好閒。」

　　　　　　　接下來
答言的是那美麗溫柔的女子；
聽見她嗓音低沉甜美，
許多人都會感到心中隱痛：
「雖說學校裡沒有這門課程，
但生為女人就理應知曉：
為求美好我們必須辛勞。」　　　　　　　　20

我說：「無疑，自從亞當墮落以來，
沒有美好的東西不需耗費大量精力。
曾有不少戀人認為，愛情應該
配合有十足高貴的禮儀；
他們常常擺出博學的面孔，
嘆息著從古籍中博引旁徵；
但如今那不過像是無聊的交易。」

提到愛情我們便沉默不語；
看夕陽最後一縷金輝燃盡；
在蒼穹瑟瑟抖顫的碧色中，　　　　　　　　30
一瓣殘月，歲歲年年，
似空貝浮沉在群星之間，

About the stars and broke in days and years.

I had a thought for no one's but your ears:
That you were beautiful, and that I strove
To love you in the old high way of love;
That it had all seemed happy, and yet we'd grown
As weary-hearted as that hollow moon.

The Old Men admiring Themselves in the Water

I heard the old, old men say,
'Everything alters,
And one by one we drop away.'
They had hands like claws, and their knees
Were twisted like the old thorn-trees
By the waters.
I heard the old, old men say,
'All that's beautiful drifts away
Like the waters.'

任時光的潮水磨損蝕裂。

我有一個念頭，只能對你說：
你美麗動人，我也盡心竭力
用古老的崇高方式把你熱愛：
那似曾很幸福，然而我們已經
像那空洞的殘月一樣心灰意冷。

水中自我欣賞的老人

我聽很老的老人說：
「萬物都變易，
我們也一個個凋落。」
他們手如雀爪，雙膝
似水邊的老荊棘樹枝，
疤節生累累。
我聽很老的老人語：
「美好的一切終逝去，
就像這流水。」

O do not Love Too Long

Sweetheart, do not love too long:
I loved long and long,
And grew to be out of fashion
Like an old song.

All through the years of our youth
Neither could have known
Their own thought from the other's,
We were so much at one.

But O, in a minute she changed —
O do not love too long,   10
Or you will grow out of fashion
Like an old song.

呵，別愛得太久

心肝喲，別愛得太久：
我曾久久地愛過，
但結果華年流逝，
像一首過時的歌。

在全部青春歲月裡，
我們誰也分不清
彼此糾纏的思緒；
我們簡直像一人。

可是呵，她一下變了——
呵，別愛得太久，
不然你華年流逝，
像一支過時的曲。

10

1910
The Green Helmet and Other Poems
選自《綠盔及其他》

Words

I had this thought a while ago,
'My darling cannot understand
What I have done, or what would do
In this blind bitter land.'

And I grew weary of the sun
Until my thoughts cleared up again,
Remembering that the best I have done
Was done to make it plain;

That every year I have cried, 'At length
My darling understands it all,   10
Because I have come into my strength,
And words obey my call';

That had she done so who can say
What would have shaken from the sieve?
I might have thrown poor words away
And been content to live.

文字

不久前我曾經這樣思想：
「我的愛人怕不能理解
在這盲目苦難的土地上
我做過或將要做什麼。」

於是我對太陽漸生倦意
直到我思緒重新清晰，
憶想起我最優良的行為
就是曾經誠實地坦白；

每年我都曾哭訴：「終於
我愛人理解了這一切，
因為我已經把力量攢足，
文字也聽從我的驅策」；

假如她理解了誰又能說
篩子中會漏下些什麼？
我也許把蹩腳文字拋却，
心滿意足地去過生活。

10

No Second Troy

Why should I blame her that she filled my days
With misery, or that she would of late
Have taught to ignorant men most violent ways,
Or hurled the little streets upon the great,
Had they but courage equal to desire!
What could have made her peaceful with a mind
That nobleness made simple as a fire,
With beauty like a tightened bow, a kind
That is not natural in an age like this,
Being high and solitary and most stern!   10
Why, what could she have done, being what she is!
Was there another Troy for her to burn?

Reconciliation

Some may have blamed you that you took away
The verses that could move them on the day
When, the ears being deafened, the sight of the eyes blind
With lightning, you went from me, and I could find
Nothing to make a song about but kings,

沒有第二個特洛伊

我何必怪她，說她使我的日子
充滿了不幸，或者說她近來會
教給無知群眾極端狂暴的方式，
或煽動小百姓去與大人物作對，
只要他們有著大如慾望的勇氣？
什麼又能使她安靜？既然生就
被高貴鍛鍊得單純如火的心地，
長得有如滿弓似的美貌，具有
高傲、孤獨和極其嚴肅的品格，
在這樣的時代裡顯得很不協調。　　　　10
嗨，她就這樣，又能做出什麼？
難道還有一個特洛伊供她焚燒？

和解

有的人也許會責怪你，說是你奪走了
那些能夠在那一天感動他們的詩歌，
當時，霹靂把雙耳震聾，閃電把兩眼
耀盲，你離我而去，於是我尋不見
可以製作一首詩歌的素材，除了君主、

Helmets, and swords, and half-forgotten things
That were like memories of you — but now
We'll out, for the world lives as long ago;
And while we're in our laughing, weeping fit,
Hurl helmets, crowns, and swords into the pit.   10
But, dear, cling close to me; since you were gone,
My barren thoughts have chilled me to the bone.

A Drinking Song

Wine comes in at the mouth
And love comes in at the eye;
That's all we shall know for truth
Before we grow old and die.
I lift the glass to my mouth,
I look at you, and I sigh.

頭盔和刀劍，以及半已遺忘的事物——
彷彿是關於你的記憶——但此時此際
我們將退出，因世人生活一如往昔；
我們將在陣陣發作的大笑、大哭之中，
把頭盔、王冠和刀劍統統扔進深坑。　　　　　10
可是，親愛的，抱緊我；自從你走後，
我的貧瘠的思想已寒徹了我的骨頭。

祝酒歌

美酒口中飲，
愛情眼角傳；
我們所知唯此真，
在老死之前。
舉杯至雙唇，
眼望你，我輕嘆。

The Coming of Wisdom with Time

Though leaves are many, the root is one;
Through all the lying days of my youth
I swayed my leaves and flowers in the sun;
Now I may wither into the truth.

The Mask

'Put off that mask of burning gold
With emerald eyes.'
'O no, my dear, you make so bold
To find if hearts be wild and wise,
And yet not cold.'

'I would but find what's there to find,
Love or deceit.'
'It was the mask engaged your mind,
And after set your heart to beat,
Not what's behind.'   10

'But lest you are my enemy,
I must enquire.'

智慧隨時間到來

葉子雖然繁多，根莖却只一條；
在青年時代說謊的日子裡，
我把我的花和葉在陽光裡招搖；
現在，我不妨凋萎成眞理。

面具

「摘下那眼窩鑲嵌翡翠、
閃耀的黃金面具。」
「哦不，親愛的，你如此冒昧
想要知道心兒是否狂野而睿智，
却又不冷不灰。」

「我只要知道應該知道的，
是愛還是欺騙。」
「正是這面具佔據著你的頭腦，
後來又撥動你的心弦，
而不是它後面的眞貌。」

「可是以免你我成爲仇敵，
我一定要求你照辦。」

10

'O no, my dear, let all that be;
What matter, so there is but fire
In you, in me?'

All Things can tempt Me

All things can tempt me from this craft of verse:
One time it was a woman's face, or worse —
The seeming needs of my fool-driven land;
Now nothing but comes readier to the hand
Than this accustomed toil. When I was young,
I had not given a penny for a song
Did not the poet sing it with such airs
That one believed he had a sword upstairs;
Yet would be now, could I but have my wish,
Colder and dumber and deafer than a fish.   10

「哦不，親愛的，讓一切如此；
只要有一團火在你我心中燒燃，
這樣又有什麼關係？」

凡事都能誘使我

凡事都能誘使我拋開這詩歌藝術：
從前是一女人的臉，或更其不如——
我那傻瓜治理的國土貌似的需要；
如今什麼也不比這已習慣的辛勞
來得更得心應手。在我年輕之時，
我從來不曾花一分錢聽一支歌子，
除非那詩人是以那樣的曲調歌唱，
能令人相信他有一把劍藏在樓上；
可是現在，只要我能夠隨心所欲，
我寧願又冷又聾又啞甚於一條魚。　10

Brown Penny

I whispered, 'I am too young,'
And then, 'I am old enough';
Wherefore I threw a penny
To find out if I might love.
'Go and love, go and love, young man,
If the lady be young and fair.'
Ah, penny, brown penny, brown penny,
I am looped in the loops of her hair.

And the penny sang up in my face,
'There is nobody wise enough   10
To find out all that is in it,
For he would be thinking of love
That is looped in the loops of her hair,
Till the loops of time had run.'
Ah, penny, brown penny, brown penny.
One cannot begin it too soon.

銅分幣

我喃喃自語：「我太年輕，」
轉念又想：「我已不算小」；
為此我拋起一枚分幣
占卜戀愛是否還嫌早。
「去愛，去愛，小伙子，
如果姑娘年輕又美好。」
啊，分幣，銅分幣，銅分幣，
我陷入了她的鬈髮圈套。

那分幣面對著我唱起來：
「沒有誰聰明絕頂，　　　　　　　　　　　10
足以窺透其中的奧祕，
那陷入她鬈髮圈套的人
得把愛情久久思尋，
直到時光線圈不再纏繞。」
啊，分幣，銅分幣，銅分幣，
開始戀愛怎麼都不嫌早。

1914
Responsibilities
選自《責任》

To a Friend whose Work has come to Nothing

Now all the truth is out,
Be secret and take defeat
From any brazen throat,
For how can you compete,
Being honour bred, with one
Who, were it proved he lies,
Were neither shamed in his own
Nor in his neighbours' eyes?
Bred to a harder thing
Than Triumph, turn away   10
And like a laughing string
Whereon mad fingers play
Amid a place of stone,
Be secret and exult,
Because of all things known
That is most difficult.

致一位徒勞無功的朋友

如今眞理全淪喪，
對於任何如簧之舌
最好是緘默投降；
你出身高貴，豈可
與那等人物競爭？
縱然是謊言被揭露，
他也會旁若無人，
自己也不覺得害羞。
熟習一件比爭戰
更難之事，轉過臉；　　　　　　　　　　10
好像大笑的琴弦
在亂石成堆的地方
任瘋狂手指撥弄，
默默無語心中狂歡，
因爲已知萬事中
這是最困難的一件。

To a Shade

If you have revisited the town, thin Shade,
Whether to look upon your monument
(I wonder if the builder has been paid)
Or happier-thoughted when the day is spent
To drink of that salt breath out of the sea
When grey gulls hit about instead of men,
And the gaunt houses put on majesty:
Let these content you and be gone again;
For they are at their old tricks yet.

       A man
Of your own passionate serving kind who had brought   10
In his full hands what, had they only known,
Had given their children's children loftier thought,
Sweeter emotion, working in their veins
Like gentle blood, has been driven from the place,
And insult heaped upon him for his pains,
And for his open-handedness, disgrace;
Your enemy, an old foul mouth, had set
The pack upon him.

      Go, unquiet wanderer,
And gather the Glasnevin coverlet
About your head till the dust stops your ear,   20
The time for you to taste of that salt breath

致一個幽魂

如果你曾經重遊故城，瘦鬼，
不論是爲了瞻仰你的紀念碑
（不知工匠是否拿到了薪水）
還是在日暮時帶著更快樂的思憶
來啜飲那來自海上的鹹腥的氣息，
當人聲闃然唯見灰色的海鷗飛舞，
荒涼的屋脊披上晚霞的莊嚴之時：
就讓這些使你滿足然後重新逝去；
因爲他們仍在玩弄故伎。

　　　　　　一個男子
像你那樣熱心爲公，曾雙手滿捧——　　　　　10
但願他們知道——拿出的那些東西，
給予了他們的子孫更爲美好的感情，
更爲高尚的思想，有如溫和的血液
作用於他們的血脈裡，却被逐出此地，
他的辛苦換來了成堆的污穢，
他的慷慨換來了成堆的羞恥；
你的敵人，一張老臭嘴，唆使了群狗
去撕咬他。

　　　　　去吧，不安的遊魂，
用格拉斯內文的被單裹住你的頭，
直到塵土封住你的耳輪，　　　　　　　　　20
你品嚐那鹹腥的海風，在僻靜處

And listen at the corners has not come;

You had enough of sorrow before death —

Away, away! You are safer in the tomb.

September 29, 1913

When Helen lived

We have cried in our despair

That men desert,

For some trivial affair

Or noisy, insolent sport,

Beauty that we have won

From bitterest hours;

Yet we, had we walked within

Those topless towers

Where Helen walked with her boy,

Had given but as the rest   10

Of the men and women of Troy,

A word and a jest.

傾聽的時刻還沒有到來呢；
你生前已有過足夠的憂傷悲苦──
去吧，去吧！你在墓中更安全些。

1913 年 9 月 29 日

海倫在世時

在絕望中我們曾號泣：
為了一點瑣事
或喧鬧、野蠻的競技，
人們竟然放棄
我們歷盡了千辛萬苦
贏得的美人兒；
然而，假如我們漫步
在那些高塔裡，
遇見海倫和她的情侶，
我們也只不過   10
一如特洛伊別的男女，
打個招呼，逗個樂。

Beggar to Beggar cried

'Time to put off the world and go somewhere
And find my health again in the sea air,'
Beggar to beggar cried, being frenzy-struck,
'And make my soul before my pate is bare.'

'And get a comfortable wife and house
To rid me of the devil in my shoes,'
Beggar to beggar cried, being frenzy-struck,
'And the worse devil that is between my thighs.'

'And though I'd marry with a comely lass,
She need not be too comely — let it pass,'   10
Beggar to beggar cried, being frenzy-struck,
'But there's a devil in a looking-glass.'

'Nor should she be too rich, because the rich
Are driven by wealth as beggars by the itch,'
Beggar to beggar cried, being frenzy-struck,
'And cannot have a humorous happy speech.'

'And there I'll grow respected at my ease,
And hear amid the garden's nightly peace,'
Beggar to beggar cried, being frenzy-struck,
'The wind-blown clamour of the barnacle-geese.'   20

乞丐對著乞丐喊

「現在該脫離人世去某個地方
在海風裡重新尋找我的健康，」
瘋狂發作，乞丐對著乞丐喊，
「把靈魂造就趁腦袋尚未禿光。」

「得到一個稱心的老婆和房子，
以便趕跑我鞋子裡面的魔鬼，」
瘋狂發作，乞丐對著乞丐喊，
「和我兩腿之間的更惡的魔鬼。」

「雖然我想娶一個漂亮的女孩，
但不必太漂亮——這沒關係，」
瘋狂發作，乞丐對著乞丐喊，
「可是鏡子裡却現出一個魔鬼。」

「她也不應太富有，因為富人
累於財產猶如乞丐瘙癢難忍，」
瘋狂發作，乞丐對著乞丐喊，
「不可能有風趣談吐令人歡欣。」

「在那裡我將變得悠閒且可敬，
在花園中夜晚的寧靜裡傾聽」
瘋狂發作，乞丐對著乞丐喊，
「北極黑雁御風飛行的擊翅聲。」

10

20

The Mountain Tomb

Pour wine and dance if manhood still have pride,
Bring roses if the rose be yet in bloom;
The cataract smokes upon the mountain side,
Our Father Rosicross is in his tomb.

Pull down the blinds, bring fiddle and clarionet
That there be no foot silent in the room
Nor mouth from kissing, nor from wine unwet;
Our Father Rosicross is in his tomb.

In vain, in vain; the cataract still cries;
The everlasting taper lights the gloom;   10
All wisdom shut into his onyx eyes,
Our Father Rosicross sleeps in his tomb.

山墓

斟酒起舞，如果男兒精力仍旺健，
採來玫瑰，如果玫瑰還在盛開；
那奔流的瀑布嫋嫋生煙在山邊，
我們的羅西克勞斯神父在墓穴裡。

拉下百葉窗，取來提琴和單簧管，
好讓沒有一雙腳沉默在房間裡，
也沒有嘴唇不接吻，酒也不沾；
我們的羅西克勞斯神父在墓穴裡。

徒勞，徒勞；那瀑布依然在吶喊；
那照亮這幽暗的燭光長明不熄；　　　　　　　　10
一切智慧都關進了他石化的眼，
我們的羅西克勞斯神父在墓穴裡。

Fallen Majesty

Although crowds gathered once if she but showed her face,
And even old men's eyes grew dim, this hand alone,
Like some last courtier at a gypsy camping-place
Babbling of fallen majesty, records what's gone.

The lineaments, a heart that laughter has made sweet,
These, these remain, but I record what's gone. A crowd
Will gather, and not know it walks the very street
Whereon a thing once walked that seemed a burning cloud.

The Magi

Now as at all times I can see in the mind's eye,
In their stiff, painted clothes, the pale unsatisfied ones
Appear and disappear in the blue depth of the sky
With all their ancient faces like rain-beaten stones,
And all their helms of silver hovering side by side,
And all their eyes still fixed, hoping to find once more,
Being by Calvary's turbulence unsatisfied,
The uncontrollable mystery on the bestial floor.

亡國之君

雖說，只要她一露面，群眾就會立即聚集，
連老頭子的眼睛也變朦朧，但唯有這隻手，
就像某位前朝遺老在一個吉卜賽人宿營地
喋喋敍說著亡國之君，把逝去的一切記錄。

那容貌，一顆被笑聲薰陶甜美的心，這些，
這些還存在，但我記錄逝去的一切。人群
還會聚集，却不知道他們走過的那條大街，
從前有一尤物就在那兒走，像朵燃燒的雲。

東方三賢

此刻，正如我時時在內心中所見，
那些蒼白的不滿者身穿僵硬的彩衣
在那湛藍幽深的天穹裡時隱時現：
他們蒼老的容顏都好似雨打的岩石，
他們銀製的頭盔在空中聯翩飛舞；
卡爾佛里山的暴行並不使他們滿意，
他們的雙眼仍在凝望，希望再度
在獸性的地面上找到那莫測的神祕。

A Coat

I made my song a coat
Covered with embroideries
Out of old mythologies
From heel to throat;
But the fools caught it,
Wore it in the world's eyes
As though they'd wrought it.
Song, let them take it,
For there's more enterprise
In walking naked.   10

一件外套

我為我的歌兒縫就
一件長長的外套，
上面綴滿剪自古老
神話的花邊刺繡；
但蠢人們把它搶去，
穿上在人前炫示，
儼然出自他們之手。
歌，讓他們拿去，
因為要有更大魄力
才敢於赤身行走。　　　　10

1919
The Wild Swans at Coole
選自《庫勒的野天鵝》

An Irish Airman foresees his Death

I know that I shall meet my fate
Somewhere among the clouds above;
Those that I fight I do not hate,
Those that I guard I do not love;
My country is Kiltartan Cross,
My countrymen Kiltartan's poor,
No likely end could bring them loss
Or leave them happier than before.
Nor law, nor duty bade me fight,
Nor public men, nor cheering crowds,   10
A lonely impulse of delight
Drove to this tumult in the clouds;
I balanced all, brought all to mind,
The years to come seemed waste of breath,
A waste of breath the years behind
In balance with this life, this death.

Men improve with the Years

I am worn out with dreams;

一位愛爾蘭飛行員預見自己的死

我知道我將要遭逢厄運
在頭頂上的雲間的某處；
我對所抗擊者並不仇恨，
我對所保衛者也不愛慕；
我的故鄉是在基爾塔坦，
那裡的窮人是我的同胞，
結局既不會使他們損減，
也不會使他們過得更好。
不是聞人或歡呼的群眾，
或法律或義務使我參戰，
是一股寂寞的愉快衝動
長驅直入這雲中的騷亂；
我回想一切，權衡一切，
未來的歲月似毫無意義，
毫無意義的是以往歲月，
二者平衡在這生死之際。

10

人隨歲月長進

我因多夢而憔悴衰減；

A weather-worn, marble triton
Among the streams;
And all day long I look
Upon this lady's beauty
As though I had found in a book
A pictured beauty,
Pleased to have filled the eyes
Or the discerning ears,
Delighted to be but wise,   10
For men improve with the years;
And yet, and yet,
Is this my dream, or the truth!
O would that we had met
When I had my burning youth!
But I grow old among dreams,
A weather-worn, marble triton
Among the streams.

The Collar-bone of Hare

Would I could cast a sail on the water
Where many a king has gone
And many a king's daughter,

像一尊風雨剝蝕的石雕海神
在溪流中間；
整整一天我都在凝看
這位女士的美貌，
好像在一本書裡發現
一幅畫中美人兒，
因眼睛或聰敏的耳朵
充實而歡欣，
因僅僅智慧而愉悅，　　　　　　　10
因為人隨歲月長進；
可是，可是，
這是我的夢，還是真實？
呵，但願我們相識
在我青春如火時！
但是，我在夢中已變衰殘，
像一尊風雨剝蝕的石雕海神
在溪流中間。

野兔的鎖骨

但願我能夠揚帆遠航，
去眾多君王和君王之女
曾經前去的海上，

And alight at the comely trees and the lawn,

The playing upon pipes and the dancing,

And learn that the best thing is

To change my loves while dancing

And pay but a kiss for a kiss.

I would find by the edge of that water

The collar-bone of a hare   10

Worn thin by the lapping of water,

And pierce it through with a gimlet and stare

At the old bitter world where they marry in churches,

And laugh over the untroubled water

At all who marry in churches,

Through the white thin bone of a hare.

Solomon to Sheba

Sang Solomon to Sheba,

And kissed her dusky face,

'All day long from mid-day

We have talked in the one place,

All day long from shadowless noon

We have gone round and round

抵達那秀美的樹林和草地，
到風笛的樂音和舞蹈中間，
得知最好的事情乃是
在跳舞時頻頻把愛人更換，
僅以一吻回報一吻。

我願在那海岸邊撿到
一隻野兔的鎖骨——   10
被拍岸的浪濤磨薄——
用鑽子把它洞穿，然後
透過那白而且薄的兔骨凝望
那苦難的舊世界——在那裡他們
在教堂裡成婚；且在平靜的海面上
嘲笑所有在教堂裡成婚的人。

所羅門對示巴

所羅門對示巴唱，
吻著她微黑的臉：
「從日中起一整天來
我們都在同一地方交談，
從無影的正午起，整日裡
都圍著愛這狹窄話題

In the narrow theme of love
Like an old horse in a pound.'

To Solomon sang Sheba,
Planted on his knees,   10
'If you had broached a matter
That might the learned please,
You had before the sun had thrown
Our shadows on the ground
Discovered that my thoughts, not it,
Are but a narrow pound.'

Said Solomon to Sheba,
And kissed her Arab eyes,
'There's not a man or woman
Born under the skies   20
Dare match in learning with us two,
And all day long we have found
There's not a thing but love can make
The world a narrow pound.'

一直在轉啊轉，
就像一匹老馬在圈裡。」

穩坐在他膝頭上，
示巴對所羅門唱：   10
「如果你提出一個話題
可以讓博學者歡暢，
在太陽把我們的身影
投到地上之前，你會發現
並非那話題，而是我的思想，
才是一個狹窄的馬圈。」

吻著她的阿拉伯眼睛，
所羅門對示巴說：
「在這天下出生的
男人或女人沒有一個   20
敢與我們倆較量學識，
而一整天來我們發現
除了愛，什麼也不能把世界
變成一個狹窄的馬圈。」

The Scholars

Bald heads forgetful of their sins,
Old, learned, respectable bald heads
Edit and annotate the lines
That young men, tossing on their beds,
Rhymed out in love's despair
To flatter beauty's ignorant ear.

All shuffle there; all cough in ink;
All wear the carpet with their shoes;
All think what other people think;
All know the man their neighbour knows.   10
Lord, what would they say
Did their Catullus walk that way?

His Phoenix

There is a queen in China, or maybe it's in Spain,
And birthdays and holidays such praises can be heard
Of her unblemished lineaments, a whiteness with no stain,
That she might be that sprightly girl trodden by a bird;

學究

禿頭們總不記得他們的罪孽，
年邁、博學、可尊敬的禿頭們，
他們編輯和註釋的那些詩歌
不過是往昔愛情失意的年輕人
在床上輾轉反側之時的傑作：
爲的是奉承美人兒無知的耳朵。

都步履蹣跚；在墨水裡咳嗽；
都在用他們的鞋底把地毯磨損；
都思想著別人所思想的念頭；
都認識他們的鄰居所認識的人。　　　　　10
他們將會說些什麼，我的主，
假如他們的卡圖魯斯那樣走路？

他的不死鳥

在中國有一位王后，或者也許是在西班牙，
每逢壽誕和節慶日都能聽見對她的潔白
無瑕，那無可挑剔的如玉容顏的如此讚誇：
她也許是那被一隻鳥兒踩踏的活潑女孩；

And there's a score of duchesses, surpassing womankind,

Or who have found a painter to make them so for pay

And smooth out stain and blemish with the elegance of his mind:

I knew a phoenix in my youth, so let them have their day.

The young men every night applaud their Gaby's laughing eye,

And Ruth St. Denis had more charm although she had poor luck;   10

From nineteen hundred nine or ten, Pavlova's had the cry,

And there's a player in the States who gathers up her cloak

And flings herself out of the room when Juliet would be bride

With all a woman's passion, a child's imperious way,

And there are — but no matter if there are scores beside:

I knew a phoenix in my youth, so let them have their day.

There's Margaret and Marjorie and Dorothy and Nan,

A Daphne and a Mary who live in privacy;

One's had her fill of lovers, another's had but one,

Another boasts, 'I pick and choose and have but two or three.'   20

If head and limb have beauty and the instep's high and light

They can spread out what sail they please for all I have to say,

Be but the breakers of men's hearts or engines of delight:

I knew a phoenix in my youth, so let them have their day.

There'll be that crowd, that barbarous crowd, through all the centuries,

And who can say but some young belle may walk and talk men wild

Who is my beauty's equal, though that my heart denies,

But not the exact likeness, the simplicity of a child,

還有一大群公爵夫人，風頭出眾的女人們，
或者說她們曾找來一位畫師，爲了酬金
而使她們如此，以靈巧的心思把瑕疵弄平：
我年輕時認識一隻不死鳥，那就讓她們走運。

小伙子們每夜都爲他們的嘉碧的笑眼喝彩；
露絲‧聖德尼斯更有魅力儘管時乖命苦；　　　　　　10
從一九〇九或一〇起，帕夫洛娃獲得青睞；
在美國當茱麗葉即將以一個女人的全部
熱情、一個孩子的蠻橫舉止成爲新娘之時，
有一個演員攏起自己的斗篷，衝出房門，
還有——但此外是否還有一大群也沒關係：
我年輕時認識一隻不死鳥，那就讓她們走運。

還有瑪格瑞特、瑪蕎蕊、多蘿茜、楠等等，
過著隱居生活的一位黛芙妮和一位瑪瑞；
這位有過盡量多的，那位只有過一個情人，
另一位自吹：「我挑來揀去只選中兩三位。」　　　　20
假如頭臉和四肢長得美，腳面又高又輕盈，
她們就會不顧我說的一切任意張開帆篷，
一味去做男人的心的傷害者或快樂的引擎：
我年輕時認識一隻不死鳥，那就讓她們走運。

世世代代都會有那樣一群，那野蠻的人群，
誰能說只有某個年輕美妞會使男人發昏，
堪與我的美人相比——儘管我的心不承認——
却不完全相似，沒有一種童稚般的單純，

And that proud look as though she had gazed into the burning sun,
And all the shapely body no tittle gone astray.   30
I mourn for that most lonely thing; and yet God's will be done:
I knew a phoenix in my youth, so let them have their day.

A Thought from Propertius

She might, so noble from head
To great shapely knees
The long flowing line,
Have walked to the altar
Through the holy images
At Pallas Athena's side,
Or been fit spoil for a centaur
Drunk with the unmixed wine.

Broken Dreams

There is grey in your hair.
Young men no longer suddenly catch their breath

和那彷彿凝神注視燃燒的太陽的驕傲目光，
以及那沒有一絲一毫走樣的體形和風韻。　　　　30
我傷悼那最孤寂的尤物；但天意難以違抗：
我年輕時認識一隻不死鳥，那就讓她們走運。

得自普羅佩提烏斯的一個想法

她，從頭到絕美的
雙膝，那流動的長線條
如此高貴，大可
穿過帕拉斯‧雅典娜
身旁眾多的神聖形象
走向那祭壇，
或者成為一匹醉於醇酒的
人頭馬怪的稱心的獵物。

殘破的夢

你的頭髮裡有灰白色。
你走過時，

When you are passing;

But maybe some old gaffer mutters a blessing

Because it was your prayer

Recovered him upon the bed of death.

For your sole sake — that all heart's ache have known,

And given to others all heart's ache,

From meagre girlhood's putting on

Burdensome beauty — for your sole sake   10

Heaven has put away the stroke of her doom,

So great her portion in that peace you make

By merely walking in a room.

Your beauty can but leave among us

Vague memories, nothing but memories.

A young man when the old men are done talking

Will say to an old man, 'Tell me of that lady

The poet stubborn with his passion sang us

When age might well have chilled his blood.'

Vague memories, nothing but memories,   20

But in the grave all, all, shall be renewed.

The certainty that I shall see that lady

Leaning or standing or walking

In the first loveliness of womanhood,

And with the fervour of my youthful eyes,

Has set me muttering like a fool.

年輕人不再突然屏住他們的呼吸；
但也許某個老頭子會咕噥一句祝福，
因為是你的祈禱
使他在垂死的床上康復。
唯獨為了你──你了解所有的心痛，
並給予別人所有的心痛，
自從細瘦的少女背負起
累贅的美的時候起──唯獨為了你，　　　　　　　10
天國放棄了她那厄運的鐘聲，
在那寧靜中她佔有那麼大一份，
你僅僅在屋子裡走動便製造了那寧靜。

你的美只能在我們中間留下
模糊的記憶，僅僅是記憶。
老人們說完後，一個年輕人
會對一個老人說：「給我講講
雖然老之將至、早已氣血冰涼，
却還硬逗激情的詩人為我們歌唱的女郎。」

模糊的記憶，僅僅是記憶，　　　　　　　　　20
但在墳墓裡，一切，一切都將重來。
確定無疑，我將看見那女郎
或倚靠，或站立，或行走，
帶著成熟女人最初的嫵媚，
和我年輕的雙眼中的熱情：
這使我像傻瓜似地開始囁囁嚅嚅。

You are more beautiful than any one,
And yet your body had a flaw:
Your small hands were not beautiful,
And I am afraid that you will run   30
And paddle to the wrist
In that mysterious, always brimming lake
Where those that have obeyed the holy law
Paddle and are perfect. Leave unchanged
The hands that I have kissed,
For old sake's sake.

The last stroke of midnight dies.
All day in the one chair
From dream to dream and rhyme to rhyme I have ranged
In rambling talk with an image of air: 40
Vague memories, nothing but memories.

A Deep-sworn Vow

Others because you did not keep
That deep-sworn vow have been friends of mine;
Yet always when I look death in the face,
When I clamber to the heights of sleep,

現在你比任何人都美麗，
但你的身上曾有瑕疵：
你的小手以前並不美麗，
我怕你會跑去，　　　　　　　　　　　　30
在那神祕的、永遠充盈的湖裡
玩水，讓湖水浸及手腕：
那些依從了神聖律法者在那裡
嬉水且臻於完美。爲了舊緣故的緣故，
讓那雙我吻過的手
保持不變。

午夜的最後一聲鐘鳴沉寂。
整天都坐在同一張椅子裡，
我從夢想到夢想，從詩韻到詩韻漫遊，
與一個虛幻的影像閒談：　　　　　　　40
模糊的記憶，僅僅是記憶。

深沉的誓言

因爲你不守那深沉的誓言，
別的人就成了我的朋友；
但每當我面對面審視死亡，
每當我攀上睡眠的峰巔，

Or when I grow excited with wine,
Suddenly I meet your face.

The Balloon of the Mind

Hands, do what you're bid:
Bring the balloon of the mind
That bellies and drags in the wind
Into its narrow shed.

On being asked for a War Poem

I think it better that in times like these
A poet's mouth be silent, for in truth
We have no gift to set a statesman right;
He has had enough of meddling who can please
A young girl in the indolence of her youth,
Or an old man upon a winter's night.

或每當我縱酒狂放的時候，
突然我就遇見你的臉龐。

心意的氣球

雙手啊，聽從我的請求：
快把那在風中脹鼓，
冉冉上升的心意的氣球
塞回它狹窄的小屋。

有人求作戰爭詩有感

我想在這樣的時代裡最好
讓詩人緘默，因為事實上
我們沒有天賦以糾正政客；
管夠了閒事的他只會討好
一個青春慵懶的年輕女郎，
或一個寒冬之夜裡的老爹。

Ego Dominus Tuus

Hic. On the grey sand beside the shallow stream
        Under your old wind-beaten tower, where still
        A lamp burns on beside the open book
        That Michael Robartes left, you walk in the moon
        And though you have passed the best of life still trace,
        Enthralled by the unconquerable delusion,
        Magical shapes.
Ille.   By the help of an image
        I call to my own opposite, summon all
        That I have handled least, least looked upon.
Hic. And I would find myself and not an image.   10
Ille. That is our modern hope and by its light
        We have lit upon the gentle, sensitive mind
        And lost the old nonchalance of the hand;
        Whether we have chosen chisel, pen or brush,
        We are but critics, or but half create,
        Timid, entangled, empty and abashed,
        Lacking the countenance of our friends.
Hic.   And yet
        The chief imagination of Christendom,
        Dante Alighieri, so utterly found himself
        That he has made that hollow face of his   20
        More plain to the mind's eye than any face

吾乃爾主

希克：在你那風吹雨打的古塔下面，淺溪
　　　岸邊的灰色沙灘上，一盞燈火猶自
　　　燃亮，在麥克爾·羅巴蒂斯留下的
　　　攤開的書本旁邊；你漫步在月下，
　　　雖然你的最好年華已逝，却依然
　　　被那不可征服的幻想所迷惑，描畫著
　　　祕法的圖符。

伊勒：　　　　借助於一個圖像，
　　　我召喚自己的對立面，召集一切
　　　我一向最少接觸，最少正視者。

希克：我却寧願找到自我，而不是一個圖像。　　　　10

伊勒：那是我們的現代希望，藉它的光亮
　　　我們啓發了高雅、敏感的頭腦
　　　却喪失了古老的手的冷靜；
　　　無論我們選擇鑿子、鵝毛筆還是畫筆，
　　　我們都不過是評論者，或只半具創造性，
　　　又羞怯、又困惑、又空虛、又慚愧，
　　　缺乏朋友們的鼓勵支持。

希克：　　　　　　　　可是
　　　基督教世界的想像主力，
　　　但丁·阿利蓋里，完全地找到了他自己，
　　　竟至於使他那凹陷的臉面　　　　20
　　　比除基督的尊容以外任何面孔

But that of Christ.

Ille.   And did he find himself

Or was the hunger that had made it hollow

A hunger for the apple on the bough

Most out of reach? and is that spectral image

The man that Lapo and that Guide knew?

I think he fashioned from his opposite

An image that might have been a stony face

Staring upon a Bedouin's horse-hair roof

From doored and windowed cliff, or half upturned   30

Among the coarse grass and the camel-dung.

He set his chisel to the hardest stone.

Being mocked by Guide for his lecherous life,

Derided and deriding, driven out

To climb that stair and eat that bitter bread,

He found the unpersuadable justice, he found

The most exalted lady loved by a man.

Hic. Yet surely there are men who have made their art

Out of no tragic war, lovers of life,

Impulsive men that look for happiness   40

And sing when they have found it.

Ille   No, not sing,

For those that love the world serve it in action,

Grow rich, popular and full of influence,

And should they paint or write, still it is action:

The struggle of the fly in marmalade.

都易於在人的心目中顯現。

伊勒： 是他找到了自己，

還是那使他的臉頰凹陷的飢餓

乃是對那最不可及的枝頭上的

蘋果的渴望？那鬼怪似的形象

可就是拉波和基多認識的那個人？

我想，他把他的對立面塑造成

一個形象，那或許曾經是一張

石刻的人面，自鑿有門窗的峭壁

凝望貝都因人的馬毛帳頂，或在 30

粗糙的草莽和駝糞中間半仰朝天。

他把鑿子使在了最硬的石頭上。

雖因生活淫蕩而受到基多嘲笑，

被人嘲笑也嘲笑別人，被逐出

去爬那樓梯，吃那苦麵包，

但他找到了不可動搖的正義，他找到了

那為一個男人所愛、備受讚美的女人。

希克：但確還有人不用悲慘的戰爭為題材

而造就了他們的藝術：他們是

生活的熱愛者、感情衝動的人們， 40

他們尋找歡樂且在找到時歌唱。

伊勒： 不，並不歌唱，

因為那些熱愛塵世的人以行動為它服務，

變得有錢財、有名望且有權勢，

即使他們繪畫或寫作，那仍然是行動：

橘皮醬裡的蒼蠅的掙扎。

The rhetorician would deceive his neighbours,

The sentimentalist himself; while art

Is but a vision of reality.

What portion in the world can the artist have

Who has awakened from the common dream   50

But dissipation and despair?

Hic.   And yet

No one denies to Keats love of the world;

Remember his deliberate happiness.

Ille. His art is happy, but who knows his mind?

I see a schoolboy when I think of him,

With face and nose pressed to a sweet-shop window,

For certainly he sank into his grave

His senses and his heart unsatisfied,

And made — being poor, ailing and ignorant,

Shut out from all the luxury of the world,   60

The coarse-bred son of a livery-stable keeper —

Luxuriant song.

Hic.   Why should you leave the lamp

Bunning alone beside an open book,

And trace these characters upon the sands?

A style is found by sedentary toil

And by the imitation of great masters.

Ille. Because I seek an image, not a book.

Those men that in their writings are most wise

Own nothing but their blind, stupefied hearts.

巧言善辯者會欺騙他的鄰人，

濫情感傷者則欺騙他自己；而藝術

不過是現實的一個幻景。

從平庸的夢裡醒來的藝術家

除了放浪和絕望，還能擁有　　　　　　　　　　　50

世界的哪一部分？

希克：　　　　　　　可是，

沒有誰拒絕濟慈熱愛人世；

想想他那故做的歡樂。

伊勒：他的藝術是歡樂的，但誰了解他的心思？

當我想起他的時候，我就看見一個學童，

臉蛋和鼻子貼在一家糖果店的櫥窗上，

因為無疑，他沉入了墓穴之中，

感官和心都沒有得到滿足，

却製作出——身為一個車馬行看守的

教養粗鄙的兒子，貧窮、病弱、無知，　　　　　60

被排斥在人間的一切奢侈之外——

奢華的歌。

希克：　　　　你何必要把那燈火留在

一本攤開的書旁邊獨自燃燒，

却在沙灘上追尋這些人物？

一種風格通過伏案辛勞

和摹仿大師就找得到。

伊勒：因為我尋找一個圖像，而非一本書。

那些在他們的著作中顯得最聰明的人

除了盲目、呆滯的心什麼也沒有。

I call to the mysterious one who yet   70
  Shall walk the wet sands by the edge of the stream
And look most like me, being indeed my double,
And prove of all imaginable things
The most unlike, being my anti-self,
And standing by these characters disclose
All that I seek; and whisper it as though
He were afraid the birds, who cry aloud
Their momentary cries before it is dawn,
Would carry it away to blasphemous men.

A Prayer on going into my House

God grant a blessing on this tower and cottage
And on my heirs, if all remain unspoiled,
No table or chair or stool not simple enough
For shepherd lads in Galilee; and grant
That I myself for portions of the year
May handle nothing and set eyes on nothing
But what the great and passionate have used
Throughout so many varying centuries
We take it for the norm; yet should I dream
Sinbad the sailor's brought a painted chest,   10

我召喚那神祕的一位——他仍將　　　　　　　70
漫步在那溪邊潮濕的沙灘上，
與我極其相像，確是我的副本；
却原來在所有可以想見的事物中
最與我不同，是我的反自性；
並且站在這些人物旁邊揭示出
我所尋求的一切；低聲陳說，好像
他害怕那些鳥兒——破曉前
它們大聲啼叫暫時的啼叫——
會把它銜去送給不敬神的人們。

入宅祈禱

上帝，請賜福給這塔堡和農舍，
給我的繼嗣，如果一切都保留完好，
桌子、椅子或凳子無不簡單得足以
招待加利利的牧童；請恩准
我自己在一年裡的若干時候
可以什麼也不處理，什麼也不過目，
除了風雲變幻的許多世紀以來，偉大
和富有激情的人物一直沿用，以至
被我們奉為典範的東西；可是，假如
我夢見水手辛巴達從磁山那邊　　　　　　　10

Or image, from beyond the Loadstone Mountain,
That dream is a norm; and should some limb of the devil
Destroy the view by cutting down an ash
That shades the road, or setting up a cottage
Planned in a government office, shorten his life,
Manacle his soul upon the Red Sea bottom.

The Phases of the Moon

An old man cocked his ear upon a bridge;
He and his friend, their faces to the South,
Had trod the uneven road. Their boots were soiled,
Their Connemara cloth worn out of shape;
They had kept a steady pace as though their beds,
Despite a dwindling and late risen moon,
Were distant still. An old man cocked his ear.

Aherne. What made that sound!
Robartes.   A rat or water-hen
    Splashed, or an otter slid into the stream.
    We are on the bridge; that shadow is the tower,   10
    And the light proves that he is reading still.
    He has found, after the manner of his kind,

攜來一個彩繪的匣子或圖像的話，

那夢就是一個典範；而假如魔鬼的

某個爪牙砍倒一棵蔭覆道路的梣樹，

或建起一座在政府機關裡設計的別墅，

破壞了風景，就請縮短他的壽命，

把他的靈魂鎮鎖在紅海底下。

月相

一個老人在一座橋上豎起他的耳朵；

他和他的朋友，他們的臉朝南方，

走過了不平的道路。他們的靴子很髒，

他們的康吶瑪拉布袍破損得不成形狀；

他們一直保持從容的步伐，不顧那

一爿漸虧的初升的月亮，似乎他們的臥榻

仍在遠方。一個老人豎起他的耳朵。

阿赫恩：是什麼發出那聲響？

羅巴蒂斯： 一隻老鼠或水雞

濺水，或一隻水獺滑進了溪水裡。

我們是在橋上；那影子是那座塔， 10

那燈光證明他還在讀書。

他照他那類人的方式，僅僅找到了

Mere images; chosen this place to live in

Because, it may be, of the candle-light

From the far tower where Milton's Platonist

Sat late, or Shelley's visionary prince:

The lonely light that Samuel Palmer engraved,

An image of mysterious wisdom won by toil;

And now he seeks in book or manuscript

What he shall never find.   20

Aherne.   Why should not you

Who know it all ring at his door, and speak

Just truth enough to show that his whole life

Will scarcely find for him a broken crust

Of all those truths that are your daily bread;

And when you have spoken take the roads again?

Robartes. He wrote of me in that extravagant style

He had learned from Pater, and to round his tale

Said I was dead; and dead I choose to be.

Aherne. Sing me the changes of the moon once more;

True song, though speech: 'mine author sung it me'.   30

Robartes. Twenty-and-eight the phases of the moon,

The full and the moon's dark and all the crescents,

Twenty-and-eight, and yet but six-and-twenty

The cradles that a man must needs be rocked in;

For there's no human life at the full or the dark.

From the first crescent to the half, the dream

But summons to adventure, and the man

形象；選擇了這個地方居住，

也許，是由於來自彌爾頓的柏拉圖主義者

或雪萊幻想的王子在其中熬夜的

那遙遠的塔樓裡的燭火：

塞繆爾・帕爾默刻畫的那寂寞的燈光，

一個靠辛勞贏得的神祕智慧的形象；

而現在，他在書籍或手稿中尋找

他將永遠也找不到的東西。　　　　　　20

阿赫恩：　　　　　　　　　你洞知一切，

何不去搖響他的門鈴，說出

適當的真理，便足以顯示他畢生

都難以為自己找到所有那些

充當你日常食糧的真理的一塊碎屑；

說完後你再重新上路？

羅巴蒂斯：他以那種學自佩特的浮華

風格寫我，且為了使他的故事圓滿

而說我死了；我倒寧願是死了。

阿赫恩：再給我唱一遍月相的變化吧；

雖是言辭，實為真歌：「造吾者為吾歌此」。　30

羅巴蒂斯：二十八種，月之變相，

月望月晦和種種盈虧之相，

共計二十八，但只有二十六種

是人必須育於其中的搖籃；

因為月望月晦時沒有人類生命。

從初一新月到上弦月，夢

只是召喚人去歷險，人

Is always happy like a bird or a beast;

But while the moon is rounding towards the full

He follows whatever whim's most difficult   40

Among whims not impossible, and though scarred,

As with the cat-o'-nine-tails of the mind,

His body moulded from within his body

Grows comelier. Eleven pass, and then

Athena takes Achilles by the hair,

Hector is in the dust, Nietzsche is born,

Because the hero's crescent is the twelfth.

And yet, twice born, twice buried, grow he must,

Before the full moon, helpless as a worm.

The thirteenth moon but sets the soul at war   50

In its own being, and when that war's begun

There is no muscle in the arm; and after,

Under the frenzy of the fourteenth moon,

The soul begins to tremble into stillness,

To die into the labyrinth of itself!

Aherne. Sing out the song; sing to the end, and sing

The strange reward of all that discipline.

Robartes. All thought becomes an image and the soul

Becomes a body: that body and that soul

Too perfect at the full to lie in a cradle,   60

Too lonely for the traffic of the world:

Body and soul cast out and cast away

Beyond the visible world.

就像鳥獸一樣永遠快樂；

但是隨著月亮漸臻圓滿，

他遵從並非不可能的異想中   40

任何最困難的異想；雖有疤痕，

就好像被心意的九尾貓所撓，

他那從他身體內部翻鑄出的身體

越來越俊美。十一相過去，於是

雅典娜揪住阿基里斯的頭髮，

赫克特在塵埃裡，尼采降生，

因爲英雄的月相是第十二。

但是，在滿月之前，他必兩度出生，

兩度入葬，變得像蠕蟲般柔弱無助。

第十三相只是使靈魂在其自身   50

存在中開戰，那戰爭開始後，

手臂却無肌肉；然後，

在第十四相的狂亂之下，

靈魂開始顫巍巍步入寧靜，

死在其自身的迷宮之中！

阿赫恩：把那歌唱出來；唱到結尾，唱

    那全部戒行的奇異果報。

羅巴蒂斯：一切思想都變成一個形象，靈魂

    則變成一個肉體：那肉體和那靈魂

    在滿月時太完美而無法躺在搖籃裡，   60

    太寂寞而不適合人世的熙來攘往：

    被驅逐和被拋棄到現實世界

    之外的肉體和靈魂。

Aherne.   All dreams of the soul

    End in a beautiful man's or woman's body.

Robartes. Have you not always known it?

Aherne   The song will have it

    That those that we have loved got their long fingers

    From death, and wounds, or on Sinai's top,

    Or from some bloody whip in their own hands.

    They ran from cradle to cradle till at last

    Their beauty dropped out of the loneliness   70

    Of body and soul.

Robartes.   The lover's heart knows that.

Aherne. It must be that the terror in their eyes

    Is memory or foreknowledge of the hour

    When all is fed with light and heaven is bare.

Robartes. When the moon's full those creatures of the full

    Are met on the waste hills by country men

    Who shudder and hurry by: body and soul

    Estranged amid the strangeness of themselves,

    Caught up in contemplation, the mind's eye

    Fixed upon images that once were thought,   80

    For perfected, completed, and immovable

    Images can break the solitude

    Of lovely, satisfied, indifferent eyes.

    And thereupon with aged, high-pitched voice

    Aherne laughed, thinking of the man within,

阿赫恩：　　　　　　　　靈魂的所有夢想

　都歸結於一個俊男或美女的肉體之中。

羅巴蒂斯：難道你不總是知道這一點嗎？

阿赫恩：　　　　　　　　　　　　歌裡將唱到

　我們曾經愛戀過的那些人兒從死亡和創傷，

　或西奈的山頂上，或從她們自己手中

　血淋淋的鞭子，得到纖長的手指。

　她們從搖籃跑到搖籃，直到最後

　她們的美由於肉體和靈魂的　　　　　　　　　70

　寂寞而隕落。

羅巴蒂斯：　　戀人的心知道這個。

阿赫恩：無疑，她們眼神中的恐怖

　是對那一切都沐浴著光、天空

　毫無遮掩的時刻的記憶或預知。

羅巴蒂斯：月圓之時，在荒山野嶺上，

　瑟瑟發抖、匆匆跑過的鄉下人會遇見

　那些圓月的產物：肉體和靈魂

　在他們自身的陌生之中疏離，

　陷入沉思觀想，心目

　凝注於從前是思想的形象，　　　　　　　　　80

　因為彼此分離、完美無缺且不可動搖的

　形象能夠打破美麗、

　滿足、超然的眼睛的孤寂。

　此時，阿赫恩想起那塔裡的人、

　他那不眠的燭火和辛勤的筆，

His skepless candle and laborious pen.

Robartes. And after that the crumbling of the moon:

　　The soul remembering its loneliness

　　Shudders in many cradles; all is changed.

　　It would be the world's servant, and as it serves,　　　　90

　　Choosing whatever task's most difficult

　　Among tasks not impossible, it takes

　　Upon the body and upon the soul

　　The coarseness of the drudge.

Aherne.　　　　　　　　　　Before the full

　　It sought itself and afterwards the world.

Robartes. Because you are forgotten, half out of life,

　　And never wrote a book, your thought is clear.

　　Reformer, merchant, statesman, learned man,

　　Dutiful husband, honest wife by turn,

　　Cradle upon cradle, and all in flight and all　　　　100

　　Deformed, because there is no deformity

　　But saves us from a dream.

Aherne.　　　　　　　　　　And what of those

　　That the last servile crescent has set free?

Robartes. Because all dark, like those that are all light,

　　They are cast beyond the verge, and in a cloud,

　　Crying to one another like the bats;

　　But having no desire they cannot tell

　　What's good or bad, or what it is to triumph

遂發出蒼老、尖銳的大笑聲。

羅巴蒂斯：然後是月亮破碎：

　　仍記得其寂寞的靈魂

　　在許多搖籃裡顫抖；一切都變了。

　　它願做塵世的奴僕，在它選擇　　　　　　90

　　並非不可能的差使中任何

　　最困難的差使服役時，它給

　　肉體和靈魂都加上了

　　苦役的粗鄙。

阿赫恩：　　　　在月圓之前

　　它尋求自己，之後則追求塵世。

羅巴蒂斯：因為你被人遺忘，半出離生活，

　　又從未寫過一本書，所以你的思想清晰。

　　改良者、商賈、政治家、博學者、

　　有責任心的丈夫、忠實的妻子等

　　輪流出入一個又一個搖籃，都在逃亡，　　100

　　都被毀容變形，因為醜陋的畸形

　　無不把我們從幻夢中驚醒。

阿赫恩：　　　　　　那最後的

　　奴性的月相所釋放的那些又怎樣？

羅巴蒂斯：因為全晦暗者，猶如那些全光明者，

　　他們被拋到了邊緣以外，在一團雲霧中

　　像蝙蝠一樣朝著彼此叫喚；

　　但是由於沒有慾望，他們無法分辨

　　孰善孰惡，也不知道在自己的

At the perfection of one's own obedience;

And yet they speak what's blown into the mind;   110

Deformed beyond deformity, unformed,

Insipid as the dough before it is baked,

They change their bodies at a word.

Aherne.   And then?

Robartes. When all the dough has been so kneaded up

That it can take what form cook Nature fancies,

The first thin crescent is wheeled round once more.

Aherne. But the escape; the song's not finished yet.

Robartes. Hunchback and Saint and Fool are the last crescents.

The burning bow that once could shoot an arrow

Out of the up and down, the wagon-wheel   120

Of beauty's cruelty and wisdom's chatter —

Out of that raving tide — is drawn betwixt

Deformity of body and of mind.

Aherne. Were not our beds far off I'd ring the bell,

Stand under the rough roof-timbers of the hall

Beside the castle door, where all is stark

Austerity, a place set out for wisdom

That he will never find; I'd play a part;

He would never know me after all these years

But take me for some drunken country man;   130

I'd stand and mutter there until he caught

'Hunchback and Saint and Fool', and that they came

Under the three last crescents of the moon,

臣服臻於極致時有什麼可得意；

而且他們道聽途說，人云亦云； 110

形容損無可損，簡直無形可言，

就好像麵團烤熟之前一樣淡而無味，

他們說話間就能變化形體。

阿赫恩： 然後呢？

羅巴蒂斯：當整個麵團都被如此揉好，

能夠塑成造化廚娘所喜歡的任何形狀時，

初一的細芽新月又再一次輪轉。

阿赫恩：但有所遺漏；這歌還沒有唱完。

羅巴蒂斯：駝背、聖人、傻子是最後的殘月。

出自那盛衰盈虧、從前能夠

射箭的燃燒的弓、美之殘酷 120

和智慧之饒舌的車輪——

出自那咆哮的浪潮——被拖入

肉體與心靈的醜陋畸形之間。

阿赫恩：要不是我們的臥榻遙遠，我就會搖響那門鈴，

站在那塔堡門邊大廳的粗糙的

屋椽下面，那裡一切都十分

簡樸，是一個為他永遠也找不到的

智慧佈置的地方；我要演一齣戲；

過了這麼多年，他絕不會認出我來，

只會把我當做某個喝醉了的鄉下人； 130

我會站在那裡咕咕噥噥，等他聽到

「駝背、聖徒、傻子」，以及他們在

最後的三種月相之下出世，

And then I'd stagger out. He'd crack his wits
Day after day, yet never find the meaning.

And then he laughed to think that what seemed hard
Should be so simple — a bat rose from the hazels
And circled round him with its squeaky cry,
The light in the tower window was put out.

那時我就蹣跚而出。他將日復一日
傷腦筋，却永遠想不出其中含義。

於是他大笑，想到，似乎困難的事情
竟如此簡單——一隻蝙蝠從榛樹叢中飛起，
尖銳地叫著，繞著他盤旋；
那塔樓窗戶裡的燭光熄滅了。

1921
Michael Robartes and the Dancer
選自《麥克爾‧羅巴蒂斯與舞蹈者》

Michael Robartes and the Dancer

He. Opinion is not worth a rush;

    In this altar-piece the knight,

    Who grips his long spear so to push

    That dragon through the fading light,

    Loved the lady; and it's plain

    The half-dead dragon was her thought,

    That every morning rose again

    And dug its claws and shrieked and fought.

    Could the impossible come to pass

    She would have time to turn her eyes,   10

    Her lover thought, upon the glass

    And on the instant would grow wise.

She. You mean they argued.

He.   Put it so;

    But bear in mind your lover's wage

    Is what your looking-glass can show,

    And that he will turn green with rage

    At all that is not pictured there.

She. May I not put myself to college?

He. Go pluck Athena by the hair;

    For what mere book can grant a knowledge   20

    With an impassioned gravity

    Appropriate to that beating breast,

麥克爾・羅巴蒂斯與舞蹈者

他：意見不值一根燈芯草；
　　在這祭壇畫上，那騎士——
　　他那樣緊握長矛
　　透過暮色向那惡龍猛刺——
　　愛那淑女；顯然
　　那半死的龍是她的思想，
　　每天早晨重新醒轉，
　　張牙舞爪、咆哮抵抗。
　　假如不可能之事也會發生，
　　她的愛人想，她就有時間　　　　　　　　　10
　　把目光轉向梳妝鏡，
　　剎那間變得聰明淑賢。
她：你是說他們彼此爭論。
他：　　　　　　　　　　　可以這麼說；
　　但是要記住，你的愛人所得薪金
　　就是你的梳妝鏡所能顯示的一切；
　　而他會變得臉色鐵青，
　　對那裡映不出的一切怒氣勃發。
她：難道我不可以去上學？
他：去拔雅典娜的頭髮吧！
　　什麼樣的書本能傳授一種？　　　　　　　20
　　知識，既熱情又莊重，
　　適合那跳動的胸部、

That vigorous thigh, that dreaming eye?

And may the devil take the rest.

She. And must no beautiful woman be

　　Learned like a man!

He. 　　　　　　　　Paul Veronese

　　And all his sacred company

　　Imagined bodies all their days

　　By the lagoon you love so much,

　　For proud, soft, ceremonious proof　　　　　　　30

　　That all must come to sight and touch;

　　While Michael Angelo's Sistine roof,

　　His 'Morning' and his 'Night' disclose

　　How sinew that has been pulled tight,

　　Or it may be loosened in repose,

　　Can rule by supernatural right

　　Yet be but sinew.

She. 　　　　　　I have heard said

　　There is great danger in the body.

He. Did God in portioning wine and bread

　　Give man His thought or His mere body?　　　　40

She. My wretched dragon is perplexed.

He. I have principles to prove me right.

　　It follows from this Latin text

　　That blest souls are not composite,

　　And that all beautiful women may

　　Live in uncomposite blessedness,

　　那健壯的大腿、那朦朧的眼睛？

　　但願魔鬼把其餘的都拿去。

她：難道就不許有美女

　　像男人一樣博學？

他：　　　　　　　保羅‧維若奈斯

　　和他所有虔誠的伴侶

　　畢其一生都在你熱愛的

　　鹹水湖邊構思種種肉體，

　　它們都必須變得摸得著看得清，　　　　　30

　　作為驕傲、溫柔、堂皇的證據；

　　而米開朗基羅的西斯廷穹頂、

　　他的《晨》和《夜》都昭揭

　　那被拉緊，或在休息時

　　可能放鬆的筋肉如何

　　能夠憑超自然的權力統治，

　　却又不過是筋肉而已。

她：　　　　　　　我聽說

　　肉體中有極大的危機。

他：上帝在分酒和麵包的時刻

　　給人的是思想還是僅僅肉體？　　　　　40

她：我可憐的龍已被弄糊塗。

他：我有原理可證明我正確。

　　從這拉丁文本中可以得出：

　　有福的靈魂不是混合的；

　　假如她們願意摒棄各種思想，

　　所有美女就都可能會

And lead us to the like — if they
Will banish every thought, unless
The lineaments that please their view
When the long looking-glass is full,   50
Even from the foot-sole think it too.
She. They say such different things at school.

Easter, 1916

I have met them at close of day
Coming with vivid faces
From counter or desk among grey
Eighteenth-century houses.
I have passed with a nod of the head
Or polite meaningless words,
Or have lingered awhile and said
Polite meaningless words,
And thought before I had done
Of a mocking tale or a gibe   10
To please a companion
Around the fire at the club,
Being certain that they and I
But lived where motley is worn:

生活在單純的幸福之鄉，
且引導我們趨向類似境界，除非
當長形的梳妝鏡映滿時，
那使她們得意的曲線體形　　　　　　　　　　50
甚至從腳底也認為如此。
她：人家學校裡講的是那麼不同。

1916 年復活節

日暮時分我曾遇見他們，
一張張生動活潑的臉
來自十八世紀的灰房中
辦公桌或櫃台的後面。
擦肩而過時，我點點頭
或談些無意義的閒話，
或偶爾稍事盤桓說幾句
禮貌而無意義的閒話，
而話未說完我就想出了
一個諷刺故事或趣聞，　　　　　　　　　　10
好去俱樂部裡擁火而坐
講給一個伙伴來開心，
因為，我確信他們和我
不過像丑角一樣生活：

All changed, changed utterly:
A terrible beauty is born.

That woman's days were spent
In ignorant good-will,
Her nights in argument
Until her voice grew shrill.   20
What voice more sweet than hers
When, young and beautiful,
She rode to harriers?
This man had kept a school
And rode our winged horse;
This other his helper and friend
Was coming into his force;
He might have won fame in the end,
So sensitive his nature seemed,
So daring and sweet his thought.   30
This other man I had dreamed
A drunken, vainglorious lout.
He had done most bitter wrong
To some who are near my heart,
Yet I number him in the song;
He, too, has resigned his part
In the casual comedy;
He, too, has been changed in his turn,
Transformed utterly:

一切都變了，徹底變了：
一個可怕的美誕生了。

那個女人的白晝都耗費
在無知的良好意願裡，
在夜晚則與人辯論爭執
直到她嗓音變得尖厲。　　　　　　　　　　20
當年她也曾年輕又美麗，
在她騎馬打獵的時光，
那甜美的嗓音誰能相比？
這個男人曾開辦學堂，
而且也乘騎我們的飛馬；
這另一位是他的友人，
將與他聯合幫助他謀劃；
他的天性如此地銳敏，
他的思想既大膽又清新，
最終他也許贏得名氣。　　　　　　　　　　30
我所想到的這另一個人
是個虛榮粗鄙的醉鬼。
他曾經對我貼心的人兒
做過極端刻薄的事情，
而我在歌裡仍把他提起；
他也辭去了在那即興
喜劇中他所扮演的角色；
在輪到他時也改變了，
他已被徹底地改弦易轍：

A terrible beauty is born.   40

Hearts with one purpose alone
Through summer and winter seem
Enchanted to a stone
To trouble the living stream.
The horse that comes from the road,
The rider, the birds that range
From cloud to tumbling cloud,
Minute by minute they change;
A shadow of cloud on the stream
Changes minute by minute;   50
A horse-hoof slides on the brim,
And a horse plashes within it;
The long-legged moor-hens dive,
And hens to moor-cocks call;
Minute by minute they live:
The stone's in the midst of all.

Too long a sacrifice
Can make a stone of the heart.
O when may it suffice?
That is Heaven's part, our part   60
To murmur name upon name,
As a mother names her child
When sleep at last has come
On limbs that had run wild.

一個可怕的美誕生了。　　　　　　　　　40

眾多的心只有一個目的，
經過盛夏和嚴冬似乎
中了魔法被變成了頑石，
要把活潑的溪流攔阻。
大路上奔馳而來的馬匹、
騎馬的人、翻飛盤旋
在翻滾的層雲間的鳥兒，
一分鐘一分鐘地變幻；
溪水上倒映的雲影一片
變幻，一分又一分鐘；　　　　　　　　50
一隻馬蹄滑陷在溪水邊，
一匹馬濺水在溪流中；
長腿雌水雞向水裡跳躍，
雌雞把雄雞聲聲呼喚；
一分鐘一分鐘它們生活：
那頑石在這一切中間。

一場犧牲奉獻太長太久
能夠把心靈變成頑石。
呵，什麼時候才算個夠？
那是天命；我們的事　　　　　　　　　60
是低喚一個又一個名姓，
像母親呼喚她的孩子，
當昏沉的睡意終於降臨
在野跑的肢體之上時。

What is it but nightfall?
No, no, not night but death;
Was it needless death after all?
For England may keep faith
For all that is done and said.
We know their dream; enough   70
To know they dreamed and are dead;
And what if excess of love
Bewildered them till they died?
I write it out in a verse —
MacDonagh and MacBride
And Connolly and Pearse
Now and in time to be,
Wherever green is worn,
Are changed, changed utterly:
A terrible beauty is born.   80

      September 25, 1916

On a Political Prisoner

She that but little patience knew,
From childhood on, had now so much
A grey gull lost its fear and flew

要不是夜色那又是什麼？
不，不是黑夜而是死；
畢竟那死亡是否不值得？
因為英國可能守信義，
對於所做和所說的一切。
我們知道他們的夢寐；　　　　　　　　　　　70
知道他們夢過且已死了，
足矣；如果過度的愛
把他們迷惑至死又如何？
我把一切用詩寫出來──
麥克多納和麥克布萊德，
康諾利和皮爾斯之輩，
無論是現在還是在將來，
只要有地方佩戴綠色，
他們都會變，變得徹底：
一個可怕的美誕生了。　　　　　　　　　　　80

　　　1916 年 9 月 25 日

關於一名政治犯

她從小就不大有耐心，
如今竟能使一隻灰鷗
丟掉它的恐懼，飛進

Down to her cell and there alit,
And there endured her fingers' touch
And from her fingers ate its bit.

Did she in touching that lone wing
Recall the years before her mind
Became a bitter, an abstract thing,
Her thought some popular enmity: 10
Blind and leader of the blind
Drinking the foul ditch where they lie?

When long ago I saw her ride
Under Ben Bulben to the meet,
The beauty of her country-side
With all youth's lonely wildness stirred,
She seemed to have grown clean and sweet
Like any rock-bred, sea-borne bird:

Sea-borne, or balanced on the air
When first it sprang out of the nest   20
Upon some lofty rock to stare
Upon the cloudy canopy,
While under its storm-beaten breast
Cried out the hollows of the sea.

她的小小囚室內棲止，
在那裡接受她的愛撫，
從她指尖上頻頻啄食。

撫摸著那孤獨的翅膀，
她可曾憶起往昔歲月，
在心靈變得苦澀抽象，
思想變成了公敵之前：　　　　　　　　　　　10
群盲和群盲的領導者
躺在臭水溝裡喝得歡？

多年前我看見她騎馬
經布爾本山下去會獵，
鄉間的美人兒引得那
青年人寂寞的心狂跳，
她已出落得甜美皎潔
好像山育海生的鷗鳥：

出自波濤，翱翔空際，
第一次它從高高山岩　　　　　　　　　　　20
某處的窠巢飛躍出來，
凝望濃雲密佈的天幕，
風暴擊打的胸膛下面
是大海的波谷在號呼。

The Second Coming

Turning and turning in the widening gyre
The falcon cannot hear the falconer;
Things fall apart; the centre cannot hold;
Mere anarchy is loosed upon the world,
The blood-dimmed tide is loosed, and everywhere
The ceremony of innocence is drowned;
The best lack all conviction, while the worst
Are full of passionate intensity.

Surely some revelation is at hand;
Surely the Second Coming is at hand.   10
The Second Coming! Hardly are those words out
When a vast image out of *Spiritus Mundi*
Troubles my sight: somewhere in sands of the desert
A shape with lion body and the head of a man,
A gaze blank and pitiless as the sun,
Is moving its slow thighs, while all about it
Reel shadows of the indignant desert birds.
The darkness drops again; but now I know
That twenty centuries of stony sleep
Were vexed to nightmare by a rocking cradle,   20
And what rough beast, its hour come round at last,
Slouches towards Bethlehem to be born?

再度降臨

盤旋盤旋在漸漸開闊的螺旋中，
獵鷹再聽不見馴鷹人的呼聲；
萬物崩散；中心難再維繫；
世界上散布著一派狼籍，
血污的潮水到處氾濫，
把純真的禮俗吞噬；
優秀的人們缺乏信念，
卑劣之徒却狂囂一時。

確乎有某種啓示近在眼前；
確乎「再度降臨」近在眼前。   10
「再度降臨」！這幾個字尚未出口，
驀地一個巨大形象出自「世界靈魂」，
闖入我的眼界：在大漠的塵沙裡，
一個獅身人面的形體，
目光似太陽茫然而冷酷，
正挪動著遲鈍的腿股；它周圍處處
旋舞著憤怒的沙漠野禽的陰影。
黑暗重新降臨；但如今我明白
那兩千年僵臥如石的沉睡
已被一隻搖籃攪擾成惡夢，   20
於是何等惡獸——它的時辰終於到來——
懶洋洋走向伯利恆去投生？

A Prayer for my Daughter

Once more the storm is howling, and half hid
Under this cradle-hood and coverlid
My child sleeps on. There is no obstacle
But Gregory's wood and one bare hill
Whereby the haystack- and roof-levelling wind,
Bred on the Atlantic, can be stayed;
And for an hour I have walked and prayed
Because of the great gloom that is in my mind.

I have walked and prayed for this young child an hour
And heard the sea-wind scream upon the tower,   10
And under the arches of the bridge, and scream
In the elms above the flooded stream;
Imagining in excited reverie
That the future years had come,
Dancing to a frenzied drum,
Out of the murderous innocence of the sea.

May she be granted beauty and yet not
Beauty to make a stranger's eye distraught,
Or hers before a looking-glass, for such,
Being made beautiful overmuch,   20
Consider beauty a sufficient end,
Lose natural kindness and maybe

爲我女兒的祈禱

風暴又一次咆哮；半掩
在這搖籃的篷罩和被巾下面，
我的孩子依然安睡。除去
葛列格里的樹林和一座禿丘，
再沒有任何屏障足以阻擋
那起自大西洋上的掀屋大風；
我踱步祈禱已一個時辰，
因爲那巨大陰影籠罩在我心上。

爲這幼女我踱步祈禱了一個時辰，
耳聽著海風呼嘯在高塔頂，   10
在橋拱下，在氾濫的溪水上，
在溪邊的楡樹林中迴盪；
在興奮的幻想中自認
未來的歲月已經來到：
踏著狂亂的鼓點舞蹈，
來自大海的兇殘的天眞。

願她天生美麗，但不至
美得使陌生人的眼光癡迷，
或使自己在鏡前得意，因爲
這種人由於生得過分艷麗，   20
便把美看作是自足的目的，
從而喪失天性的善良，還可能

The heart-revealing intimacy
That chooses right, and never find a friend.

Helen being chosen found life flat and dull
And later had much trouble from a fool,
While that great Queen, that rose out of the spray,
Being fatherless could have her way
Yet chose a bandy-leggèd smith for man.
It's certain that fine women eat   30
A crazy salad with their meat
Whereby the Horn of Plenty is undone.

In courtesy I'd have her chiefly learned;
Hearts are not had as a gift but hearts are earned
By those that are not entirely beautiful;
Yet many, that have played the fool
For beauty's very self, has charm made wise,
And many a poor man that has roved,
Loved and thought himself beloved,
From a glad kindness cannot take his eyes.   40

May she become a flourishing hidden tree
That all her thoughts may like the linnet be,
And have no business but dispensing round
Their magnanimities of sound,
Nor but in merriment begin a chase,
Nor but in merriment a quarrel.

失去推心置腹、擇善而從的交情，
永遠也找不到一個伴侶。

海倫命定要感到生活平淡，
後來因一個蠢漢惹來許多麻煩，
而那從浪花中升起的偉大女王，
因沒有生父便可以自做主張，
却選中了一個瘸腿鐵匠做男人。
無疑，嬌貴的女人們喜歡　　　　　　　　　　　　　30
喫肉時佐以瘋狂的生菜冷盤，
豐饒角因此而被糟蹋罄盡。

我要讓她首先精通禮節；
心不可視為天賜，而是被那些
並不十分美麗的人所掙得；
而許多曾為美而甘當傻瓜者
已經將魅力變成了智慧，
還有不少曾經漫遊的窮漢，
愛戀過並自認為曾被愛戀，
如今却注目於一種令人愉快的和藹。　　　　　　　40

願她長成一株繁茂而隱蔽的樹，
她全部的思緒就可以像紅雀鳥族，
沒有勞形的事務，只是
四處播送著它們宏亮的鳴啼，
只是在歡樂中相互嬉逐，
只是在歡樂中你吵我爭。

O may she live like some green laurel
Rooted in one dear perpetual place.

My mind, because the minds that I have loved,
The sort of beauty that I have approved,   50
Prosper but little, has dried up of late,
Yet knows that to be choked with hate
May well be of all evil chances chief.
If there's no hatred in a mind
Assault and battery of the wind
Can never tear the linnet from the leaf.

An intellectual hatred is the worst,
So let her think opinions are accursed.
Have I not seen the loveliest woman born
Out of the mouth of Plenty's horn,   60
Because of her opinionated mind
Barter that horn and every good
By quiet natures understood
For an old bellows full of angry wind!

Considering that, all hatred driven hence,
The soul recovers radical innocence
And learns at last that it is self-delighting,
Self-appeasing, self-affrighting,
And that its own sweet will is Heaven's will;
She can, though every face should scowl   70

呵，但願她像月桂那樣長青
植根在一個可愛的永恆之處。

近來，由於我曾喜愛的那些心意
和我曾讚賞的那種美麗　　　　　　　　　50
皆如曇花一現，我的心靈已枯竭，
但知道若爲仇恨所壅塞
才定然是最可怕的厄運。
假如心靈中毫無仇恨，
那厲風的襲擊再烈再猛，
也絕不能將紅雀和綠葉撕分。

理智的仇恨爲害最甚，
那就教她把意見視爲可憎。
難道我不曾目睹那誕生
自豐饒角之口的絕色美人，　　　　　　　60
只因她固執己見的心腸，
便用那只羊角和爲溫和的
天性所了解的每一種美德
換取了一隻充滿怒氣的舊風箱？

想到此，一切仇恨被驅逐散盡，
靈魂恢復了根本的天眞，
終於得知它是在自娛自樂，
自慰自安，自驚自嚇，
它自己的美好願望就是天意；
儘管每一張面孔都會怒惱，　　　　　　　70

And every windy quarter howl
Or every bellows burst, be happy still.

And may her bridegroom bring her to a house
Where all's accustomed, ceremonious;
For arrogance and hatred are the wares
Peddled in the thoroughfares.
How but in custom and in ceremony
Are innocence and beauty born?
Ceremony's a name for the rich horn,
And custom for the spreading laurel tree.   80

     June 1919

A Meditation in Time of War

For one throb of the artery,
While on that old grey stone I sat
Under the old wind-broken tree,
I knew that One is animate,
Mankind inanimate phantasy.

每一處風源都會咆哮，或每一套
風箱都會脹破，她都會常歡喜。

還願她的新郎引她入洞房，
那裡一切尋常，莊重堂皇；
因為傲慢和仇恨都不過
是大路兩旁零售的雜貨。
若非自風俗和禮儀之中，
純眞和美又如何誕生？
禮儀是豐饒角的一個別名，
風俗是紛披的月桂樹的名稱。　　　　　　80

　　　1919 年 6 月

戰時冥想

在被風吹折的老樹蔭中
靜坐在那古老的青石上之時，
由於脈搏的猛一下跳動，
我悟知太一是活生生的存在，
人類則是無生命的幻影。

1928
The Tower
選自《塔堡》

Sailing to Byzantium

I

That is no country for old men. The young
In one another's arms, birds in the trees,
— Those dying generations — at their song,
The salmon-falls, the mackerel-crowded seas,
Fish, flesh, or fowl, commend all summer long
Whatever is begotten, born, and dies.
Caught in that sensual music all neglect
Monuments of unageing intellect.

II

An aged man is but a paltry thing,
A tattered coat upon a stick, unless   10
Soul clap its hands and sing, and louder sing
For every tatter in its mortal dress,
Nor is there singing school but studying
Monuments of its own magnificence;
And therefore I have sailed the seas and come
To the holy city of Byzantium.

III

O sages standing in God's holy fire

航往拜占庭

一

那絕非老年人適宜之鄉。彼此
擁抱的年輕人、那些漸趨滅絕
在樹林中婉轉放歌的鳥類、
鮭魚溯洄的瀑布、鯖魚麇集的海河、
水族、走獸、飛禽，整夏讚美
成孕、出生和死亡的一切。
全都沉湎於那感性的音樂，
而忽視不朽理性的豐碑傑作。

二

年老之人不過是件無用之物，
一根竿子撐著的破衣裳，　　　　　　　　　　10
除非穿著凡胎肉體的靈魂爲全部
破衣裳拍手歌唱，愈唱愈響；
而所有歌詠學校無不研讀
獨具自家輝煌的豐碑樂章；
因此我揚帆出海駕舟航行，
來到這神聖之城拜占庭。

三

呵，佇立在上帝的聖火之中

As in the gold mosaic of a wall,

Come from the holy fire, perne in a gyre,

And be the singing-masters of my soul.   20

Consume my heart away; sick with desire

And fastened to a dying animal

It knows not what it is; and gather me

Into the artifice of eternity.

IV

Once out of nature I shall never take

My bodily form from any natural thing,

But such a form as Grecian goldsmiths make

Of hammered gold and gold enamelling

To keep a drowsy Emperor awake;

Or set upon a golden bough to sing   30

To lords and ladies of Byzantium

Of what is past, or passing, or to come.

   1927

一如在嵌金壁畫中的聖賢們，
請走出聖火來，在螺旋中轉動，
來教導我的靈魂學習歌吟。　　　　　　　　　20
請耗盡我的心；它思欲成病，
緊附於一具垂死的動物肉身，
迷失了本性；請把我收集
到那永恆不朽的技藝裡。

四

一旦超脫塵凡，我絕不再採用
任何天然之物做我的身體軀殼，
而只要那種造型，一如古希臘手工
藝人運用鎏金和鍍金的方法製作，
以使睡意昏沉的皇帝保持清醒；
或安置於一根金色的枝上唱歌，　　　　　30
把過去，現在，或未來的事情
唱給拜占庭的諸侯和貴婦們聽。

　　1927 年

The Stare's Nest by My Window

The bees build in the crevices
Of loosening masonry, and there
The mother birds bring grubs and flies.
My wall is loosening; honey-bees,
Come build in the empty house of the stare.

We are closed in, and the key is turned
On our uncertainty; somewhere
A man is killed, or a house burned,
Yet no clear fact to be discerned:
Come build in the empty house of the stare.   10

A barricade of stone or of wood;
Some fourteen days of civil war;
Last night they trundled down the road
That dead young soldier in his blood:
Come build in the empty house of the stare.

We had fed the heart on fantasies,
The heart's grown brutal from the fare;
More substance in our enmities
Than in our love; O honey-bees,
Come build in the empty house of the stare.   20

我窗邊的燕雀巢

蜜蜂在鬆動的石壁隙縫
中間營巢築居；而在那裡，
母鳥銜去些蠕蟲和飛蟲。
我的牆壁鬆動了；蜜蜂，
來，築居在燕雀的空房裡。

我們被鎖起，不能肯定
門鎖何時才會打開；某地
一人被殺，一所房遭焚，
但沒有事實可以說得清：
來，築居在燕雀的空房裡。　　　　　　10

石頭或木頭壘起的路障；
十四天左右內戰尚未停息；
昨夜他們推車沿路送葬，
年輕的兵在血泊中死亡：
來，築居在燕雀的空房裡。

我們曾用幻想把心供奉，
心變得野蠻，皆因這伙食；
我們的敵意比愛意之中
有更多實質；呵，蜜蜂，
來，築居在燕雀的空房裡。　　　　　　20

The Wheel

Through winter-time we call on spring,
And through the spring on summer call,
And when abounding hedges ring
Declare that winter's best of all;
And after that there's nothing good
Because the spring-time has not come —
Nor know what disturbs our blood
Is but its longing for the tomb.

Youth and Age

Much did I rage when young,
Being by the world oppressed,
But now with flattering tongue
It speeds the parting guest.

1924

輪

在整個多季裡我們呼喚春季，
在整個春天裡又呼喚夏天，
當繁茂的樹籬搖響風鈴之時
又宣稱其中最好的是多天；
在那以後不再有什麼好季節，
因為春的時刻還沒有來臨──
却不知那煩擾我們的生命者
不過是生命對墓地的憧憬。

青年與老年

年輕時被這世界壓抑，
我曾經憤激狂狷，
可如今它滿口諂媚辭，
祝過客一路平安。

　　　1924 年

Leda and the Swan

A sudden blow: the great wings beating still
Above the staggering girl, her thighs caressed
By the dark webs, her nape caught in his bill,
He holds her helpless breast upon his breast.

How can those terrified vague fingers push
The feathered glory from her loosening thighs?
And how can body, laid in that white rush,
But feel the strange heart beating where it lies?

A shudder in the loins engenders there
The broken wall, the burning roof and tower   10
And Agamemnon dead.
                              Being so caught up,
So mastered by the brute blood of the air,
Did she put on his knowledge with his power
Before the indifferent beak could let her drop?

1923

麗達與天鵝

突然一下猛擊：那巨翼依然拍動
在蹣跚的少女頭頂，黝黑的蹼掌
摸著她大腿，硬喙銜著她的背頸，
他把她無助的胸緊貼在自己胸上。

那些驚恐不定的柔指如何能推開
她漸漸鬆弛的大腿上榮幸的羽絨？
被置於那雪白的燈心草叢的弱體
又怎能不感觸那陌生心房的悸動？

腰股間的一陣顫慄便造成在那裡
牆垣坍塌斷殘，屋頂和塔樓燒燃，
亞格曼儂慘死。

　　　　　　　就如此遭到劫持，
如此聽憑那空中獸性的生靈宰制，
趁那冷漠的喙尚未把她放下之前，
她可曾藉他的力量吸取他的知識？

　　1923 年

10

On a Picture of a Black Centaur
by Edmund Dulac

Your hooves have stamped at the black margin of the wood,

Even where horrible green parrots call and swing.

My works are all stamped down into the sultry mud.

I knew that horse-play, knew it for a murderous thing.

What wholesome sun has ripened is wholesome food to eat,

And that alone; yet I, being driven half insane

Because of some green wing, gathered old mummy wheat

In the mad abstract dark and ground it grain by grain

And after baked it slowly in an oven; but now

I bring full-flavoured wine out of a barrel found   10

Where seven Ephesian topers slept and never knew

When Alexander's empire passed, they slept so sound.

Stretch out your limbs and sleep a long Saturnian sleep;

I have loved you better than my soul for all my words,

And there is none so fit to keep a watch and keep

Unwearied eyes upon those horrible green birds.

題埃德蒙·杜拉克作
黑色人頭馬怪圖

你的蹄子曾經踩踏在黑暗的樹林邊緣，
甚至在可怕的綠鸚鵡啼叫和搖晃的地方。
我的作品全都被踩入悶熱的污泥裡面。
我知道那惡作劇，認爲那可是惡事一樁。
有益的太陽催熟的東西是有益的食品，
僅此而已；可我，由於某隻綠色的羽翮
而被逼半瘋，曾在瘋狂的茫茫夜暗中
收取古老的木乃伊小麥，一粒一粒研磨，
然後在一個爐灶裡慢慢烘烤；而如今
我從一隻在那七個以弗所醉漢酣睡之處
發現的酒桶中取出醇香的美酒：他們
睡得眞死，不知亞歷山大帝國何時逝去。
伸展你的四肢，睡上一個暢快的長覺；
不管怎麼說，我曾經愛你勝過我的靈魂，
而且沒有誰如此適合值班守望，並且
孜孜不倦地監視那些可怕的綠色的鳴禽。

10

Among School Children

I

I walk through the long schoolroom questioning;

A kind old nun in a white hood replies;

The children learn to cipher and to sing,

To study reading-books and history,

To cut and sew, be neat in everything

In the best modern way — the children's eyes

In momentary wonder stare upon

A sixty-year-old smiling public man.

II

I dream of a Ledaean body, bent

Above a sinking fire, a tale that she   10

Told of a harsh reproof, or trivial event

That changed some childish day to tragedy —

Told, and it seemed that our two natures blent

Into a sphere from youthful sympathy,

Or else, to alter Plato's parable,

Into the yolk and white of the one shell.

III

And thinking of that fit of grief or rage

在學童中間

一

我邊走邊問,從長長的教室穿過;
戴白頭巾的和藹的老修女作答解釋;
孩子們學習算術,學習唱歌,
學習閱讀語文課本和歷史故事,
學習剪裁和縫紉,一切都乾淨俐落,
以最佳的現代方式——孩子們一時
帶著好奇的神情,凝眸注目
一個六十歲的含笑的有名人物。

二

我想像一個麗達那樣的身體,低俯於
漸熄的爐火之上,她講的一個故事,　　　　　10
說的是一次嚴厲的責備,或區區
瑣事把童年的某一天變成了悲劇的事——
講過後,我們兩人的天性彷彿出於
青年人的同情而混合成了一個球體,
或者說——把柏拉圖的比喻略加修改——
成了同一蛋殼裡的蛋黃和蛋白。

三

心想著那時的一陣悲傷或怒氣,

I look upon one child or t'other there
And wonder if she stood so at that age —
For even daughters of the swan can share   20
Something of every paddler's heritage —
And had that colour upon cheek or hair,
And thereupon my heart is driven wild:
She stands before me as a living child.

IV

Her present image floats into the mind —
Did Quattrocento finger fashion it
Hollow of cheek as though it drank the wind
And took a mess of shadows for its meat?
And I though never of Ledaean kind
Had pretty plumage once — enough of that,   30
Better to smile on all that smile, and show
There is a comfortable kind of old scarecrow.

V

What youthful mother, a shape upon her lap
Honey of generation had betrayed,
And that must sleep, shriek, struggle to escape
As recollection or the drug decide,
Would think her son, did she but see that shape
With sixty or more winters on its head,
A compensation for the pang of his birth,

我在此把這個孩子瞅瞅，那個孩子看看，
不知她在這個年紀是否也這樣站立——
因為天鵝的女兒們也可能遺傳　　　　　　　　20
所有涉禽共有的某種東西——
是否也有這樣顏色的臉蛋或髮辮，
想到此，我的心簡直就像發了瘋癲：
她彷彿一個活生生的孩子站在我面前。

四

她現在的形象浮現在我的腦海中——
可是十五世紀大師的手指所塑做？
雙頰凹陷，就好像靠喝風
吃影子的雜燴當飲食過活。
而我，儘管絕非麗達的遺種，
却也有過漂亮的羽毛——夠了，　　　　　　　30
不如對所有微笑的人微笑，顯示
有一種老稻草人日子過得還舒適。

五

年輕的母親——一個形象在她膝上，
為「生殖之蜜」所捉弄，
且必將睡眠，哭叫，掙扎著要逃亡，
一如回憶或那藥物所決定——
會怎樣看她的兒子？假如她只把那形象——
它頭上有六十個或更多的寒冬——
當做對生他時劇痛的一份補償，

Or the uncertainty of his setting forth?   40

VI

Plato thought nature but a spume that plays
Upon a ghostly paradigm of things;
Solider Aristotle played the taws
Upon the bottom of a king of kings;
World-famous golden-thighed Pythagoras
Fingered upon a fiddle-stick or strings
What a star sang and careless Muses heard:
Old clothes upon old sticks to scare a bird.

VII

Both nuns and mothers worship images,
But those the candies light are not as those   50
That animate a mother's reveries,
But keep a marble or a bronze repose.
And yet they too break hearts — O Presences
That passion, piety or affection knows,
And that all heavenly glory symbolise —
O self-born mockers of man's enterprise;

VIII

Labour is blossoming or dancing where
The body is not bruised to pleasure soul,
Nor beauty born out of its own despair,

或對爲他前程擔憂的一份補償。　　　　　　40

　　　　六

柏拉圖認爲自然界不過是遊戲
在精神的萬物變化圖上的一顆泡沫；
較壯實的亞里斯多德則舞弄著鞭子
在一位萬王之王的屁股上薄施懲戒；
舉世聞名的金股畢達哥拉斯
在提琴弓或琴弦上運指彈撥
星星所唱、無心的繆斯們所聽的樂章：
用以嚇唬鳥兒的舊竿子上的舊衣裳。

　　　　七

修女和母親們都崇拜偶像，
但是那些被燭光照亮的尊容不似　　　　50
那些撩惹母親幻想的形象，
只是使大理石或青銅保持靜止。
然而它們也令人心碎──呵，種種現相，
爲熱情、虔誠或愛慕所熟知，
一切天國的榮耀所象徵的尊神──
呵，自生的人類事業的嘲笑者們；

　　　　八

只要肉體不爲取悅靈魂而損傷，
美並非生於其自身的絕望斷念，
兩眼昏花的智慧亦非出自夜半燈光，

Nor blear-eyed wisdom out of midnight oil.   60

O chestnut tree, great rooted blossomer,

Are you the leaf, the blossom or the bole?

O body swayed to music, O brightening glance,

How can we know the dancer from the dance?

The Fool by the Roadside

When all works that have

From cradle run to grave

From grave to cradle run instead;

When thoughts that a fool

Has wound upon a spool

Are but loose thread, are but loose thread;

When cradle and spool are past

And I mere shade at last

Coagulate of stuff

Transparent like the wind,   10

I think that I may find

A faithful love, a faithful love.

勞動就會綻開花朵或起舞蹁躚。 60
呵，栗樹，根鬚粗壯繁花興旺，
你究竟是葉子、花朵還是枝幹？
呵，身隨樂擺，呵，眼光照人，
我們怎能將跳舞人和舞蹈區分？

路邊的傻子

當所有從搖籃
跑進墳墓的物件
又從墳墓跑進搖籃；
當一個傻子
纏在軸上的心思
不過是鬆散的線，不過是鬆散的線；

當搖籃和線軸已成過去，
而我終於變成區區
鬼影，由某物質凝聚而成，
透明如風，那時候 10
我想，我就可以找到
一個忠誠的愛人，一個忠誠的愛人。

First Love

Though nurtured like the sailing moon
In beauty's murderous brood,
She walked awhile and blushed awhile
And on my pathway stood
Until I thought her body bore
A heart of flesh and blood.

But since I laid a hand thereon
And found a heart of stone
I have attempted many things
And not a thing is done,   10
For every hand is lunatic
That travels on the moon.

She smiled and that transfigured me
And left me but a lout,
Maundering here, and maundering there,
Emptier of thought
Than the heavenly circuit of its stars
When the moon sails out.

初戀

雖然在美的殘酷的孕育中
她出落得像滑翔的月亮，
但她時而漫步，時而臉紅，
久久佇立在我的小徑上
直到我以爲她的體內藏有
一顆有血有肉的心臟。

但是自從我伸手在那裡
發現了一顆石頭心之時起，
我已經嘗試過許多事情，
却沒有一件事成功順利，
因爲凡在月亮上摸索的手
肯定是神經出了問題。

她的微笑改變了我的面貌，
撇下我就像個小丑
這裡走走，那裡逛逛，
頭腦空空沒有念頭，
還不如天空中群星的軌跡，
在月亮滑翔出天外之後。

10

Human Dignity

Like the moon her kindness is,
If kindness I may call
What has no comprehension in't,
But is the same for all
As though my sorrow were a scene
Upon a painted wall.

So like a bit of stone I lie
Under a broken tree.
I could recover if I shrieked
My heart's agony   10
To passing bird, but I am dumb
From human dignity.

The Mermaid

A mermaid found a swimming lad,
Picked him for her own,
Pressed her body to his body,
Laughed; and plunging down

人類的尊嚴

她的好意就像月亮，
假如我可以
把其中沒有理解，而對人人
都一樣的東西叫做好意，
好像我的憂傷是一個佈景
塗畫在一面牆壁。

於是像一塊石頭我躺倒
在一棵斷樹下邊。
假如把內心的痛苦
衝著掠過的飛鳥嘶喊，　　　　　　　　　　10
我就有可能復元，但我啞然，
由於人類的尊嚴。

美人魚

美人魚發現一個游水的少年，
便把他捉過來做她的情郎，
把她的身體緊貼於他的身體，
放聲大笑；於是下潛深藏，

Forgot in cruel happiness
That even lovers drown.

The Death of the Hare

I have pointed out the yelling pack,
The hare leap to the wood,
And when I pass a compliment
Rejoice as lover should
At the drooping of an eye,
At the mantling of the blood.

Then suddenly my heart is wrung
By her distracted air
And I remember wildness lost
And after, swept from there,   10
Am set down standing in the wood
At the death of the hare.

却忘記了在殘酷的歡樂之中
即便是有情人也會被溺亡。

野兔之死

我指出那狂吠的群犬，
好讓野兔跳進樹林，
且當我叫好致意時，
猶如戀人面臨
眼皮的低垂一般，
因鮮血凝固而歡欣。

突然我的心爲她那
失神的神情絞痛起來，
遂想起野性已失，
後來，被從那裡推開，　　　　　　　10
我站在樹林裡，因
野兔之死而受到責怪。

The Empty Cup

A crazy man that found a cup,
When all but dead of thirst,
Hardly dared to wet his mouth
Imagining, moon-accursed,
That another mouthful
And his beating heart would burst.
October last I found it too
But found it dry as bone,
And for that reason am I crazed
And my sleep is gone.   10

His Memories

We should be hidden from their eyes,
Being but holy shows
And bodies broken like a thorn
Whereon the bleak north blows,
To think of buried Hector
And that none living knows.

空杯

一個瘋子找到一隻杯子，
在快要渴死的時刻，
却幾乎不敢潤一潤嘴，
精神錯亂，想像著
要是再喝一口，
他那狂跳的心就會爆裂。
去年十月我也找到了它，
但發現它乾如枯骨，
由於這原因，我發了瘋，
睡眠也隨之逝去。　　　　　　　　10

他的記憶

我們應被藏起，不讓他們看見，
只是作為聖物展示；
身體殘損，猶如
被凄厲的北風吹折的荊棘；
想想已入土的赫克特，
活著的人誰也不知。

The women take so little stock
In what I do or say
They'd sooner leave their cosseting
To hear a jackass bray;   10
My arms are like the twisted thorn
And yet there beauty lay;

The first of all the tribe lay there
And did such pleasure take —
She who had brought great Hector down
And put all Troy to wreck —
That she cried into this ear,
'Strike me if I shriek.'

The Three Monuments

They hold their public meetings where
Our most renowned patriots stand,
One among the birds of the air,
A stumpier on either hand;
And all the popular statesmen say
That purity built up the State
And after kept it from decay;

女人們一點兒也不注意
我的所做或所說，
她們寧可丟下她們的寵物
去聽一頭公驢放歌； 10
我的手臂像彎彎扭扭的荊棘，
但從前也有美人枕過；

全部落的頭號美人曾枕在上面
享受過如此的快樂——
她曾讓偉大的赫克特威風掃地
使整個特洛伊城毀滅——
她竟然衝著我這耳朵大喊，
「要是我叫喚就猛撞我。」

三座紀念雕像

他們舉行公開集會，在我們
最著名的愛國者佇立的地方，
一個高聳在空中群鳥當中，
兩個較矮些矗立在兩旁；
所有知名的政治家都說
純潔建立起國家政權，
然後又防止它腐敗墮落；

Admonish us to cling to that
And let all base ambition be,
For intellect would make us proud   10
And pride bring in impurity:
The three old rascals laugh aloud.

都告誡我們要堅持這點，
不要理睬一切卑鄙的野心，
因為才智會使我們驕傲，　　　　　　　　　　　　10
驕傲則把不純潔引進：
那三個老流氓哈哈大笑。

1933
The Winding Stair and Other Poems
選自《旋梯及其他》

In Memory of Eva Gore-Booth
and Con Markievicz

The light of evening, Lissadell,
Great windows open to the south,
Two girls in silk kimonos, both
Beautiful, one a gazelle.
But a raving autumn shears
Blossom from the summer's wreath;
The older is condemned to death,
Pardoned, drags out lonely years
Conspiring among the ignorant.
I know not what the younger dreams —   10
Some vague Utopia — and she seems,
When withered old and skeleton-gaunt,
An image of such politics.
Many a time I think to seek
One or the other out and speak
Of that old Georgian mansion, mix
Pictures of the mind, recall
That table and the talk of youth,
Two girls in silk kimonos, both
Beautiful, one a gazelle.   20

Dear shadows, now you know it all,

紀念伊娃・郭爾-布斯
和康・馬凱維奇

利薩代爾，傍晚的燈光，
朝南開的大窗戶，
兩個穿絲袍的少女，都
很美，一個像羚羊。
可是一個肅殺的秋天
把鮮花從夏日的花環上剪除；
年長者遭了死刑的判處，
遇赦後，挨過寂寞的長年，
在愚氓中間從事陰謀。
我不知年幼者夢想什麼——　　　　　　　　　　10
某種模糊的烏托邦——她彷彿，
當枯萎衰老瘦骨嶙峋的時候，
這類政治的一個鬼影。
好多次我想訪尋
這位或那位，談論
那喬治時代的舊宅，混同
心靈的圖景，回想
那桌子和青年時代的談吐，
兩個穿絲袍的少女，都
很美，一個像羚羊。　　　　　　　　　　　　20

親愛的幽靈，現在你們洞徹，

All the folly of a fight
With a common wrong or right.
The innocent and the beautiful
Have no enemy but time;
Arise and bid me strike a match
And strike another till time catch;
Should the conflagration climb,
Run till all the sages know.
We the great gazebo built,   30
They convicted us of guilt;
Bid me strike a match and blow.

     October 1927

Death

Nor dread nor hope attend
A dying animal;
A man awaits his end
Dreading and hoping all;
Many times he died,
Many times rose again.
A great man in his pride
Confronting murderous men

一切與共有的是或非
作戰的愚蠢行爲。
天眞者和美麗者
除了時光沒有仇敵；
起身，叫我劃一根火柴，
再劃一根，直到時光燃起來；
假如大火升騰而起，
就奔跑，直到所有智者都知道。
我們建築了偉大的樓台，   30
他們宣告我們有罪；
叫我劃一根火柴把火吹著。

　　　　1927 年 10 月

死

垂死的野獸不知
恐懼或希望；
臨終的人却滿懷
希冀和恐慌；
多少次他死去，
多少次又復活。
一個偉大的人物
壯年面對殺人者，

Casts derision upon
Supersession of breath;   10
He knows death to the bone —
Man has created death.

A Dialogue of Self and Soul

I

+ **My Soul.** I summon to the winding ancient stair;
      Set all your mind upon the steep ascent,
      Upon the broken, crumbling battlement,
      Upon the breathless starlit air,
      Upon the star that marks the hidden pole;
      Fix every wandering thought upon
      That quarter where all thought is done:
      Who can distinguish darkness from the soul?

  My Self. The consecrated blade upon my knees
      Is Sato's ancient blade, still as it was,   10
      Still razor-keen, still like a looking-glass
      Unspotted by the centuries;
      That flowering, silken, old embroidery, torn

把輕蔑投向

呼吸的交替；　　　　　　　　　　　　　　　　　10

他深知死亡——

是人創造了死。

自性與靈魂的對話

一

我的靈魂：我號召去那盤旋的古老樓梯；

　　　把你的全部心意都置於那陡階，

　　　置於那破裂、崩坍欲墜的雉堞，

　　　置於那無息的星光耀映的空氣，

　　　置於那標誌著隱蔽極軸的星辰；

　　　把每一縷漫遊的思緒都集中在

　　　一切思想都在那裡成熟的方位：

　　　誰又能把黑暗與靈魂分辨區分？

我的自性：橫在我膝上的這神聖的劍

　　　是佐籐的古劍，依然像從前一樣，　　　　10

　　　依然快如剃刀，依然像明鏡一樣，

　　　不曾被幾個世紀的歲月染上銹斑；

　　　扯自某位宮廷貴婦的袍衣，

From some court-lady's dress and round

The wooden scabbard bound and wound,

Can, tattered, still protect, faded adorn.

My Soul. Why should the imagination of a man

Long past his prime remember things that are

Emblematical of love and war?

Think of ancestral night that can, 20

If but imagination scorn the earth

And intellect its wandering

To this and that and t'other thing,

Deliver from the crime of death and birth.

My Self. Montashigi, third of his family, fashioned it

Five hundred years ago, about it lie

Flowers from I know not what embroidery —

Heart's purple — and all these I set

For emblems of the day against the tower

Emblematical of the night, 30

And claim as by a soldier's right

A charter to commit the crime once more.

My Soul. Such fullness in that quarter overflows

And falls into the basin of the mind

That man is stricken deaf and dumb and blind,

For intellect no longer knows

Is from the *Ought*, or *Knower* from the *Known* —

在那木製劍鞘上圍裹包纏，

那繡花的、絲織的、古老的錦緞

破損了，仍能保護，褪色了，仍能裝飾。

我的靈魂：一個人盛年久已度過，

　　爲什麼還要在想像中回顧

　　那些象徵愛情和戰爭的事物？

　　想一想祖先留傳下來的夜，　　　　　　　20

　　只要想像蔑視凡塵世界，

　　理智蔑視其從此到彼

　　又到其他事物的游移，

　　夜就能使你脫離生與死的罪惡。

我的自性：元茂，他家族的第三世，

　　五百年前造就了它，它周圍躺著

　　來自我所不知的某種刺繡的花朵——

　　像心一樣猩紅——我把這些東西

　　都當做白晝的象徵，與那象徵

　　黑夜的塔樓相互對立，　　　　　　　　30

　　並且像是以一個士兵的權利

　　要求一份再次犯罪的許可證。

我的靈魂：如此的充實在那方位流溢，

　　繼而瀉入心意的盆地之中，

　　使人震驚得又盲又啞又聾，

　　因爲理智不再能夠辨識

　　「在」與「應在」，或「能知」與「所知」——

That is to say, ascends to Heaven;

Only the dead can be forgiven;

But when I think of that my tongue's a stone.   40

II

My Self. A living man is blind and drinks his drop.

What matter if the ditches are impure?

What matter if I live it all once more!

Endure that toil of growing up;

The ignominy of boyhood; the distress

Of boyhood changing into man;

The unfinished man and his pain

Brought face to face with his own clumsiness;

The finished man among his enemies? —

How in the name of Heaven can he escape   50

That defiling and disfigured shape

The mirror of malicious eyes

Casts upon his eyes until at last

He thinks that shape must be his shape?

And what's the good of an escape

If honour find him in the wintry blast?

I am content to live it all again

And yet again, if it be life to pitch

Into the frog-spawn of a blind man's ditch,

A blind man battering blind men;   60

也就是說，不再能升天；

唯有死者能夠得到赦免；

但我想到此時，舌頭便僵硬如石。　　　　　　40

　　　　二

我的自性：活人是盲目的，且嗜飲。

　有什麼要緊？即使水溝不乾淨。

　有什麼要緊？即使我再活一次，

　忍受那成長的艱辛；

　那少年時代的恥辱；那從

　少年轉變成年的坎坷；

　那未成就的成人和被迫

　與自己的愚笨面對面的苦痛；

　那四面受敵的成就之人──

　他究竟如何才能夠逃避　　　　　　　　　　50

　那些惡意的眼睛的鏡子

　投射到他眼睛裡的那毀損

　而污穢的形象，直至終於

　他認定那形象是他的形象？

　而假如在寒風中榮譽臨降

　逃避又有什麼好處？

　我滿足於從頭再活過

　一遍又一遍，假如那是

　把一個痛打眾盲人的盲人投擲

　到盲人溝的蛙卵中間去的生活；　　　　　　60

Or into that most fecund ditch of all,

The folly that man does

Or must suffer, if he woos

A proud woman not kindred of his soul.

I am content to follow to its source

Every event in action or in thought;

Measure the lot; forgive myself the lot!

When such as I cast out remorse

So great a sweetness flows into the breast

We must laugh and we must sing,   70

We are blest by everything,

Everything we look upon is blest.

Oil and Blood

In tombs of gold and lapis lazuli

Bodies of holy men and women exude

Miraculous oil, odour of violet.

But under heavy loads of trampled clay

Lie bodies of the vampires full of blood;

Their shrouds are bloody and their lips are wet.

或是把男人所做的或不得
不忍受的蠢事——假如他追求
與他靈魂無緣的驕傲女人——擲投
到那最有繁殖力的水溝裡去的生活。

我滿足於在行動或思想中追溯
每一事件，直至其源頭根柢；
衡量一切；徹底原諒我自己！
當我這樣的人把悔恨拋出，
一股巨大的甜蜜流入胸中時，
我們必大笑，我們必歌呼，
我們備受一切事物的祝福，
我們目視的一切都有了福氣。

70

膏血

在黃金和寶石裝修的墓穴裡邊
聖潔的男人和女人們滲流出
奇蹟的油膏，紫羅蘭的香氣。

而在被夯實的泥土的重壓下面
躺著吸血鬼充滿鮮血的身軀；
它們的屍衣血污，嘴唇尚濕。

Symbols

A storm-beaten old watch-tower,
A blind hermit rings the hour.

All-destroying sword-blade still
Carried by the wandering fool.

Gold-sewn silk on the sword-blade,
Beauty and fool together laid.

Spilt Milk

We that have done and thought,
That have thought and done,
Must ramble, and thin out
Like milk spilt on a stone.

象徵

風吹雨打一座古譙樓，
一位盲隱士敲鐘報漏。

無堅不摧的長劍仍舊
背在流浪的傻子肩頭。

劍刃包裹金縷的錦衣，
美人和傻子睡在一起。

灑落的牛奶

我們曾有過作為和思索，
有過思索和作為的人士，
都必將漫流，然後稀薄，
像灑落在石頭上的牛奶。

The Nineteenth Century and After

Though the great song return no more
There's keen delight in what we have:
The rattle of pebbles on the shore
Under the receding wave.

At Algeciras—a Meditation upon Death

The heron-billed pale cattle-birds
That feed on some foul parasite
Of the Moroccan hocks and herds
Cross the narrow Straits to light
In the rich midnight of the garden trees
Till the dawn break upon those mingled seas.

Often at evening when a boy
Would I carry to a friend —
Hoping more substantial joy
Did an older mind commend —
Not such as are in Newton's metaphor,
But actual shells of Rosses' level shore.

10

十九世紀及以後

雖然偉大的歌不再回返，
我們仍擁有熱切的歡樂：
海灘上白石如卵
落潮下嘩嘩唱和。

在阿耳黑西拉斯——沉思死亡

以摩洛哥的牛羊身上
骯髒的寄生蟲為食，
喙似蒼鷺的白色牛背鷺
越過狹窄的海峽，棲止
在園林裡濃厚的夜色中，
直到曙光在交匯的海面綻进。

少年時，在傍晚時分，
我常給一個朋友帶去——
希望一個年長的慧心
推荐更具實質的樂趣——
並非牛頓的比喻中所說，
而是羅西斯平灘的真貝殼。

10

Greater glory in the sun,

An evening chill upon the air,

Bid imagination run

Much on the Great Questioner;

What He can question, what if questioned I

Can with a fitting confidence reply.

November 1928

The Choice

The intellect of man is forced to choose

Perfection of the life, or of the work,

And if it take the second must refuse

A heavenly mansion, raging in the dark.

When all that story's finished, what's the news?

In luck or out the toil has left its mark:

That old perplexity an empty purse,

Or the day's vanity, the night's remorse.

陽光裡有更大的榮耀，
空氣中一股夜寒降落，
讓想像力多多關照
那位偉大的訊問者；
他會問什麼，如果被問及，我
又能以適當的自信回答些什麼。

　　　1928 年 11 月

選擇

人的理智被迫要選擇
生活，或工作的完美，
若取後者它就得棄絕
豪宅，在黑暗中憤激。
故事結束後，消息如何？
運氣內外，辛苦留下印記：
那古老困惑是個空錢袋，
或白天的虛榮，黑夜的痛悔。

Mohini Chatterjee

I asked if I should pray,
But the Brahmin said,
'Pray for nothing, say
Every night in bed,
"I have been a king,
I have been a slave,
Nor is there anything,
Fool, rascal, knave,
That I have not been,
And yet upon my breast   10
A myriad heads have lain."'

That he might set at rest
A boy's turbulent days
Mohini Chatterjee
Spoke these, or words like these.
I add in commentary,
'Old lovers yet may have
All that time denied —
Grave is heaped on grave
That they be satisfied —   20
Over the blackened earth
The old troops parade,

摩希尼·查特基

我問是否我應當祈禱，
可是那婆羅門却說：
「什麼也不要祈禱，
只是每夜在床上說：
『我曾經是一個國王，
我曾經是一個奴隸，
傻瓜、無賴、流氓，
諸如此類的東西
我無不曾經當過，
而且我胸膛上面　　　　　　　　　　　10
曾有上萬美人枕過。』」

為使一個少年的狂亂
日子平靜下來，
摩希尼·查特基
說了這些，或類似的話。
我加以解說闡釋：
「年老的戀人還會擁有
時光所拒絕的一切——
墳墓堆積在墳墓上頭，
他們或許得到慰藉——　　　　　　　　20
在這變暗的大地之上，
那古老隊伍行進的所在；

Birth is heaped on birth

That such cannonade

May thunder time away,

Birth-hour and death-hour meet,

Or, as great sages say,

Men dance on deathless feet.'

1928

Byzantium

The unpurged images of day recede;

The Emperor's drunken soldiery are abed;

Night resonance recedes, night-walkers' song

After great cathedral gong;

A starlit or a moonlit dome disdains

All that man is,

All mere complexities,

The fury and the mire of human veins.

Before me floats an image, man or shade,

Shade more than man, more image than a shade;   10

For Hades' bobbin bound in mummy-cloth

May unwind the winding path;

誕生堆積在誕生之上，

如此連番的轟炸

有可能把時光轟跑；

生與死的時刻相遇，

或者，如偉大聖哲所說，

人們以不死的雙腳跳舞。」

　　　1928 年

拜占庭

白天的種種不潔的形象隱退；

皇帝的酒醉的士兵們上床沉睡；

夜籟沉寂：大敎堂的鑼鳴，

接著是夜行者的歌聲；

星輝或月光下的圓屋頂蔑視

人類的一切，

不過是聚合的一切，

人類血脈的怒氣和淤泥。

一個幻影、人或鬼在我眼前浮動，

說是人更像鬼，說是鬼更像幻影；　　10

因爲裏在屍布裡的哈得斯的線軸

也許會解開那纏繞的道路；

A mouth that has no moisture and no breath

Breathless mouths may summon;

I hail the superhuman;

I call it death-in-life and life-in-death.

Miracle, bird or golden handiwork,

More miracle than bird or handiwork,

Planted on the starlit golden bough,

Can like the cocks of Hades crow,   20

Or, by the moon embittered, scorn aloud

In glory of changeless metal

Common bird or petal

And all complexities of mire or blood.

At midnight on the Emperor's pavement flit

Flames that no faggot feeds, nor steel has lit,

Nor storm disturbs, flames begotten of flame,

Where blood-begotten spirits come

And all complexities of fury leave,

Dying into a dance,   30

An agony of trance,

An agony of flame that cannot singe a sleeve.

Astraddle on the dolphin's mire and blood,

Spirit after spirit! The smithies break the hood,

The golden smithies of the Emperor!

Marbles of the dancing floor

一張沒有水分也沒有氣息的嘴，
可能把眾多沒有氣息的嘴召集；
我向那超人者歡呼致意：
我稱它為死中之生、生中之死。

奇蹟、鳥或金製的玩藝，
說是鳥或玩藝不如說是奇蹟，
棲止在星光照耀的金枝上，
能像哈得斯的晨雞一樣啼唱，　　　　　　　　　20
或者被月亮所激怒，身披
不朽金屬的光華，高聲輕賤
平凡的飛鳥或花瓣，
以及一切淤泥或血液的聚合體。

夜半，皇帝的舖石街道上飄閃
不假柴薪和鋼鐮燃點，
狂風不擾，生自火焰的火焰，
血生的鬼魂來到其間，
一切怒氣的聚合體於是撤離，
消逝在一個舞，　　　　　　　　　　　　　30
一陣失神的痛苦，
一種燒不焦衣袖的火焰的痛苦裏。

跨騎著海豚的泥血之軀，
鬼魂魚貫而來！工匠們截斷那洪流，
皇帝御用的金匠們！
舞場舖地的大理石

Break bitter furies of complexity,
Those images that yet
Fresh images beget,
That dolphin-torn, that gong-tormented sea.   40

    1930

Quarrel in Old Age

Where had her sweetness gone?
What fanatics invent
In this blind bitter town,
Fantasy or incident
Not worth thinking of,
Put her in a rage.
I had forgiven enough
That had forgiven old age.

All lives that has lived;
So much is certain;   10
Old sages were not deceived:
Somewhere beyond the curtain
Of distorting days
Lives that lonely thing

截斷聚合的強烈怒氣，

那些仍在孳生

新幻影的幻影，

那被海豚劃破、鑼聲折磨的大海。　　　　　　　　40

　　1930 年

老年的爭吵

她的可愛之處哪兒去了？

在這盲目苦悶的城裡，

狂熱者們發明的一切，

不值得考慮的

幻想或事故，

使得她陷入狂熱。

我已足夠寬恕

那寬恕老年者。

從前活過者現在都活著；

只有這是確實無疑的；　　　　　　　　10

古代的聖賢不曾受欺騙：

在歪曲事實的日子的

簾幕以外某個地方，

生活著那寂寞的人：

That shone before these eyes
Targeted, trod like Spring.

Gratitude to the Unknown Instructors

What they undertook to do
They brought to pass;
All things hang like a drop of dew
Upon a blade of grass.

Stream and Sun at Glendalough

Through intricate motions ran
Stream and gliding sun
And all my heart seemed gay:
Some stupid thing that I had done
Made my attention stray.

Repentance keeps my heart impure;
But what am I that dare

她曾在我這雙眼前閃光，
帶著盾，步態宛如春神。

對不相識的導師們的謝忱

凡答應要做的事情
他們都付諸實現；
一切就像露珠晶瑩
懸掛在草葉尖端。

格倫達澇的溪水和太陽

通過複雜的機制，溪水
和滑翔的太陽奔馳；
我心中似乎充滿歡欣：
我做過的一件蠢事
却使我心神不定。

悔恨使我的心渾濁不堪；
可我算什麼，竟敢

Fancy that I can
Better conduct myself or have more
Sense than a common man?   10

What motion of the sun or stream
· Or eyelid shot the gleam
That pierced my body through?
What made me live like these that seem
Self-born, born anew?

     June 1932

Crazy Jane Reproved

I care not what the sailors say:
All those dreadful thunder-stones,
All that storm that blots the day
Can but show that Heaven yawns;
Great Europa played the fool
That changed a lover for a bull.
Fol de rol, fol de rol.

To round that shell's elaborate whorl,
Adorning every secret track
With the delicate mother-of-pearl,   10

妄想我能夠比
普通人有更好的表現
或更多的見識？　　　　　　　　　　　　　　　10

太陽或溪流或眼瞼的什麼
機制放射出那閃爍，
把我的身體洞穿？
是什麼使我再生，生活，
像這些彷彿自生的事物一般？

　　　1932 年 6 月

受責的瘋珍妮

我不在乎水手們說些什麼：
所有那些可怕的霹雷閃電，
所有那些遮天蔽日的風波
都不過顯示上天在打呵欠；
偉大的歐羅巴當了冤大頭，
她用情郎換取了一頭公牛。
缶兒得嘍兒，缶兒得嘍兒。

為磨圓那貝殼的精緻螺紋，
用那優美細巧的珍珠母殼
裝飾那每一條秘密的路徑，　　　　　　　　　10

Made the joints of Heaven crack:
So never hang your heart upon
A roaring, ranting journeyman.
Fol de rol, fol de rol.

Crazy Jane on God

That lover of a night
Came when he would,
Went in the dawning light
Whether I would or no;
Men come, men go:
All things remain in God.

Banners choke the sky;
Men-at-arms tread;
Armoured horses neigh
Where the great battle was
In the narrow pass:
All things remain in God.

Before their eyes a house
That from childhood stood
Uninhabited, ruinous,

10

曾使得天堂的接縫處開裂：
所以決不要把你的心掛在
一個咋咋呼呼的僱工身上。
岳兒得嘍兒，岳兒得嘍兒。

瘋珍妮論上帝

那一夜間的情郎
想來時他就來，
他走時天剛亮，
不管我願意與否；
男人們來，走：
萬物仍歸于上帝。

旌旗林立蔽天空；
武裝兵士相踏；
鐵甲戰馬嘶鳴；
偉大戰役爆發在
那狹窄的關隘：
萬物仍歸于上帝。

自從孩提時代起
就矗立的一座
殘破空屋蕩地

10

Suddenly lit up
From door to top:
All things remain in God.

I had wild Jack for a lover;
Though like a road   20
That men pass over
My body makes no moan
But sings on:
All things remain in God.

Crazy Jane Talks with the Bishop

I met the Bishop on the road
And much said he and I.
'Those breasts are flat and fallen now
Those veins must soon be dry;
Live in a heavenly mansion,
Not in some foul sty.'

'Fair and foul are near of kin,
And fair needs foul,' I cried.
'My friends are gone, but that's a truth
Nor grave nor bed denied,   10

在他們眼前燃起，
從屋門到屋脊：
萬物仍歸于上帝。

我有情郎野傑克；
雖然像條道路　　　　　　　　　20
任男人們經過，
我的身體不呻吟，
而是繼續歌吟：
萬物仍歸于上帝。

瘋珍妮與主教交談

我在路上遇見主教，
他和我滔滔地交談。
「這對乳房如今乾癟下垂，
那些血管很快也必定枯乾；
去住一幢豪華的宅院，
別呆在醜陋的豬圈。」

「美好和醜陋是近親，
美好需要醜陋，」我呵斥。
「我的朋友們已逝去，但這是
墳墓或床舖都不否認的真理，　　　　10

Learned in bodily lowliness
And in the heart's pride.

'A woman can be proud and stiff
When on love intent;
But Love has pitched his mansion in
The place of excrement;
For nothing can be sole or whole
That has not been rent.'

Love's Loneliness

Old fathers, great-grandfathers,
Rise as kindred should.
If ever lover's loneliness
Came where you stood,
Pray that Heaven protect us
That protect your blood.

The mountain throws a shadow,
Thin is the moon's horn;
What did we remember
Under the ragged thorn?
Dread has followed longing,

10

是在肉體的低賤
和心靈的高傲之中獲知。

「當熱衷於戀愛之時，
一個女人會驕傲而矜持；
但是愛神已把他的宅院
拋進了漚糞的土池；
因為未經分裂過的東西
都不會是完整或唯一。」

愛的寂寞

老父親們，曾祖父們，
像親人應該的，起來。
假如戀人的寂寞曾經
來到你們站立的所在，
請祈禱上天護佑我們
就像護佑你們的血脈。

山巒投下一片陰影，
細細的是月亮的角；
在那蓬亂的荊棘下
我們又想起了什麼？
恐懼已隨渴望而來，

10

And our hearts are torn.

Lullaby

Beloved, may your sleep be sound
That have found it where you fed.
What were all the world's alarms
To mighty Paris when he found
Sleep upon a golden bed
That first dawn in Helen's arms?

Sleep, beloved, such a sleep
As did that wild Tristram know
When, the potion's work being done,
Roe could run or doe could leap   10
Under oak and beechen bough,
Roe could leap or doe could run;

Such a sleep and sound as fell
Upon Eurotas' grassy bank
When the holy bird, that there
Accomplished his predestined will,
From the limbs of Leda sank
But not from her protecting care.

我們的心已被撕裂。

催眠曲

親愛的，在從前吮乳之處
入睡，願你睡得安穩舒適。
當強健的帕里斯沉緬
在海倫懷中，良宵初度，
在一張金床上酣眠之時，
全世界的警報又與他何干？

親愛的，睡一個好覺，
就像那狂野的崔斯坦所體驗，
當時，那迷藥的功用見了效，
雄鹿會奔跑，或者雌鹿會蹦跳
在橡樹和櫸樹的枝椏下面，
雄鹿會蹦跳，或者雌鹿會奔跑；
睡一個好覺，安穩猶如
降臨在歐羅塔斯河岸上的酣睡：
當時那神聖的鳥兒，在那裡
實現了他命定的意願之後，
從麗達的肢體上滾落下來，
却並沒有擺脫她的呵護關懷。

After Long Silence

Speech after long silence; it is right,
All other lovers being estranged or dead,
Unfriendly lamplight hid under its shade,
The curtains drawn upon unfriendly night,
That we descant and yet again descant
Upon the supreme theme of Art and Song:
Bodily decrepitude is wisdom; young
We loved each other and were ignorant.

Mad as the Mist and Snow

Bolt and bar the shutter,
For the foul winds blow:
Our minds are at their best this night,
And I seem to know
That everything outside us is
Mad as the mist and snow.

Horace there by Homer stands,
Plato stands below,

長久沉默之後

長久沉默之後說話；不錯——
別的戀人們或疏遠或亡故，
冷漠的燈光躲入燈罩深處，
層層窗簾擋住冷漠的夜色——
我們談論了却又再次談起
那藝術與詩歌的至高主題：
肉體衰老即智慧；年輕時
我們彼此相愛却懵懂無知。

像霧和雪一般狂

關好門牢窗門，
因為惡風逞強：
我們的頭腦今夜最靈敏，
而我彷彿知詳
我們身外的一切都是
像霧和雪一般狂。

賀瑞斯與荷馬並立，
柏拉圖站在下方，

And here is Tully's open page.

How many years ago

Were you and I unlettered lads

Mad as the mist and snow?

You ask what makes me sigh, old friend,

What makes me shudder so?

I shudder and I sigh to think

That even Cicero

And many-minded Homer were

Mad as the mist and snow.

Father and Child

She hears me strike the board and say

That she is under ban

Of all good men and women,

Being mentioned with a man

That has the worst of all bad names;

And thereupon replies

That his hair is beautiful,

Cold as the March wind his eyes.

還有圖里翻開的書頁。
多少歲月以往，   10
你我曾是不識字的少年，
像霧和雪一般狂？

你問我為何嘆息，老友，
什麼使我顫慄惶惶？
我顫慄、嘆息，是想起
就連西塞羅也一樣
和智慧過人的荷馬都曾經
像霧和雪一般狂。

父與女

她聽見我拍案訴說
所有的好男好女
都把她詛咒譴責，
一併提到的還有
一個罵名昭著的男人；
於是隨口應聲：
他的頭髮美麗，
眼波清冷像三月的風。

Before the World was Made

If I make the lashes dark
And the eyes more bright
And the lips more scarlet,
Or ask if all be right
From mirror after mirror,
No vanity's displayed:
I'm looking for the face I had
Before the world was made.

What if I look upon a man
As though on my beloved,   10
And my blood be cold the while
And my heart unmoved?
Why should he think me cruel
Or that he is betrayed?
I'd have him love the thing that was
Before the world was made.

創世之前

如果我把睫毛描黛
把眼睛襯得更明，
把嘴唇塗得更紅，
或對一面面鏡子發問，
是否一切都妥當，
那也不是爲了虛榮：
我是在尋找我在
創世之前曾有的顏容。

如果我凝視一個男人
好像凝視我的情郎，
同時我的血液冰冷，
心也不動，那又怎樣？
他何必認爲我冷酷，
或者認爲他遭到背棄？
我想讓他愛上那
創世之前存在的東西。

10

A First Confession

I admit the briar
Entangled in my hair
Did not injure me;
My blenching and trembling
Nothing but dissembling,
Nothing but coquetry.

I long for truth, and yet
I cannot stay from that
My better self disowns,
For a man's attention   10
Brings such satisfaction
To the craving in my bones.

Brightness that I pull back
From the Zodiac,
Why those questioning eyes
That are fixed upon me?
What can they do but shun me
If empty night replies?

最初的表白

我承認那糾纏在
我頭髮裡的棘刺
並不曾把我傷著；
我臉變色身抖顫
不過是喬裝遮掩
不過是撒嬌賣俏。

我渴求真理，却
無法擺脫更好的
自我所拒斥的東西，
因為男人的注目
帶來如此的滿足
給我入骨的希冀。

我從黃道帶上
扯回來的光亮，
為何這些疑問的眼睛
緊盯在我身上？
除了躲避我它們能怎樣，
假若空虛的夜作出回應？

10

Consolation

O but there is wisdom
In what the sages said;
But stretch that body for a while
And lay down that head
Till I have told the sages
Where man is comforted.

How could passion run so deep
Had I never thought
That the crime of being born
Blackens all our lot?   10
But where the crime's committed
The crime can be forgot.

Her Vision in the Wood

Dry timber under that rich foliage,
At wine-dark midnight in the sacred wood,
Too old for a man's love I stood in rage
Imagining men. Imagining that I could

慰藉

呵，但願賢哲所說的
話語裡含有智慧；
且把那身體舒展片刻，
把那腦袋低垂，
直到我告知賢哲們
人在哪裡感到安慰。

假如我從未想到
那生而為人的罪過
籠罩我們的全部命運，
情欲怎會如此深切？ 　　　　　　　10
但是罪過在哪裡犯下，
就能夠在哪裡被忘却。

她在樹林中的幻視

像那繁茂的樹葉下面的乾燥木質，
在那神聖的樹林中濃黑如酒的子夜，
太老了沒有男人愛，我憤怒地佇立，
想像著男人。想像著我能夠憑藉

A greater with a lesser pang assuage

Or but to find if withered vein ran blood,

I tore my body that its wine might cover

Whatever could recall the lip of lover.

And after that I held my fingers up,

Stared at the wine-dark nail, or dark that ran   10

Down every withered finger from the top;

But the dark changed to red, and torches shone,

And deafening music shook the leaves; a troop

Shouldered a litter with a wounded man,

Or smote upon the string and to the sound

Sang of the beast that gave the fatal wound.

All stately women moving to a song

With loosened hair or foreheads grief-distraught,

It seemed a Quattrocento painter's throng,

A thoughtless image of Mantegna's thought —   20

Why should they think that are for ever young?

Till suddenly in griefs contagion caught,

I stared upon his blood-bedabbled breast

And sang my malediction with the rest.

That thing all blood and mire, that beast-torn wreck,

Half turned and fixed a glazing eye on mine,

And, though love's bitter-sweet had all come back,

Those bodies from a picture or a coin

較小的痛苦使較大的痛苦緩和平息
或僅僅為查看枯萎的血管是否流血，　　　　　　　　30
我就撕破我的身體，好讓其中的酒液
覆蓋能讓我憶起情郎嘴唇的一切。

然後，我舉起我的手指，
凝視那濃黑如酒的指甲，或那從　　　　　　　　　10
每一根枯萎的手指尖端淌下的濃黑；
可是那濃黑變紅，只見火把通明，
震耳欲聾的音樂撼動樹葉；一列長隊
用擔架抬著一個受傷的男人，
或者猛擊琴弦，和著琴聲的伴奏
歌唱那造成這致命創傷的野獸。

所有高雅的女人伴著歌曲舞動，
長髮鬆散，或者眉頭緊鎖憂傷，
彷彿一位十五世紀畫家筆下的群眾，
曼特格納的思想中沒有思想的形象——　　　　　　20
為什麼他們竟認為她們永遠年輕？
我一直凝視著他那鮮血染污的胸膛，
與其他人一起唱著我的詛咒，
直到突然被傳染上憂傷悲愁。

那渾身血污的冤家，那野獸撕裂的廢物，
半轉過臉，目光灼灼盯著我的眼睛；
雖然愛情的苦澀甜蜜都已回歸恢復，
但那些來自一幅畫或一枚硬幣的人形

Nor saw my body fall nor heard it shriek,
Nor knew, drunken with singing as with wine,   30
That they had brought no fabulous symbol there
But my heart's victim and its torturer.

A Last Confession

What lively lad most pleasured me
Of all that with me lay?
I answer that I gave my soul
And loved in misery,
But had great pleasure with a lad
That I loved bodily.

Flinging from his arms I laughed
To think his passion such
He fancied that I gave a soul
Did but our bodies touch,   10
And laughed upon his breast to think
Beast gave beast as much.

I gave what other women gave
That stepped out of their clothes,
But when this soul, its body off,

既沒有看見我倒地，也沒有聽見我驚呼，

且醉酒般地迷醉於歌唱，也不知情　　　　　　30

他們抬到那裡的並不是神話中的象徵，

而是我的心的迫害者和受害的犧牲。

最後的表白

在所有與我共眠的活潑少年中

哪一個最使我歡快？

我回答說，我曾獻出我的靈魂，

却在不幸之中戀愛，

但是與一個少年曾共享極樂，

他是我肉體所愛。

突然掙脫他的懷抱，我大笑著，

心想他竟激動如此：

他幻想我獻出了一個靈魂，

只要我們接觸肉體；　　　　　　　　　　　　10

我在他的胸脯上大笑著心想，

禽獸對禽獸不過如此。

我給出一如別的跨出衣裙的

女人們所給出的東西，

但是當這個靈魂脫離了肉體，

Naked to naked goes,
He it has found shall find therein
What none other knows,

And give his own and take his own
And rule in his own right;   20
And though it loved in misery
Close and cling so tight,
There's not a bird of day that dare
Extinguish that delight.

Meeting

Hidden by old age awhile
In masker's cloak and hood,
Each hating what the other loved,
Face to face we stood:
'That I have met with such,' said he,
'Bodes me little good.'

'Let others boast their fill,' said I,
'But never dare to boast
That such as I had such a man
For lover in the past;   10

赤裸著走向赤裸者時，
它所找到的他將在其中發現
別人誰也不知道的東西，

給出他自己的，得到他自己的，
以他自己的權利統治；　　　　　　　　　　　20
並且，儘管它曾在不幸中戀愛，
仍把它抱得那麼緊密，
以致沒有一個白天的鳥兒敢於
聒噪而使那極樂終止。

相遇

被老年暫時掩藏在
假面人的斗篷和風帽裡，
彼此憎恨對方所愛，
面對面我們站立：
「我遇見了這種人，」他說，
「不會有什麼好事。」

「讓別人盡情吹噓，」我說，
「但從不敢誇口自衿
有誰像我一樣過去曾經有
那樣一個男人作情人；　　　　　　　　　　10

Say that of living men I hate
Such a man the most.'

'A loony'd boast of such a love,'
He in his rage declared:
But such as he for such as me —
Could we both discard
This beggarly habiliment —
Had found a sweeter word.

說在活著的男人中我現在
最恨那樣的男人。」

「傻瓜才會誇耀那樣的情人，」
他怒沖沖地斷言：
但是他這種人為我這種人——
假如我們倆都能脫換
這身乞丐的衣裳——
找到了一個更美妙的字眼。

1935
[Parnell's Funeral and Other Poems]
選自《帕內爾的葬禮及其他》

Two Songs Rewritten for the Tune's Sake

I

My Paistin Finn is my sole desire,
And I am shrunken to skin and bone,
For all my heart has had for its hire
Is what I can whistle alone and alone.
     Oro, oro!
To-morrow night I will break down the door.

What is the good of a man and he
Alone and alone, with a speckled shin?
I would that I drank with my love on my knee,
Between two barrels at the inn.   10
     Oro, oro!
To-morrow night I will break down the door.

Alone and alone nine nights I lay
Between two bushes under the rain;
I thought to have whistled her down that way,
I whistled and whistled and whistled in vain.
     Oro, oro!
To-morrow night I will break down the door.

依譜重塡的兩首歌

一

我的派絲汀·芬是我唯一所欲得，
我已憔悴消損至皮包骨頭，
因為，我的心所有供租用的一切
只是我孤苦伶仃所能嘯謳。
　　　哦咯，哦咯！
明天夜晚我要去把那屋門砸開。

一個男人，孤苦又伶仃，小腿上
還有斑痕，他有什麼本領？
我但願，我愛人坐在我的膝頭上，
在酒館的兩個酒桶間痛飲。
　　　哦咯，哦咯！
明天夜晚我要去把那屋門砸開。

孤苦伶仃孤苦伶仃我躺了九晚上
在霾雨中的兩叢灌木之間；
我原打算用口哨引她到那條路上，
我吹呀，吹呀，吹也枉然。
　　　哦咯，哦咯！
明天夜晚我要去把那屋門砸開。

10

II

I would that I were an old beggar
Rolling a blind pearl eye,
For he cannot see my lady
Go gallivanting by;

A dreary, dreepy beggar
Without a friend on the earth
But a thieving rascally cur —
O a beggar blind from his birth;

Or anything else but a rhymer
Without a thing in his head   10
But rhymes for a beautiful lady,
He rhyming alone in his bed.

Ribh at the Tomb of Baile and Aillinn

Because you have found me in the pitch-dark night
With open book you ask me what I do.
Mark and digest my tale, carry it afar
To those that never saw this tonsured head
Nor heard this voice that ninety years have cracked.

二

我但願我是一個老乞丐
轉動著珍珠似的瞽目，
因爲他看不見我的所愛
陪伴著別人招搖過路；

一個陰鬱、沮喪的乞丐，
在世上沒有一個朋友，
除了偷東西的無賴野狗——
呵，生來盲目的乞丐；

或別的什麼，除了詩人——
頭腦空空，一無所思，　　　　　　　　　10
只會爲美貌娘兒們押韻，
獨自一人在床上作詩。

瑞夫在波伊拉和艾琳之墓畔

因爲你發現了我在漆黑的夜裡
面對翻開的書本，所以你問我在做什麼。
點校和整理我的傳說，把它帶到遠方
給那些從未見過這削了髮的頭
也從未聽見過這喑啞了九十年的嗓音的人們。

Of Baile and Aillinn you need not speak,
All know their tale, all know what leaf and twig,
What juncture of the apple and the yew,
Surmount their bones; but speak what none have heard.

The miracle that gave them such a death   10
Transfigured to pure substance what had once
Been bone and sinew; when such bodies join
There is no touching here, nor touching there,
Nor straining joy, but whole is joined to whole;
For the intercourse of angels is a light
Where for its moment both seem lost, consumed.

Here in the pitch-dark atmosphere above
The trembling of the apple and the yew,
Here on the anniversary of their death,
The anniversary of their first embrace,   20
Those lovers, purified by tragedy,
Hurry into each other's arms; these eyes,
By water, herb and solitary prayer
Made aquiline, are open to that light.
Though somewhat broken by the leaves, that light
Lies in a circle on the grass; therein
I turn the pages of my holy book.

關於波伊拉和艾琳你無須說什麼，
人人都知道他們的傳說，人人都知道蘋果樹
和紫杉樹的什麼樣的枝葉、什麼樣的枝節
覆蓋他們的遺骨；而說些誰也沒聽說過的事。

賜給他們以如此死法的奇蹟　　　　　　　　　　　10
把從前是筋骨的東西變成了
純粹的物質；當這樣的身體交合時，
無所謂此處的接觸，也無所謂彼處的接觸，
也沒有緊張的歡樂，而是全體與全體結合；
因爲天使的交媾是一團光，
閃耀之際二者都彷彿迷失、消融於其中。

在此，在蘋果樹和紫杉樹的顫抖
之上的漆黑的天空中，
在此，在他們的週年忌日，
他們初次擁抱的週年紀念日，　　　　　　　　　20
那對被悲劇淨化了的戀人
急急撲入彼此的懷抱；我這雙
被清水、藥草和孤獨的祈禱鍛鍊得
像鷹眼般犀利的眼睛都不堪那亮光的炫耀。
雖然那亮光有些被樹葉割破，形成
一個圓圈落在草地上，但是在其中
我翻動我的聖經書頁。

Ribh in Ecstasy

What matter that you understood no word!
Doubtless I spoke or sang what I had heard
In broken sentences. My soul had found
All happiness in its own cause or ground.
Godhead on Godhead in sexual spasm beget
Godhead. Some shadow fell. My soul forgot
Those amorous cries that out of quiet come
And must the common round of day resume.

There

There all the barrel-hoops are knit,
There all the serpent-tails are bit,
There all the gyres converge in one,
There all the planets drop in the Sun.

瑞夫在出神狀態

即使你一字也不懂又有什麼關係！
無疑我所說或所唱是我斷斷續續
聽來的句子。我的靈魂已經找到了
有其自身原因或依據的一切快樂。
神靈與神靈在性交的痙攣中生出了
神靈。有陰影落下。我的靈魂忘却
那些來自寂靜中的動情的叫喊聲；
日子的正常循環必定要重新運行。

那裡

那裡，所有的桶箍都緊緊銜接，
那裡，所有的蛇尾都遭到咬囓，
那裡，所有螺旋體都交匯合一，
那裡，所有行星都墜入太陽裡。

What Magic Drum?

He holds him from desire, all but stops his breathing lest
Primordial Motherhood forsake his limbs, the child no longer rest,
Drinking joy as it were milk upon his breast.

Through light-obliterating garden foliage what magic drum?
Down limb and breast or down that glimmering belly move his mouth
    and sinewy tongue.
What from the forest came! What beast has licked its young?

Whence had they Come?

Eternity is passion, girl or boy
Cry at the onset of their sexual joy
'For ever and for ever'; then awake
Ignorant what Dramatis Personae spake;
A passion-driven exultant man sings out
Sentences that he has never thought;
The Flagellant lashes those submissive loins
Ignorant what that dramatist enjoins,
What master made the lash. Whence had they come,
The hand and lash that beat down frigid Rome?   10

什麼魔鳥的鼓噪聲？

他抑制住自己的慾望，幾乎停止了呼吸，
以免原始母性遺棄他的肢體，那女孩子不再偎依
在他的胸脯上暢飲歡樂，彷彿吮吸乳汁。

透進抹煞陽光的花園樹蔭裡的是什麼魔鳥的鼓噪聲？
他的嘴和韌勁的舌沿著四肢和胸脯或那光澤的小腹移動。
什麼曾來自森林？什麼野獸把它的幼崽已舐舐成形？

它們從何處來？

永恆即情欲，少女或少男
在他們交歡之始叫喊
「永遠復永遠」；然後醒來，
茫然不解劇中人所說的台詞；
被情欲驅使的狂喜之人唱出
他從未想到過的詞句；
那苦行者鞭打順從的腰股，
却茫然不知那劇作者有何吩咐，
鞭子是哪位大匠所造。它們從何處來，
那打倒了冷淡的羅馬帝國的手和鞭子？

10

What sacred drama through her body heaved
When world-transforming Charlemagne was conceived?

The Four Ages of Man

He with body waged a fight,
But body won; it walks upright.

Then he struggled with the heart;
Innocence and peace depart.

Then he struggled with the mind;
His proud heart he left behind.

Now his wars on God begin;
At stroke of midnight God shall win.

Conjunctions

If Jupiter and Saturn meet,
What a crop of mummy wheat!

什麼神聖戲劇通過她的身體開幕，
當改變世界的查理曼投胎的時候？

人的四個時期

他曾經與肉體戰鬥過一場，
但肉體贏了；它趾高氣揚。

於是，他又與心較量抗拒；
純真與和平遂都棄他而去。

然後，他與頭腦較量爭鬥；
他把驕傲的心拋在了身後。

現在，他對上帝之戰開始；
夜半鐘響時，上帝將勝利。

會合

假如朱庇特與薩圖恩相逢，
木乃伊小麥會有何等收成！

The sword's a cross; thereon He died:
On breast of Mars the goddess sighed.

Meru

Civilisation is hooped together, brought
Under a rule, under the semblance of peace
By manifold illusion; but man's life is thought,
And he, despite his terror, cannot cease
Ravening through century after century,
Ravening, raging, and uprooting that he may come
Into the desolation of reality:
Egypt and Greece good-bye, and good-bye, Rome!
Hermits upon Mount Meru or Everest,
Caverned in night under the drifted snow,   10
Or where that snow and winter's dreadful blast
Beat down upon their naked bodies, know
That day brings round the night, that before dawn
His glory and his monuments are gone.

劍是一具十字架；他死於其上：
那女神嘆息，在馬爾斯的胸上。

須彌山

文明被箍起，由多重幻想
置於一條規則，置於和平的幌子
之下；但人生即思想；
他，儘管恐懼，却無法停止
劫掠，經過一個又一個世紀，
劫掠，狂暴，滅絕，以便他
可以進入現實的荒涼裡：
埃及和希臘，別了，別了，羅馬！
在須彌山或艾佛勒斯山中，
在積雪之下的洞穴裡過夜，　　　　10
或在那大雪和嚴冬的厲風
抽打其裸體之處的隱士們了解
白晝周而復始帶來黑夜，黎明前
他的榮耀和碑銘都消逝不見。

1938
New Poems
選自《新詩》

Lapis Lazuli (For Harry Clifton)

I have heard that hysterical women say
They are sick of the palette and fiddle-bow,
Of poets that are always gay,
For everybody knows or else should know
That if nothing drastic is done
Aeroplane and Zeppelin will come out,
Pitch like King Billy bomb-balls in
Until the town lie beaten flat.

All perform their tragic play,
There struts Hamlet, there is Lear,   10
That's Ophelia, that Cordelia;
Yet they, should the last scene be there,
The great stage curtain about to drop,
If worthy their prominent part in the play,
Do not break up their lines to weep.
They know that Hamlet and Lear are gay;
Gaiety transfiguring all that dread.
All men have aimed at, found and lost;
Black out; Heaven blazing into the head:
Tragedy wrought to its uttermost.   20
Though Hamlet rambles and Lear rages,
And all the drop scenes drop at once

天青石雕（爲哈利‧克里夫頓作）

我曾聽見歇斯底里的女人們
說她們厭惡調色板和提琴弓，
厭惡那些永遠快樂的詩人們，
因爲人人皆知，否則也應該懂：
假如不採取激烈的手段，
飛機和飛艇就將會出動，
像比利王那樣投下炸彈
直到這城市被摧毀夷平。

人人都在扮演各自的悲劇，
那邊傲然走著哈姆雷特，那邊是李爾王，　　　　10
那是奧菲莉婭，那是考娣莉婭；
然而，假如竟有最後一場，
巨大的幕布即將落地，
假如他們在劇中的顯要角色還值得，
他們就不會中斷台詞而啜泣。
他們知道哈姆雷特和李爾是快樂的；
快樂改變著一切恐懼的人們。
人人都曾努力、找到和失去；
場燈熄滅；天堂之光照進頭頂：
悲劇被表演到極致。　　　　　　　　　　　　　20
儘管哈姆雷特徬徨，李爾怒狂，
所有的吊裝佈景同時降落

Upon a hundred thousand stages,
It cannot grow by an inch or an ounce.

On their own feet they came, or on shipboard,
Camel-back, horse-back, ass-back, mule-back,
Old civilisations put to the sword.
Then they and their wisdom went to rack:
No handiwork of Callimachus
Who handled marble as if it were bronze,   30
Made draperies that seemed to rise
When sea-wind swept the corner, stands;
His long lamp chimney shaped like the stem
Of a slender palm, stood but a day;
All things fall and are built again
And those that build them again are gay.

Two Chinamen, behind them a third,
Are carved in Lapis Lazuli,
Over them flies a long-legged bird
A symbol of longevity;   40
The third, doubtless a serving-man,
Carries a musical instrument.

Every discolouration of the stone,
Every accidental crack or dent
Seems a water-course or an avalanche,
Or lofty slope where it still snows

在成千上萬座舞台之上，
悲劇也不能再發展一分一毫。

他們來過：或徒步，或駕船，
或騎馬，或騎騾，或騎驢，或騎駱駝，
古老的文明遂面臨刀劍。
於是他們和他們的智慧走向毀滅：
伽里瑪科斯刻石如刻銅，
他雕琢的衣紋，當海風吹襲　　　　　　　　　30
這角落之時，彷彿飄飄飛動，
如今他的作品沒有一件完好矗立；
他那棕櫚樹形的細長燈罩
也僅僅矗立了一晝夜；
一切都傾覆又被重造，
重造一切的人們是快樂的。

天青石上雕刻著兩個中國佬，
身後跟著第三人，
他們頭頂上飛著一隻長腿鳥，
那是長生不老的象徵；　　　　　　　　　　40
第三位無疑是僕人，
隨身攜帶一件樂器。

石上每一片褪色的斑痕，
每一處偶然的凹窩或裂隙
都像是一道河流或一場雪崩，
或依然積雪的高坡峻嶺，

Though doubtless plum or cherry-branch
Sweetens the little half-way house
Those Chinamen climb towards, and I
Delight to imagine them seated there;   50
There, on the mountain and the sky,
On all the tragic scene they stare.
One asks for mournful melodies;
Accomplished fingers begin to play.
Their eyes mid many wrinkles, their eyes,
Their ancient, glittering eyes, are gay.

Sweet Dancer

The girl goes dancing there
On the leaf-sown, new-mown, smooth
Grass plot of the garden;
Escaped from bitter youth,
Escaped out of her crowd,
Or out of her black cloud.
Ah dancer, ah sweet dancer!

If strange men come from the house
To lead her away do not say

雖然杏花或櫻枝很可能

薰香了半山腰上那小小涼亭——

那些中國人正朝它攀登；我樂於

想像他們在那裡坐定；　　　　　　　50

在那裡，他們凝望山巒和天宇，

注視著一切悲劇的場景。

有一位請奏悲悼的曲子；

嫻熟的手指便開始彈撥。

他們的眼邊佈滿皺紋，他們的眼裡，

他們古老的、炯炯的眼裡，充滿快樂。

曼妙的舞女

那少女去那裡跳舞，

在那花園中落葉繽紛，

新剪修的柔滑草坪上；

逃離她苦澀的青春，

避開她周圍的人群，

或擺脫籠罩她的烏雲。

啊，舞女，曼妙的舞女！

假如陌生人從那座房子

前來把她領走，可別說

That she is happy being crazy;   10

Lead them gently astray;

Let her finish her dance,

Let her finish her dance.

Ah dancer, ah sweet dancer!

The Three Bushes

An incident from the 'Hirtoria mei Temporis'
of the Abbe Michel de Bourdeille.

Said lady once to lover,

'None can rely upon

A love that lacks its proper food;

And if your love were gone

How could you sing those songs of love!

I should be blamed, young man.

       O my dear, O my dear.

'Have no lit candles in your room,'

That lovely lady said,

'That I at midnight by the clock   10

May creep into your bed,

For if I saw myself creep in

她發起瘋來很快樂；　　　　　　　　　　　　　10
把他們悄悄拉到一側；
讓她跳完她的舞，
讓她跳完她的舞。
啊，舞女，曼妙的舞女！

三叢灌木

米歇爾·德·布爾代葉神父《我的時代的歷史》
中記載的一件事。

貴婦有一回對情郎說，
「沒有誰能夠依賴
缺乏適當資糧的愛；
假如愛人已經離開，
你又怎能唱那些情歌？
小伙子，我應受到責怪。」
　　　哦親親，哦親親。

「在你房間裡別點燈，」
那嬌美的貴婦叮囑，
「我好在夜半更深時　　　　　　　　　　　　10
偷偷爬上你的床舖，
要是我看見自己偷情，

I think I should drop dead.

    O my dear, O my dear.

'I love a man in secret,
Dear chambermaid,' said she,
'I know that I must drop down dead
If he stop loving me,
Yet what could I but drop down dead
If I lost my chastity?'   20

    O my dear, O my dear.

'So you must lie beside him
And let him think me there,
And maybe we are all the same
Where no candles are,
And maybe we are all the same
That strip the body bare.'

    O my dear, O my dear.

But no dogs barked and midnights chimed,
And through the chime she'd say,   30
'That was a lucky thought of mine,
My lover looked so gay;'
But heaved a sigh if the chambermaid
Looked half asleep all day.

    O my dear, O my dear.

'No, not another song,' said he,

我想我就會倒地死去。」
　　哦親親，哦親親。

「我祕密地愛著一個人，
親愛的侍婢，」她說，
「我知道我必倒地而死，
假如說他不再愛我，
可除了倒地而死我又能如何，
假如我失去了貞潔？」　　　　　　　　20
　　哦親親，哦親親。

「所以你得去躺在他身邊
讓他以為是我在那床上，
也許我們都一樣，
在沒有燈燭的地方；
也許我們都一樣，
一旦把身上都脫光。」
　　哦親親，哦親親。

可是沒有犬吠；夜鐘鳴響；
聽著那鐘聲，她會說：　　　　　　　　30
「我這個主意真不錯，
我的情郎看上去很快樂；」
却又長嘆一聲，如果那侍婢
整天都顯得昏昏欲睡。
　　哦親親，哦親親。

「不，不是另一首歌，」他說，

'Because my lady came
A year ago for the first time
At midnight to my room,
And I must lie between the sheets   40
When the clock begins to chime.'
      O my dear, O my dear.

'A laughing, crying, sacred song,
A leching song,' they said.
Did ever men hear such a song?
No, but that day they did.
Did ever man ride such a race?
No, not until he rode.
      O my dear, O my dear.

But when his horse had put its hoof   50
Into a rabbit hole
He dropped upon his head and died.
His lady saw it all
And dropped and died thereon, for she
Loved him with her soul.
      O my dear, O my dear.

The chambermaid lived long, and took
Their graves into her charge,
And there two bushes planted
That when they had grown large   60

「因為一年以前

我的情婦第一次

在半夜來到我的房間，

當鐘聲開始鳴響的時候　　　　　　　　　　　40

我必須躺在被單中間。」

　　　哦親親，哦親親。

「一首大笑、大叫、神聖的歌，

一首色情的歌，」他們說。

可有人曾聽過這樣一首歌？

沒有，除了那天他們聽見過。

可有人曾跑過這樣一回馬？

沒有，直到他跑過。

　　　哦親親，哦親親。

可是當他的馬把一隻蹄子　　　　　　　　　　　50

陷入一個兔子洞時，

他一頭栽到地上而死去。

他的情婦全都看在眼裡，

立時便倒地而死，因為她

以她的靈魂把他熱愛。

　　　哦親親，哦親親。

那侍婢活了很久，

照管著他們的墳墓，

並在那裡種了兩叢灌木，

以便它們長大後　　　　　　　　　　　　　　　60

Seemed sprung from but a single root
So did their roses merge.

    O my dear, O my dear.

When she was old and dying,
The priest came where she was;
She made a full confession.
Long looked he in her face,
And O, he was a good man
And understood her case.

    O my dear, O my dear.   70

He bade them take and bury her
Beside her lady's man,
And set a rose-tree on her grave.
And now none living can
When they have plucked a rose there
Know where its roots began.

    O my dear, O my dear.

The Lady's First Song

I turn round
Like a dumb beast in a show,

就好像生自一條根，
它們的玫瑰花也混在一處。

    哦親親，哦親親。

在她衰老臨死的時候，
牧師來到了她的身旁；
她做了徹底的坦白懺悔。
久久地他盯著她的臉龐，
哦，他是個善心人，
理解她的情況。

    哦親親，哦親親。　　　　　　　　70

他吩咐他們把她抬去，葬在
她女主人的男人一側，
並在她的墓上種下一叢玫瑰。
現在活著的人在那裡
摘玫瑰時，誰也不會
知道它的根莖始於哪裡。

    哦親親，哦親親。

貴婦的第一支歌

我轉身四顧，
像一隻表演的啞巴動物，

Neither know what I am
Nor where I go,
My language beaten
Into one name;
I am in love
And that is my shame.
What hurts the soul
My soul adores,   10
No better than a beast
Upon all fours.

The Lady's Second Song

What sort of man is coming
To lie between your feet!
What matter we are but women.
Wash; make your body sweet;
I have cupboards of dried fragrance
I can strew the sheet.
　　The Lord have mercy upon us.

He shall love my soul as though
Body were not at all,

既不知我是什麼
也不知要去何處，
我的語言被錘鍊
成一個名字；
我在戀愛中，
而這是我的羞恥。
傷害靈魂者
為我靈魂所愛慕，10
還不如一個
四條腿的動物。

貴婦的第二支歌

什麼樣的男人即將前來
隈躺在你的雙腳之間？
我們除了女人還是什麼！
沐浴；使你的身體香甜；
我有一櫃櫃乾品香料
可以用來點綴床單。

　　　　願主憐憫我們。

他將愛我的靈魂，彷彿
肉體全然不存在；

He shall love your body   10
Untroubled by the soul,
Love cram love's two divisions
Yet keep his substance whole.
    The Lord have mercy upon us.

Soul must learn a love that is
Proper to my breast,
Limbs a love in common
With every noble beast.
If soul may look and body touch
Which is the more blest?   20
    The Lord have mercy upon us.

The Lady's Third Song

When you and my true lover meet
And he plays tunes between your feet,
Speak no evil of the soul,
Nor think that body is the whole
For I that am his daylight lady
Know worse evil of the body;
But in honour split his love

他將愛你的肉體，　　　　　　　　　　10
不受靈魂的干擾；
愛填充愛的兩個部分，
却保持他的實體完好。
　　　願主憐憫我們。

靈魂必須學習一種
適合我胸房的愛；
肢體則學習一種與所有
高等動物共同的愛。
假如靈魂會看肉體會觸，
哪一個更有福氣？　　　　　　　　　20
　　　願主憐憫我們。

貴婦的第三支歌

假若你和我的真情郎相遇，
他在你的雙腳間彈奏樂曲，
請不要妄說靈魂的壞處，
也不要以爲肉體就是全部，
因爲我是他白天的女人，
了解肉體有更多的弊病；
但是爲了名譽請劈分他的愛情，

Till either neither have enough,
That I may hear if we should kiss
A contrapuntal serpent hiss,
You, should hand explore a thigh,   10
All the labouring heavens sigh.

The Lover's Song

Bird sighs for the air,
Thought for I know not where,
For the womb the seed sighs.
Now sinks the same rest
On mind, on nest,
On straining thighs.

The Chambermaid's First Song

How came this ranger
Now sunk in rest,
Stranger with stranger,

直到二者都不享有足夠的一份，
好讓我聽見——假如我們竟吻成
對位的毒蛇似的嘶嘶聲——　　　　　　10
你；假如手竟摸索大腿，
辛勞的一切諸天都會嘆息。

情郎的歌

鳥雀嚮往天空，
思緒嚮往我所不知的地方，
精子嚮往子宮。
此刻同樣的休息降落
在心意，在巢窠，
在繃緊的大腿上。

侍婢的第一支歌

怎麼搞的，這流浪漢
此刻沉陷於休養——
陌生人與陌生人——

On my cold breast.
What's left to sigh for,
Strange night has come;
God's love has hidden him
Out of all harm,
Pleasure has made him
Weak as a worm.   10

The Chambermaid's Second Song

From pleasure of the bed,
Dull as a worm,
His rod and its butting head
Limp as a worm,
His spirit that has fled
Blind as a worm.

An Acre of Grass

Picture and book remain,

在我冰涼的胸上。
還剩下什麼可企盼，
既然陌生的夜已到來；
上帝的愛已把他蔽遮，
使他免受一切災害，
歡樂已使他變得
虛弱得像條蟲豸。　　　　　　　　　　　　10

侍婢的第二支歌

由於床第的歡樂，
遲鈍得像條蟲；
他的棍子及其突出的頭
疲軟得像條蟲；
他那已逃走的魂魄
盲目得像條蟲。

一畝草地

圖畫和書籍仍在；

An acre of green grass
For air and exercise,
Now strength of body goes;
Midnight an old house
Where nothing stirs but a mouse.

My temptation is quiet.
Here at life's end
Neither loose imagination,
Nor the mill of the mind   10
Consuming its rag and bone,
Can make the truth known.

Grant me an old man's frenzy.
Myself must I remake
Till I am Timon and Lear
Or that William Blake
Who beat upon the wall
Till truth obeyed his call;

A mind Michael Angelo knew
That can pierce the clouds   20
Or inspired by frenzy
Shake the dead in their shrouds;
Forgotten else by mankind
An old man's eagle mind.

一畝地青草
用以養氣和運動；
如今體力衰耗；
夜半，一幢老屋，
毫無動靜，除了一隻鼠。

我已不爲外物所動。
在這生命的盡頭，
鬆弛的想像力
或消耗著骨頭   10
和破布的頭腦之磨
都不能使眞理傳播。

請賜予我老年人的狂熱。
我必須爲自己重鑄
一顆爲米開朗基羅所熟知，
能夠穿透重重雲霧，
或受了狂熱的激動，
能夠把僵屍撼醒的心靈，

一顆老年人雄鷹似的心靈，
直到我成爲泰門和李爾   20
或那位擊打牆壁，
直到眞理聽從召喚的
威廉·布雷克，
否則就會被人類忘却。

To Dorothy Wellesley

Stretch towards the moonless midnight of the trees

As though that hand could reach to where they stand,

And they but famous old upholsteries

Delightful to the touch; tighten that hand

As though to draw them closer yet.

                                   Rammed full

Of that most sensuous silence of the night

(For since the horizon's bought strange dogs are still)

Climb to your chamber full of books and wait,

No books upon the knee and no one there

But a great dane that cannot bay the moon   10

And now lies sunk in sleep.

                            What climbs the stair?

Nothing that common women ponder on

If you are worth my hope! Neither Content

Nor satisfied Conscience, but that great family

Some ancient famous authors misrepresent,

The Proud Furies each with her torch on high.

致多蘿茜·韋爾斯利

伸向那樹林裡沒有月光的中夜，
彷彿那隻手能達到它們林立之處；
它們不過是著名的古舊室內陳設，
摸起來令人愉悅；握緊那隻手，
彷彿要把它們拉得更近些。
　　　　　　　　內心
充滿了夜晚的那最感性的靜寂
（購得地平線，陌生的狗便安靜），
上樓去到你滿是書籍的臥室等待，
膝頭上沒有書，也沒有人在那裡，
只有一隻丹麥大狗，無月可吠，
此刻正躺倒沉睡。
　　　　　　是什麼在登樓梯？
絕不是平庸女人們所想得到的東西，
如果你不負我的期望！既不是滿足
也不是滿意的良心，而是某些古代
著名作家誤寫訛傳的那偉大的家族——
個個高舉火炬的驕傲的復仇三女神。

10

The Spur

You think it horrible that lust and rage
Should dance attendance upon my old age;
They were not such a plague when I was young;
What else have I to spur me into song?

A Drunken Man's Praise of Sobriety

Come swish around my pretty punk
And keep me dancing still
That I may stay a sober man
Although I drink my fill.
Sobriety is a jewel
That I do much adore;
And therefore keep me dancing
Though drunkards lie and snore.
O mind your feet, O mind your feet,
Keep dancing like a wave,   10
And under every dancer
A dead man in his grave.
No ups and downs, my Pretty,

刺激

你認爲可怕的是情欲和憤怒
竟然向我的暮年殷勤獻舞；
我年輕時它們不算什麼禍殃；
如今還有什麼刺激我歌唱？

一個醉漢對清醒的讚美

來，圍著我漂亮的婊子搖擺，
使我不停地舞蹈，
好讓我仍舊是個清醒的人，
儘管我往往喝飽。
清醒是一件珍寶，
我確實非常羨慕；
所以請使我不停地舞蹈，
雖然醉鬼躺倒且打呼嚕。
哦，注意腳步，哦，注意腳步，
不停地舞蹈像海浪翻滾，
每一個跳舞的人腳下
都有一個墳墓裡的死人。
沒有浮沉起伏，我的靚妞兒，

10

A mermaid, not a punk;
A drunkard is a dead man
And all dead men are drunk.

The Pilgrim

I fasted for some forty days on bread and buttermilk
For passing round the bottle with girls in rags or silk,
In country shawl or Paris cloak, had put my wits astray,
And what's the good of women for all that they can say
Is fol de rol de rolly O.

Round Lough Derg's holy island I went upon the stones,
I prayed at all the Stations upon my marrow bones,
And there I found an old man and though I prayed all day
And that old man beside me, nothing would he say
But fol de rol de rolly O.   10

All know that all the dead in the world about that place are stuck
And that should mother seek her son she'd have but little luck
Because the fires of Purgatory have ate their shapes away;
I swear to God I questioned them and all they had to say
Was fol de rol de rolly O.

是個美人魚，不是個婊子；
一個醉鬼就是個死人，
所有的死人都是醉鬼。

朝聖者

我只吃麵包喝淡奶，齋戒了大約四十天，
因為與身穿破布或絲綢，身披鄉土披肩
或巴黎大氅的姑娘傳瓶輪飲，曾令我神昏智迷；
女人們有什麼用處，因為她們會說的一切只是
呋兒得嘍兒得咯哩噢。

我腳踏著礫石走遍德戈湖中的聖島周遭；
我五體投地在所有的聖蹟供養龕前祈禱；
在那裡我發現了一個老人；儘管我整天都祈禱，
但是我旁邊的那個老人，他什麼也不說，除了
呋兒得嘍兒得咯哩噢。

大家都知道世上死者全都滯留在那附近，
假如母親要尋兒子，她不會有什麼好運；
因為那煉獄的烈火已經把他們的形骸盡行吞噬；
我對上帝發誓我問過他們，他們所說的不過是
呋兒得嘍兒得咯哩噢。

10

A great black ragged bird appeared when I was in the boat;

Some twenty feet from tip to tip had it stretched rightly out,

With flopping and with flapping it made a great display

But I never stopped to question, what could the boatman say

But fol de rol de rolly O.   20

Now I am in the public house and lean upon the wall,

So come in rags or come in silk, in cloak or country shawl,

And come with learned lovers or with what men you may

For I can put the whole lot down, and all I have to say

Is fol de rol de rolly O.

A Model for the Laureate

On thrones from China to Peru

All sorts of kings have sat

That men and women of all sorts

Proclaimed both good and great;

And what's the odds if such as these

For reason of the State

Should keep their lovers waiting,

    Keep their lovers waiting.

Some boast of beggar-kings and kings

我在船上時一隻毛蓬蓬的巨大黑鳥出現；
從翅尖到翅尖它伸展開來足有二十尺寬，
劈劈啪啪扇動著翅膀，它大大地一番賣弄炫耀，
但是我還是不停地問，那船工能說什麼，除了
吠兒得嘍兒得咯哩噢。   20

如今我呆在酒吧裡，身子倚靠在牆壁上，
那麼來吧，身穿破布或絲綢，身披大氅
或鄉土披肩，和博學的情郎或隨便什麼人一起，
因為我可以把一切都放下，我所要說的不過是
吠兒得嘍兒得咯哩噢。

桂冠詩人的楷模

從中國到秘魯的寶座上
坐過各種各樣的皇帝，
被各種各樣的男人女人
讚頌為既偉大又仁慈；
那又有什麼要緊，假如
這樣的人們為了國事
竟然讓他們的愛人等待，
　　　讓他們的愛人等待。

有人誇讚乞丐王和黑白

Of rascals black and white   10
That rule because a strong right arm
Puts all men in a fright,
And drunk or sober live at ease
Where none gainsay their right,
And keep their lovers waiting,
    Keep their lovers waiting.

The Muse is mute when public men
Applaud a modern throne:
Those cheers that can be bought or sold
That office fools have run,   20
That waxen seal, that signature.
For things like these what decent man
Would keep his lover waiting?
    Keep his lover waiting?

Those Images

What if I bade you leave
The cavern of the mind?
There's better exercise
In the sunlight and wind.

惡棍的王，他們統治　　　　　　　　　10
是因為一條強壯的右臂
把所有人置於恐懼裡，
無論醉醒都悠閒地生活——
無人否認他們的權力——
並且讓他們的愛人等待，
　　　讓他們的愛人等待。

詩神默然，當社會名流
歡呼一個現代王權時：
那些能被買或賣的喝采，
那傻瓜們管理的科室，　　　　　　　20
那火漆封印，花押簽名。
為這樣的事正人君子
誰願意讓他的愛人等待？
　　　讓他的愛人等待？

那些形象

假如我叫你離開
心靈的洞穴如何？
在陽光和清風裡
運動鍛鍊更適合。

I never bade you go
To Moscow or to Rome,
Renounce that drudgery,
Call the Muses home.

Seek those images
That constitute the wild,
The lion and the virgin,
The harlot and the child.

Find in middle air
An eagle on the wing,
Recognise the five
That make the Muses sing.

10

我從來不曾叫你
去莫斯科或羅馬；
放棄那乏味勞作，
把繆斯們喚回家。

去尋覓那些形象：
它們構成猖狂人，
構成獅子和處女，
構成娼妓和孩童。

去在半空中發現
一隻展翅的鷹隼，
認清那五種形象，
它們使繆斯歌吟。

10

1938-1939
[Last Poems]
選自《最後的詩》

Under Ben Bulben

I

Swear by what the Sages spoke
Round the Mareotic Lake
That the Witch of Atlas knew,
Spoke and set the cocks a-crow.

Swear by those horsemen, by those women,
Complexion and form prove superhuman,
That pale, long visaged company
That airs an immortality
Completeness of their passions won;
Now they ride the wintry dawn   10
Where Ben Bulben sets the scene.

Here's the gist of what they mean.

II

Many times man lives and dies
Between his two eternities,
That of race and that of soul,
And ancient Ireland knew it all.
Whether man dies in his bed
Or the rifle knocks him dead,

布爾本山下

一

以那些聖賢所言起誓——
在阿特拉斯女巫所知，
那馬萊奧提克湖濱，
聖賢曾開言，令晨雞啼鳴。

以那些騎者，那些女人起誓——
他們的形容超凡絕世；
那面孔白皙瘦長的一群
面帶一種不朽的神情，
曾贏得過情熱的完成；
如今踏著寒冬的黎明　　　　　　　　　10
他們馳過布爾本山下。

以下是他們所示意的精華。

二

多少回人死而復生，
在種族和靈魂的永恆
這兩極之間輪迴；
古老的愛爾蘭早已知此。
無論是壽終正寢於床榻，
還是橫遭殘暴死槍下，

A brief parting from those dear
Is the worst man has to fear.   20
Though grave-diggers' toil is long,
Sharp their spades, their muscle strong,
They but thrust their buried men
Back in the human mind again.

III

You that Mitchel's prayer have heard
'Send war in our time, O Lord!'
Know that when all words are said
And a man is fighting mad,
Something drops from eyes long blind
He completes his partial mind,   30
For an instant stands at ease,
Laughs aloud, his heart at peace,
Even the wisest man grows tense
With some sort of violence
Before he can accomplish fate
Know his work or choose his mate.

IV

Poet and sculptor do the work
Nor let the modish painter shirk
What his great forefathers did,
Bring the soul of man to God,   40

人最爲懼怕的却是
與親愛者短暫別離。　　　　　　　　　20
鐵鍬鋒利，肌肉強健，
儘管掘墓人苦作不斷，
他們也不過將下葬的屍體
重新拋回人類的精神裡。

三

「主啊，給我們時代降下戰爭！」
聽到過米切爾祈禱的人們，
你們深知當話都說盡時，
當一個人瘋狂戰鬥之時，
久瞎的眼中有物墜落，
他完善了殘缺的心魄，　　　　　　　30
悠然佇立一時片刻，
放聲大笑，心氣平和。
連那聰明絕頂之人亦因
某種暴力而變得緊張萬分，
在他得以完成定數，熟練
業藝或選定終身伴侶之前。

四

詩人和雕塑家，請努力，
也勿讓時髦的畫家偏離
他的偉大祖先們的業績；
把人類的靈魂引向上帝，　　　　　　40

Make him fill the cradles right.

Measurement began our might:
Forms a stark Egyptian thought,
Forms that gentler Phidias wrought.

Michael Angelo left a proof
On the Sistine Chapel roof,
Where but half-awakened Adam
Can disturb globe-trotting Madam
Till her bowels are in heat,
Proof that there's a purpose set   50
Before the secret working mind:
Profane perfection of mankind.

Quattrocento put in paint,
On backgrounds for a God or Saint,
Gardens where a soul's at ease;
Where everything that meets the eye
Flowers and grass and cloudless sky
Resemble forms that are, or seem
When sleepers wake and yet still dream,
And when it's vanished still declare,   60
With only bed and bedstead there,
That Heavens had opened.

                    Gyres run on;
When that greater dream had gone

讓他把搖籃填充得恰當。

我們的力量始於度量：
一位古板的埃及人構思的形式，
那溫文的菲狄亞斯造就的形式。

在西斯廷教堂的穹頂，
米開朗基羅留下了證明；
那裡唯有半醒的亞當
能撩撥周遊世界的女郎，
直到她禁不住慾火中燒；
證明那祕密運作的頭腦　　　　　　　　　50
早有一個意圖確定在先：
冒瀆神聖而使人類完善。

在襯托上帝或聖徒的背景裡，
十五世紀畫家用色彩添置
供靈魂自在棲息的花園；
那裡一切目光可遇的東西，
鮮花、綠草、無雲的天際，
都肖似實在或彷彿的形式，
當時眠者已醒却仍在夢裡，
待到只剩下床架和床墊，　　　　　　　　60
夢魂散盡時，依然斷言：
天堂的大門曾經開敞。

　　　　　　　　螺旋轉動不休；
那更偉大的夢幻逝去之後，

Calvert and Wilson, Blake and Claude
Prepared a rest for the people of God,
Palmer's phrase, but after that
Confusion fell upon our thought.

V

Irish poets learn your trade
Sing whatever is well made,
Scorn the sort now growing up   70
All out of shape from toe to top,
Their unremembering hearts and heads
Base-born products of base beds.
Sing the peasantry, and then
Hard-riding country gentlemen,
The holiness of monks, and after
Porter-drinkers' randy laughter;
Sing the lords and ladies gay
That were beaten into the clay
Through seven heroic centuries;   80
Cast your mind on other days
That we in coming days may be
Still the indomitable Irishry.

VI

Under bare Ben Bulben's head
In Drumcliff churchyard Yeats is laid,

卡爾佛、威爾遜、布雷克和克勞德
為上帝的子民準備了安息之所，
帕爾莫的名言；但在那以後，
混亂降臨在我們的思想上頭。

五

愛爾蘭詩人，把藝業學好，
歌唱一切優美的創造；
鄙棄時興的那種從頭至足　　　　　　　　70
全然不成形狀的怪物，
他們不善記憶的頭和心
是齷齪床上卑賤的私生。
歌唱田間勞作的農民，
歌唱四野奔波的鄉紳，
歌唱僧侶的虔誠清高，
歌唱酒徒的放蕩歡笑；
也歌唱快樂的公侯命婦——
經過崢嶸的春秋七百度，
他們的屍骨已化作塵泥；　　　　　　　　80
把你們的心思拋向往昔，
以使我們在未來歲月裡可能
依然是不可征服的愛爾蘭人。

六

在光禿的布爾本山頭下面，
葉慈被安葬在竺姆克利夫墓園；

An ancestor was rector there
Long years ago; a church stands near,
By the road an ancient Cross.
No marble, no conventional phrase,
On limestone quarried near the spot   90
By his command these words are cut:

> Cast a cold eye
> On life, on death.
> Horseman, pass by!

September 4, 1938

The Black Tower

Say that the men of the old black tower
Though they but feed as the goatherd feeds
Their money spent, their wine gone sour,
Lack nothing that a soldier needs,
That all are oath-bound men
Those banners come not in.

There in the tomb stand the dead upright
But winds come up from the shore

古老的十字架矗立道旁，
鄰近座落的是一幢教堂，
昔時祖上曾在此住持講經。
不用大理石，也不用傳統碑銘，
只就近採一方石灰岩石，⁣   90
遵他的遺囑鐫刻如下文字：

　　　冷眼一瞥
　　　生與死。
　　　騎者，去也！

1938 年 9 月 4 日

黑塔

假如說那古老黑塔中的人們——
雖然他們不過像牧羊人一樣吃喝，
他們的錢花光，他們的酒變酸——
並不缺乏一個士兵所需的一切，
假如說他們都是立過誓約的人物；
那些旗幟就不會進入。

在那墳墓中死者筆直挺立，
但是大風起自海岸；

They shake when the winds roar
Old bones upon the mountain shake.   10

Those banners come to bribe or threaten
Or whisper that a man's a fool
Who when his own right king's forgotten
Cares what king sets up his rule.
If he died long ago
Why do you dread us so?

There in the tomb drops the faint moonlight
But wind comes up from the shore
They shake when the winds roar
Old bones upon the mountain shake.   20

The tower's old cook that must climb and clamber
Catching small birds in the dew of the morn
When we hale men lie stretched in slumber
Swears that he hears the king's great horn.
But he's a lying hound;
Stand we on guard oath-bound.

There in the tomb the dark grows blacker
But wind comes up from the shore
They shake when the winds roar
Old bones upon the mountain shake.   30

大風咆哮時死者搖顫，
老骨頭在山上顫慄。　　　　　　　　　　　　10

那些旗幟前來行賄或恫嚇，
或悄聲說，在自家
君王被遺忘之後還關心有何
君王建立統治的人是傻瓜。
如果他久已逝去，
你為何對我們還如此畏懼？

在那墳墓中淡淡月光滴瀝，
但是大風起自海岸。
大風咆哮時死者搖顫，
老骨頭在山上顫慄。　　　　　　　　　　　　20

當我們拖拽橫臥沉睡的人們之時，
塔中那必定在晨露中
攀上爬下捉小鳥兒的老廚子
發誓說他聽見了那偉大君王的號角聲。
可是他是個愛撒謊的傢伙；
我們謹守誓約立正警戒！

在那墳墓中黑暗變得更黑，
但是大風起自海岸。
大風咆哮時死者搖顫，
老骨頭在山上顫慄。　　　　　　　　　　　　30

In Tara's Halls

A man I praise that once in Tara's Halls
Said to the woman on his knees, 'Lie still,
My hundredth year is at an end. I think
That something is about to happen, I think
That the adventure of old age begins.
To many women I have said "lie still"
And given everything that a woman needs
A roof, good clothes, passion, love perhaps
But never asked for love, should I ask that
I shall be old indeed.'   10
                    Thereon the king
Went to the sacred house and stood between
The golden plough and harrow and spoke aloud
That all attendants and the casual crowd might hear:
'God I have loved, but should I ask return
Of God or women the time were come to die.'

He bade, his hundred and first year at end,
Diggers and carpenters make grave and coffin,
Saw that the grave was deep, the coffin sound,
Summoned the generations of his house
Lay in the coffin, stopped his breath and died.   20

在塔拉宮殿中

我讚頌的一個男人那次在塔拉宮殿中
對橫陳在他膝上的女人說:「靜靜躺著,
我的一百歲就要過了。我想,
有什麼事情即將發生;我想,
老年的冒險歷程開始了。
我曾經對許多女人說過『靜靜躺著』,
且給予她們女人所需要的一切:
房子、好衣服、情欲、也許還有愛情,
但從未要求過愛情;如果我要求,
我就真的老了。」   10
　　　　　　於是,那國王
走到那神聖大殿中,站在金犁耙之間,
為了讓所有侍從和偶然聚集的群眾
都能聽見,大聲地說道:
「我曾經愛過上帝,但如果我要求
上帝或女人的回報,死亡的時刻就到了。」

他命令──他的一百零一歲即將結束──
掘墓人和木匠修造陵墓和棺槨,
眼見陵墓深邃,棺槨牢固,
遂召集起宮中的男女老幼,
然後躺進棺槨中,停息而逝。   20

News for the Delphic Oracle

I

There all the golden codgers lay,
There the silver dew,
And the great water sighed for love
And the wind sighed too.
Man-picker Niamh leant and sighed
By Oisin on the grass;
There sighed amid his choir of love
Tall Pythagoras.
Plotinus came and looked about,
The salt flakes on his breast,   10
And having stretched and yawned awhile
Lay sighing like the rest.

II

Straddling each a dolphin's back
And steadied by a fin
Those Innocents re-live their death,
Their wounds open again.
The ecstatic waters laugh because
Their cries are sweet and strange,
Through their ancestral patterns dance,

作爲德爾斐神諭的消息

一

那裡，躺著所有金膚的老傢伙，
那裡，銀色的露滴
和浩淼的海水爲愛情嘆息，
風也嘆息。
勾引男人的尼婭芙在草地上
倚在烏辛身邊嘆息；
那裡，高大的畢達哥拉斯在他的
愛情合唱隊中間嘆息。
普羅提諾到來，四下張望，
胸上沾著鹹澀的浪漬，   10
在欠伸了片刻之後，
也像其他人一樣躺下來，嘆息。

二

各自騎在一隻海豚背上，
扶一片背鰭穩坐，
那些天眞者再度經歷死亡，
他們的傷口再度綻破。
狂喜的海水因他們的喊聲
美妙和陌生而大笑，
以它們祖傳的樣式舞蹈；

And the brute dolphins plunge   20
Until in some cliff-sheltered bay
Where wades the choir of love
Proffering its sacred laurel crowns,
They pitch their burdens off.

III

Slim adolescence that a nymph has stripped,
Peleus on Thetis stares,
Her limbs are delicate as an eyelid,
Love has blinded him with tears;
But Thetis' belly listens.
Down the mountain walls   30
From where Pan's cavern is
Intolerable music falls.
Foul goat-head, brutal arm appear,
Belly, shoulder, bum,
Flash fishlike; nymphs and satyrs
Copulate in the foam.

野性的海豚上下躍跳，   20
直到一處為峭壁掩蔽的海灣，
拋下它們背上的負擔；
愛情合唱隊在那裡涉水相迎，
獻上其神聖的桂冠。

三

被山林仙女剝光衣服的細瘦少年，
珀琉斯對忒提斯凝眸注目，
她的四肢像眼皮一樣嬌嫩，
愛情使他淚眼模糊。
但是忒提斯用肚子傾聽。
從潘的洞穴所在之處   30
到層層峭壁之下，
瀉落難以忍受的音樂之瀑。
醜陋的羊頭、粗野的手臂出現，
肚皮、肩膀、屁股，
閃亮似魚；眾山林仙女與半羊怪
在那水花裡交媾。

Long-legged Fly

That civilisation may not sink
Its great battle lost,
Quiet the dog, tether the pony
To a distant post.
Our master Caesar is in the tent
Where the maps are spread,
His eyes fixed upon nothing,
A hand under his head.

Like a long-legged fly upon the stream
His mind moves upon silence.   10

That the topless towers be burnt
And men recall that face,
Move most gently if move you must
In this lonely place.
She thinks, part woman, three parts a child,
That nobody looks; her feet
Practise a tinker shuffle
Picked up on the street.

Like a long-legged fly upon the stream
Her mind moves upon silence.   20

That girls at puberty may find

長足虻

爲使偉大戰役不失敗，
文明不至於淪喪，
讓狗兒安靜，把馬駒栓在
一根遠遠的柱子上。
我們的主將凱撒在營帳裡，
那裡攤開著一幅幅地圖，
他的雙眼茫然無睹，
一隻手托著頭顱。

像一隻溪水上的長足虻，
他的心思游動在靜寂之上。　　　　　　　10

爲使那高不見頂的塔樓遭焚，
人們懷念那面龐，
假如你必須，請極輕地走動
在這寂寞的地方。
她，一分婦人，三分孩子，以爲
沒有人窺視；她的雙腳
練習著一種從街頭學來的
流浪者的滑步舞蹈。

像一隻溪水上的長足虻，
她的心思游動在靜寂之上。　　　　　　　20

爲使懷春少女發現

The first Adam in their thought,
Shut the door of the Pope's chapel,
Keep those children out.
There on the scaffolding reclines
Michael Angelo.
With no more sound than the mice make
His hand moves to and fro.

Like a long-legged fly upon the stream
His mind moves upon silence.   30

A Stick of Incense

Whence did all that fury come,
From empty tomb or Virgin womb?
St Joseph thought the world would melt
But liked the way his finger smelt.

她們心目中的第一位亞當，
請關起教皇的聖堂大門，
把那些孩子阻擋。
在那裡，絞首架上
仰躺著米開朗基羅。
動靜輕如鼠爪弄出的一般，
他的手來回移動著。

像一隻溪水上的長足虻
他的心思游動在靜寂之上。　　　　　30

一炷香

那所有的騷動都來自何處，
來自空墳還是聖處女之腹？
聖約瑟心想這世界將消亡，
却喜歡他手指散發的馨香。

John Kinsella's Lament
for Mrs. Mary Moore

I

A bloody and a sudden end,
    Gunshot or a noose,
For death who takes what man would keep,
    Leaves what man would lose.
He might have had my sister
    My cousins by the score,
But nothing satisfied the fool
    But my dear Mary Moore,
None other knows what pleasures man
    At table or in bed.   10
What shall I do for pretty girls
    Now my old bawd is dead?

II

Though swift to strike a bargain
    Like an old Jew man,
Her bargain struck we laughed and talked
    And emptied many a can;
And O! but she had stories
    Though not for the priest's ear,

約翰‧金塞拉對
瑪麗‧穆爾太太的哀悼

一

槍擊或絞索帶來一個
　　血腥而突然的結局，
死神奪去人想保留的東西，
　　或留下人所願失去。
他本可以佔有我的妹妹，
　　我的一大群表姐妹，
可是什麼也滿足不了那老傻瓜，
　　除了我親愛的瑪麗‧穆爾；
別人誰也不知道如何使男人
　　在桌前或床上快意。　　　　　10
我能爲漂亮妞兒做些什麼，
　　旣然我的老鴇兒已死？

二

雖說在討價還價時比任何
　　老猶太人都難纏，
她一旦講定，我們便大笑歡談，
　　倒空了許多壇罐；
哦！唯有她有許多故事──
　　儘管不適合牧師聽聞──

To keep the soul of man alive
   Banish age and care,
And being old she put a skin
   On everything she said.
What shall I do for pretty girls
   Now my old bawd is dead?

20

III

The priests have got a book that says
   But for Adam's sin
Eden's garden would be there
   And I there within.
No expectation fails there
   No pleasing habit ends
No man grows old, no girl grows cold,
   But friends walk by friends.
Who quarrels over halfpennies
   That plucks the trees for bread.
What shall I do for pretty girls
   Now my old bawd is dead?

30

可保持人的靈魂活躍
　　或驅除衰老和愁悶，　　　　　　　　　　20
而年老時她給她說過的一切
　　又披上了一層表皮。
我能爲漂亮妞兒做些什麼，
　　既然我的老鴇兒已死？

　　　三

我曾經在教堂裡聽說
　　要不是亞當的罪愆，
伊甸樂園應當依然存在，
　　而我也會在那裡邊。
那裡沒有期望會落空，
　　沒有愜意的習慣會結束，　　　　　　　　30
沒有男人變老，沒有少女變冷，
　　只有朋友常伴著朋友走；
那裡沒有爲了半分錢的爭吵，
　　人們從樹上摘麵包吃。
我能爲漂亮妞兒做些什麼，
　　既然我的老鴇兒已死？

High Talk

Processions that lack high stilts have nothing that catches the eye.

What if my great-granddad had a pair that were twenty foot high,

And mine were but fifteen foot, no modern stalks upon higher,

Some rogue of the world stole them to patch up a fence or a fire.

Because piebald ponies, led bears, caged lions, make but poor shows,

Because children demand Daddy-long-legs upon his timber toes,

Because women in the upper stories demand a face at the pane

That patching old heels they may shriek, I take to chisel and plane.

Malachi Stilt-Jack am I, whatever I learned has run wild,

From collar to collar, from stilt to stilt, from father to child.   10

All metaphor, Malachi, stilts and all. A barnacle goose

Far up in the stretches of night; night splits and the dawn breaks loose;

I, through the terrible novelty of light, stalk on, stalk on;

Those great sea-horses bare their teeth and laugh at the dawn.

The Apparitions

Because there is safety in derision

高談

缺少高蹺的遊行隊伍沒有什麼可引人注目。
假如說，我太爺爺有過高達二十尺的一副，
我的不過十五尺，現代就沒人踩得更高了，
怎奈世間某無賴把它們偷去修籬笆或燒了。

因為花斑馬、鏈牽熊、籠中獅只會拙劣表演，
因為孩子們要求長腿爹爹踮起他的木頭腳尖，
因為樓上的女人們要求有一張臉在窗口嬉鬧，
好讓在補舊襪跟的她們驚叫，我便操起鑿和刨。

我乃瑪拉基·高蹺傑克，我所學都已不拘形式，
從護肩到項圈，從高蹺到鷸鳥，從父親到孩子。　10

全是比喻，瑪拉基、高蹺及一切。一隻北極黑雁
高高飛翔在遼闊夜空之中；夜幕撕裂，曙光迸濺；
我，穿過那極新鮮的畫色，闊步前行，闊步前行；
那些龐大的海象露出它們的牙齒，大肆嘲笑黎明。

鬼影

因為調侃嘲弄安全無害

I talked about an apparition,
I took no trouble to convince,
Or seem plausible to a man of sense,
Distrustful of that popular eye
Whether it be bold or sly.
Fifteen apparitions have I seen;
The worst a coat upon a coat-hanger.

I have found nothing half so good
As my long-planned half solitude,   10
Where I can sit up half the night
With some friend that has the wit
Not to allow his looks to tell
When I am unintelligible.
Fifteen apparitions have I seen;
The worst a coat upon a coat-hanger.

When a man grows old his joy
Grows more deep day after day,
His empty heart is full at length
But he has need of all that strength   20
Because of the increasing Night
That opens her mystery and fright.
Fifteen apparitions have I seen;
The worst a coat upon a coat-hanger.

所以我談論起一個鬼怪；
我不屑於費力說服，
或對理智之人顯得道理充足，
不信任那尋常的眼光，
無論它是狡黠還是狂妄。
我看見過十五個鬼影；
最壞的是一具衣架撐著一件衣裳。

我還不曾發現什麼事物
有我長期經營的半獨居的一半好處，　　　　　10
我可以和某個朋友
半夜不眠，而他具有
當我玄而又玄之時，
他却不動聲色的本事。
我看見過十五個鬼影；
最壞的是一具衣架撐著一件衣裳。

一個人變老了，他的歡樂
也一天比一天變得更深刻，
他空虛的心終於充實，
但他需要那全部力氣，　　　　　　　　　　20
因為漸漸濃厚的夜幕
敞開她的神祕和恐怖。
我看見過十五個鬼影；
最壞的是一具衣架撐著一件衣裳。

Man and the Echo

Man. In a cleft that's christened Alt
    Under broken stone I halt
    At the bottom of a pit
    That broad noon has never lit,
    And shout a secret to the stone.
    All that I have said and done,
    Now that I am old and ill,
    Turns into a question till
    I lie awake night after night
    And never get the answers right.   10
    Did that play of mine send out
    Certain men the English shot?
    Did words of mine put too great strain
    On that woman's reeling brain?
    Could my spoken words have checked
    That whereby a house lay wrecked?
    And all seems evil until I
    Sleepless would lie down and die.
Echo. Lie down and die.
Man.   That were to shirk
    The spiritual intellect's great work   20
    And shirk it in vain. There is no release
    In a bodkin or disease,

人與回聲

人：在一個名叫奧特的裂谷中，
　　在崩裂的石崖下，我暫停
　　在正午的陽光從來不
　　曾照到的一個洞穴底部，
　　向那岩石喊出一個祕密。
　　既然我現在已年老多疾，
　　我所說和所做過的一切
　　就都變成一個疑問，使得
　　我夜復一夜不能成眠，
　　永遠也得不到正確答案。　　　　　　　　　10
　　是否我的那部劇本曾驅使
　　一些漢子出去讓英國人槍斃？
　　是否我的文字曾給那女子
　　暈眩的頭腦施加太大壓力？
　　是否我的發言本可以阻止
　　造成一幢宅第毀圮的動力？
　　一切都顯得是罪惡，直到
　　我夜不能寐寧願躺下死掉。

回聲：躺下死掉。

人：　　　　　　　那是逃避
　　精神理智的偉大勞役，　　　　　　　　　20
　　而逃避也屬徒勞。短劍或
　　疾病都無法帶來解脫，

Nor can there be a work so great

As that which cleans man's dirty slate.

While man can still his body keep

Wine or love drug him to sleep,

Waking he thanks the Lord that he

Has body and its stupidity,

But body gone he sleeps no more

And till his intellect grows sure   30

That all's arranged in one clear view

Pursues the thoughts that I pursue,

Then stands in judgment on his soul,

And, all work done, dismisses all

Out of intellect and sight

And sinks at last into the night.

Echo. Into the night.

Man.   O rocky voice

Shall we in that great night rejoice?

What do we know but that we face

One another in this place?   40

But hush, for I have lost the theme

Its joy or night seem but a dream;

Up there some hawk or owl has struck

Dropping out of sky or rock,

A stricken rabbit is crying out

And its cry distracts my thought.

也不可能有功德偉大如此，
能清除人的污行穢跡。
當人還能保有他的肉體時，
醇酒或愛欲使他麻醉昏睡；
醒來時，他感謝上帝
讓他擁有肉體及其愚蠢行為，
但肉體消亡後，他不再沉睡，
直到他的理智漸漸確知　　　　　　　　　30
一切都排列成一個清晰景象，
並探求我所探求的思想，
然後立等對其靈魂的判決；
諸事都做完後，把一切
遣散出理智和眼界，
最後沉入黑夜。

回聲：沉入黑夜。

人：　　　　　　　呵，岩石的聲音，
我們能否在那偉大的夜裡歡欣？
除了在此地彼此面對著，
我們還知道些什麼？　　　　　　　　　40
但噤聲，因為我丟失了那主題，
其樂趣或黑夜不過像一場夢憶；
在那高處，一隻鷹或梟自天際
或崖頂俯衝而下，搏擊；
一隻受傷的兔子發出慘叫；
它的叫聲把我的思緒攪擾。

The Circus Animals' Desertion

I

I sought a theme and sought for it in vain,
I sought it daily for six weeks or so.
Maybe at last being but a broken man
I must be satisfied with my heart, although
Winter and summer till old age began
My circus animals were all on show,
Those stilted boys, that burnished chariot,
Lion and woman and the Lord knows what.

II

What can I but enumerate old themes,
First that sea-rider Oisin led by the nose   10
Through three enchanted islands, allegorical dreams,
Vain gaiety, vain battle, vain repose,
Themes of the embittered heart, or so it seems,
That might adorn old songs or courtly shows;
But what cared I that set him on to ride,
I, starved for the bosom of his fairy bride.

And then a counter-truth filled out its play,
'The Countess Cathleen' was the name I gave it,

馴獸的逃逸

一

我尋求一個主題但徒勞無功，
六七星期來我天天尋它不斷。
或許最終，只有成爲衰頹之人，
我才必將心滿意足，雖然
冬去夏來直到垂暮之齡，
我的馴獸都在人前表演，
那些踩高蹺的男孩，那鋥亮的馬車，
獅子和女人，還有上帝知道的一切。

二

除了列舉舊的主題我更有何能？
首先是那海上騎士烏辛被牽著鼻子　　　　　10
穿越了三座魔島，寓言的幻夢，
虛幻的歡樂，虛幻的戰鬥，虛幻的休憩，
心靈受苦的主題，或彷彿如此的類型，
倒可以裝點古老歌謠或宮廷獻藝；
是我讓他馳騁，可什麼令我掛心？
我，渴望他那仙女新娘的酥胸！

其次，一個反眞理充斥在戲劇中，
「女伯爵凱瑟琳」是我給它取的名；

She, pity-crazed, had given her soul away
But masterful Heaven had intervened to save it.　　　　20
I thought my dear must her own soul destroy
So did fanaticism and hate enslave it,
And this brought forth a dream and soon enough
This dream itself had all my thought and love.

And when the Fool and Blind Man stole the bread
Cuchulain fought the ungovernable sea;
Heart mysteries there, and yet when all is said
It was the dream itself enchanted me:
Character isolated by a deed
To engross the present and dominate memory.　　　　30
Players and painted stage took all my love
And not those things that they were emblems of.

III

Those masterful images because complete
Grew in pure mind but out of what began?
A mound of refuse or the sweepings of a street,
Old kettles, old bottles, and a broken can,
Old iron, old bones, old rags, that raving slut
Who keeps the till. Now that my ladder's gone
I must lie down where all the ladders start
In the foul rag and bone shop of the heart.　　　　40

她，醉心於憐憫，放棄了靈魂，
可專橫的上天却插手把它救拯。　　　　　　　　　20
我想我的愛人定會毀掉自己的靈魂，
同樣狂熱和仇恨也把它奴役踐躪，
這便產生出一個幻夢，一轉瞬
這夢本身佔據了我全部思想和愛情。

還有，當傻子和瞎子竊取麵包時，
庫胡林却在與無羈的大海拼博；
種種心靈的神祕，然而歸根結蒂，
還是那夢幻本身使我著魔：
人物性格被一種事業與世隔離
而專注於目前且把記憶掌握。　　　　　　　　　30
佔據我全部愛情的是演員和舞台
而不是他們所象徵的那些東西。

　　　　三

因爲是在純淨的心境中成長完善，
那些形象絕妙，却自何處肇始？
街上清掃的垃圾或一大堆破爛，
舊水壺、舊酒瓶、一隻破罐子，
廢鐵、殘骨、破布、那櫃上收錢的
長舌婦。既然我的梯子已丟失，
我只得躺倒在所有梯子起始之處，
在這心靈的污穢的廢舊物品舖。　　　　　　　　40

Politics

'In our time the destiny of man presents its meanings in
political terms.'   THOMAS MANN.

How can I, that girl standing there,
My attention fix
On Roman or on Russian
Or on Spanish politics,
Yet here's a travelled man that knows
What he talks about,
And there's a politician
That has both read and thought,
And maybe what they say is true
Of war and war's alarms,   10
But O that I were young again
And held her in my arms.

政治

「在我們的時代，人類的命運在政治術語中
展現其含義。」　　　——湯瑪斯・曼

那女孩站在那裡，我怎能
集中思想
在羅馬或俄羅斯
或西班牙的政治上？
這兒倒有一位多識之士明白
他談論的是什麼；
那兒還有一位既博學
又有思想的政客；
也許他們說的都是真的——
關於戰爭和戰爭警報；　　　　　　　　　　10
可是啊，但願我再度年輕，
把她摟在我的懷抱。

註釋

＊編按：註釋號碼係為詩行行數。

阿娜殊雅與維迦亞（21 頁）

　　葉慈原註：「那個小小的印度戲劇場景原是打算作為一齣關於一個男人為兩個女人所愛的劇本的第一幕的。他在她們之間有一個靈魂，一個女人醒著時另一個睡著，一個只知道白天另一個只知道黑夜。當我在羅西斯角看見一個男人拎著兩條鮭魚時，這念頭來到我腦海中。『一個人有兩個靈魂，』我說，然後又補充說，『哦不，兩個人有一個靈魂。』現在我在《幻景》中再次忙於這種思想：晝與夜、日與月的對立」（1925；《葉慈詩集新編》589 頁）。阿娜殊雅：梵語意為「無怨」，在印度神話裡是一仙女的名字，亦為印度古劇《沙恭達羅》中一人物；維迦亞：意為「得勝」。「黃金時代」傳統指人類的最初時代。

13. 阿沐麗塔：在印度神話裡意為不死仙藥。
14. 梵天：印度神話中三大神之一，是世界的創造者。
26. 欲天：又稱「無形」，印度神話中的性愛之神，持五支花朵製成的箭，因引誘濕婆而被濕婆用神火燒死。
66. 指印度神話中的始祖神迦葉波和他的妻子們。

被拐走的孩子（37 頁）

1. 斯利什森林：在史萊果郡吉爾湖南岸。
13. 羅西斯角：史萊果附近一海濱漁村。葉慈原註說：「這裡有一塊多岩石之地，如果有人在那裡睡著了，就有醒來變癡呆的危險，因為仙女們拿走了他們的靈魂」（1888；《校刊本》797 頁）。
28. 格倫卡：蓋爾語，意為「紀念碑之谷」，史萊果附近一湖泊名。

經柳園而下（41 頁）

　　葉慈說：「這是根據史萊果郡巴利索代爾村的一個經常自哼自唱的老農婦記不完全的三行老歌詞重寫的嘗試」（1889；《校刊本》90頁）。

老漁夫的幽思(43 頁)

葉慈稱:「此詩所根據的是一個從史萊果灣捕魚歸來的漁夫對我說的一些話」(1895;《校刊本》797 頁)。

佛格斯與祭司(47 頁)

葉慈原註:「我是根據羅埃之子佛格斯的事蹟塑造『那驕傲的好做夢的國王』的,但是在我寫作這首詩和我早年的書《現在誰願跟佛格斯同驅》中的歌時,我僅從斯丹迪什・歐格拉蒂先生的作品中得知他,我的想像力當時自由地處理我所知的,今天我則不大會贊同」。葉慈還解釋說,佛格斯是「紅枝系列中的詩人……他曾經是全愛爾蘭的王,據佛格森所整理的傳說,他放棄了王位,以便能在森林裡過平靜的狩獵生活」(1889;《校刊本》,795 頁)。這裡所指是塞繆爾・佛格森爵士(1810-86)所作〈羅埃之子佛格斯的退位〉。但是這篇作品在很大程度上是佛格森想像的產物。在北愛爾蘭或紅枝英雄傳說故事中,佛格斯不是詩人,也從未做過全愛爾蘭的王,而是北愛爾蘭王,紅枝英雄的首領。被他的寡嫂兼王后耐絲用計哄騙,而讓位給她的兒子康納哈。耐絲原是北愛爾蘭王「巨人」法赫納之妻,生子康納哈。法赫納死後,其異母弟佛格斯繼位,因為康納哈尚年幼。佛格斯甚愛耐絲,欲娶之。她乘機提出條件說:「讓吾子享位一年,好讓他的後裔為王者種」。佛格斯同意了。但是,一年期滿,由於康納哈統治聖明,人民要求他繼續在位;而佛格斯又耽於宴飲射獵,於是他就到林中去隱居,以靜修和夢術等方法獲取詩人和哲人的痛苦智慧。祭司(Druid)音譯為「督伊德」,特指古凱爾特人的祭司、巫師,他們精通占卜、魔法、醫術等,在古愛爾蘭等地享有崇高地位。

2-7. 祭司施展變化之術。

11. 康納哈是佛格斯的繼子和繼承者,紅枝英雄傳說中的北愛爾蘭王。

31-36. 靈魂的輪迴轉世。

37. 生命銷蝕,而智慧增長。

38. 祭司的夢使佛格斯洞知一切,但覺自身空無。

39. 指夢。

40. 指盛夢的魔袋。

和平的玫瑰（49 頁）

2. 米迦勒是天使長，曾率眾天使與龍戰鬥，並征服撒旦。

14. 上帝創世時所說。見《舊約・創世記》第一章。

仙謠（51 頁）

葉慈解釋說，格拉妮婭是「一個美女，爲逃避年邁的芬的愛情而與狄阿米德私奔。她從一個地方逃到另一個地方，跑遍了愛爾蘭，但是最終狄阿米德被殺於史萊果布爾本山朝海的一角。芬贏得了她的愛情，把倚靠在他頸上的她帶回到芬尼亞勇士集會之處，大伙兒爆發出經久不息的歡笑聲」（1895；《校刊本》795 頁）。老英雄芬・邁庫阿爾是芬尼亞系列傳奇中的主角，他手下的勇士統稱芬尼亞勇士；狄阿米德是他的姪兒，是其中的美男子，被野豬觸死。石柵欄：係愛爾蘭史前墓葬。

湖島因尼斯弗里（53 頁）

因尼斯弗里：蓋爾語，意爲「石楠島」；是史萊果郡吉爾湖中一小島。

搖籃曲（55 頁）

7. 七曜：指日、月、金、木、水、火、土星；或說指昴宿星團的七星。

愛的悲傷（57 頁）

5. 指古希臘美女海倫。

7. 奧德修斯：古希臘傳說英雄，獻木馬計破特洛伊城，凱旋回國途中歷盡艱險，歷時十年之久才到家。

8. 普里阿摩：特洛伊老王，城破後被希臘人殺死。

當你年老時（59 頁）

仿法國詩人彼埃爾・德・龍沙（1524-85）的同名十四行詩。寫給茉德・岡。

白鳥（59 頁）

葉慈解釋說：「仙境的鳥像雪一樣白。『姐娜的海濱』當然是『青春永駐之邦』，或仙境」（1892；《校刊本》799 頁）。

3. 藍星：指金星，西方以愛神維納斯之名稱之。藍色則是悲傷之色。

5. 玫瑰：女性的象徵；百合：男性的象徵。

女伯爵凱瑟琳在天堂（63 頁）

此詩原爲葉慈劇作《女伯爵凱瑟琳》1892 年版第五幕中的一首歌。

誰跟佛格斯同去？（65 頁）

見〈佛格斯與祭司〉一詩註。

夢想仙境的人（65 頁）

1. 竺瑪海爾：利陲姆郡一鄉村。

13. 利薩代爾莊園：葉慈的朋友康斯坦絲（1868-1927）和伊娃（1870-1926）・郭爾-布斯姐妹的家宅。

25. 斯卡納文井在史萊果郡。

37. 盧格納郭爾：史萊果郡格倫卡谷地中一小鎮，蓋爾語義爲「異鄉人谷地」。

退休老人的哀傷（71 頁）

葉慈自註說：「這首小詩基本上是韋克婁的一位老農的原話翻譯」（1895；《校刊本》799 頁）。1908 年他又解釋說此詩是源自「在雙岩山上一個人對我的一位朋友所說的話」（《校刊本》844 頁）。雙岩山在都柏林郡附近；那位朋友是作家喬治・W・拉塞爾（1867-1935）。

致曾與我擁火而談的人（77 頁）

1. 姐娜，或姐奴是古愛爾蘭傳說中的諸神之母。後來有學問的基督徒即用「姐娜之民」稱呼愛爾蘭早期居民。

10. 「大眾」指眾天使。

12. 「不可道的名號」指上帝的名號。

魚（83 頁）

致茉德・岡。

到曙光裡來（83 頁）

5. 愛爾：蓋爾語，即愛爾蘭。

漫遊的安格斯之歌（85 頁）

　　葉慈解釋說：「妲奴女神的部族能夠隨意變化，那些居住在水裡的常常化身為魚。……在別的時候它們則是美麗的女人；……此詩是受一首希臘民歌所啓發的；但是希臘的民間信仰與愛爾蘭的非常相似；在寫作此詩時，我當然想到的是愛爾蘭以及愛爾蘭的那些精靈。……」（1899；《校刊本》806 頁）。關於安格斯，葉慈說他是「青春、美和詩歌之神。他統治著青春之邦」（1895；《校刊本》794 頁）。

1.　　榛樹：在愛爾蘭被視為神聖的生命之樹。
22-23.　　指日光、月光透過樹蔭灑在地面上的圓形光斑，採擷它們喩不可能的事情。

戀人傷悼失戀（91 頁）

2.　　女友：指奧麗薇亞・莎士比亞（1867-1938）。1894 年，正當葉慈陷於對茉德・岡的無望的愛情旋渦中之時，詩友萊奧內爾・約翰生把表妹奧麗薇亞介紹給了他。葉慈與她始終保持著密切關係，只因她丈夫不肯離婚而未能與她結合。
3.　　舊日的絕望：葉慈自 1889 年結識茉德・岡後，屢次向她求婚均遭拒絕。
6.　　你：指茉德・岡。

他傷嘆他和愛人所遭遇的變故並渴望世界末日的來臨（91 頁）

　　葉慈原註說：「我的鹿和獵犬恰當地與亞瑟王傳奇的各種說法中閃入閃出、引導不同騎士歷險的鹿和獵犬有關，也與所有關於烏辛的青春之鄉之旅的說法開頭部分中的獵犬和無角鹿有關。這獵犬當然與安溫或哈得斯的獵犬有關──它們是白色的，長著紅耳朵；威爾士農民過去，也許現在仍然聽見它們在夜風中追趕某種飛行物；很可能也與愛爾蘭鄉民所認為的，如果你過於大聲或過早地哀悼死者，就會叫醒並抓走其靈魂的那些獵犬有關。……我是從一首上個世紀的關於烏辛的青春之鄉之旅的蓋爾語詩中得到我的獵犬和鹿的。在對無角鹿的追獵把他引到那海灘上之後，在他與尼婭芙一同馳騁在海面上之時，他在波濤中看見──我手頭沒有那首蓋爾語詩，僅憑記憶描述──一個少年追逐著一個手持金蘋果的少女，後來又見一條有一隻紅耳朵的獵犬追逐著一頭無角鹿。這條獵犬和這

頭鹿似乎是『爲了女人的』慾望和『爲了男人的慾望的女人的慾望』以及所有類似的慾望的單純意象。……我詩中的持榛木杖的人原本是愛神安格斯；我使無鬃的野豬來自西方，因爲在愛爾蘭，一如在其他國家，日落之處過去是象徵性的黑暗和死亡之地」(1899)。安溫，威爾士傳說中的地獄。關於男女慾望的引語出自塞繆爾‧柯立芝的《桌邊談話》。

他讓愛人平靜下來 (93 頁)

葉慈解釋說：「十一月，舊時的冬季之始，或佛魔羅，亦即死亡、陰鬱、寒冷、黑暗之力量的得勝之始，是被愛爾蘭人與馬形的普卡——它們現在是頑皮的精靈，但曾經是佛魔羅神祇——相聯繫的。我想它們也許與曼南南的群馬有某種聯繫，曼南南統治著死者之國，而佛魔羅的特什拉也統治著那裡。曼南南的群馬常常與海浪相關聯，雖然它們也能同樣輕易地跑過陸地。某位新柏拉圖主義者——我忘了是誰——把大海描寫成生命的漂浮不定的苦難，而我相信，在許多愛爾蘭關於航行去魔島的傳說中含有類似的象徵，或者在形成這些故事的神話學中多少含有一些。我大體仿傚愛爾蘭和其他神話學以及巫術傳統，把北方與夜晚和睡眠相聯繫，把日出之處東方與希望相聯繫，把日盛之處南方與熱情和慾望相聯繫，把日落之處西方與衰亡和夢幻事物相聯繫」(1899；《校刊本》808 頁)。普卡：愛爾蘭傳說中的「孤獨精靈」之一，形狀多變，時而爲馬，時而爲驢，時而爲牛，時而爲鷹。特什拉：佛魔羅之王。曼南南：屬於「妲奴之部族」，爲海神。此詩是寫給奧麗薇亞‧莎士比亞的。

致他的心，讓它不要懼怕 (97 頁)

5. 「金色黎明祕術修道會」入會儀式用語。

飾鈴帽 (99 頁)

葉慈原註：「我夢見這故事，完全如我所寫，隨後又做了另一個長夢，試圖想出它的意思，以及我將用散文還是用詩寫。第一個夢與其說是夢，不如說是幻視，因爲它美麗而一貫，給我以人們得自幻景的啓示和昇華，而第二個夢則混亂而無意義。此詩對於我總有豐富的含義，雖然作爲象徵性的詩，它不是總是意味相同。布雷克會說：『作者們在永恆之中，』我肯定他們只有在夢中才能被懷疑」

（1899；《葉慈詩集新編》591 頁）。飾鈴帽：馬戲團丑角所戴的飾有鈴鐺的尖帽。

1. 弄臣：宮廷中服務的伶人，通常扮演丑角以博國王一樂。

受難之苦（105 頁）

此詩是寫給奧麗薇亞・莎士比亞的。以耶穌受難故事爲意象，是克麗斯蒂娜・羅塞蒂風格。

5. 基仲溪：《聖經》中經常提到的一條流經耶路撒冷和橄欖山之間的小溪。

詩人祈求四大之力（105 頁）

「四大」，古人所謂構成世界的四大元素，即地、水、火、風。

2-4. 葉慈自註說：「我讓大熊座的七星哀悼那玫瑰的失竊，我還讓天龍座的巨龍充當玫瑰的守護者，因爲這些星座圍繞著天軸——許多國家古時候的生命樹，常常與神話學中的生命樹相聯繫——旋轉。我就是把這生命樹以其常見的作爲榛樹的愛爾蘭形式放進了『蒙根之歌』〔按：〈他想起前世作爲天上星宿之一的偉大〉的舊題〕一詩；因爲它有時以星星爲果實，所以我給它掛上『彎曲的犁鏵』和『導航者』星——操蓋爾語的愛爾蘭人對大熊星和北極星的稱謂」（《校刊本》811-12 頁）。

都尼的提琴手（111 頁）

都尼岩位於史萊果郡吉爾湖畔。

3. 基爾瓦內：史萊果郡巴里那卡羅村附近的一個小鎮。

4. 莫卡拉比：史萊果鎮西南郊馬格拉波依鄉鎮。

7. 史萊果位於愛爾蘭西北部，是葉慈外祖父母家所在地，葉慈在那裡度過了童年的大部分時間。

10. 在基督教傳統中，聖彼得被描繪爲天堂的守門人。

箭（115 頁）

此詩寫葉慈對於 1889 年初遇茉德・岡的回憶。

1. 箭鏃：象徵情欲。

樹枝的枯萎（117 頁）

6. 埃赫蒂：據傳說是「妲奴部族」中的一員，亦即一女神。埃赫蒂

山在戈爾韋和克萊爾郡境內。

12. 姐奴：見〈致曾與我擁火而談的人〉一詩註。

17-21. 初版的《在那七片樹林裡》(1903)收有敘事詩《波伊拉與艾琳》，葉慈對該詩的原註說：「……在安格斯頭頂上飛翔的鳥兒是他用他的吻造出的四只天鵝；當波伊拉和艾琳變成被金鏈拴在一起的天鵝時，他們採取古老故事中中了魔法的戀人們所採取的形體。彌迪爾是仙境之民，即希神的一個國王；他的妻子艾闈被一個妒忌的女人所逐，一度與安格斯一起在一座玻璃房子裡避難……」(《葉慈詩集新編》686 頁)。

19. 國王和王后：波伊拉和艾琳。

亞當所受的詛咒(119 頁)

上帝因亞當偷吃禁果而把他逐出伊甸園並詛咒他說：「你必終身勞苦，才能從地裡得吃的。……你必汗流滿面才得餬口，直到你歸了土……」(《舊約·創世記》第 3 章第 17-19 節)。

2. 「你」：指茉德·岡；「密友」：指茉德·岡之妹凱瑟琳。

沒有第二個特洛伊(131 頁)

據希臘神話，特洛伊王子帕里斯誘走斯巴達王后海倫，引起十年戰爭，最終特洛伊城被希臘人攻陷焚燬。葉慈此處以海倫比茉德·岡。

3-4. 茉德·岡在愛爾蘭政治活動中鼓吹暴力革命，葉慈對此持不贊同態度。

和解(131 頁)

此詩作於 1908 年。

3. 1903 年，葉慈在都柏林正要做講演時，聽說了茉德·岡在法國結婚的消息。他雖照例做了講演，但不知道自己都說了些什麼。

祝酒歌(133 頁)

葉慈稱此詩和〈面具〉一詩的靈感得自梅寶·狄金生。

凡事都能誘使我(137 頁)

2. 暗示對茉德·岡的迷戀。

3. 暗示對政治運動的熱衷。

4. 暗示劇院事務的經營管理。

銅分幣（139 頁）

9-14. 另本作：「啊，愛情是個曲折的東西，／沒有誰聰明絕頂／足
以窺透其中的奧祕，／他得把愛情久久思尋，／直到群星都已
飛逝，／陰影把明月吞噬掉。」

致一位徒勞無功的朋友（143 頁）

葉慈 1922 年自註：「葛列格里夫人在她的《休·雷恩爵士傳》中
認為那首以『如今真理全淪喪』開頭的詩是寫給他的。其實不是；那
是寫給她自己的」。1903 年，葛列格里夫人的侄子休·雷恩爵士決定
把他收藏的一批近代法國繪畫捐贈給都柏林市，條件是須建永久性
美術館專門收藏。由於新館設計者愛德華·路廷斯爵士是英國人以
及建館資金不足，該計劃遭到以《先驅晚報》和《獨立愛爾蘭人報》總
裁威廉·馬丁·莫菲為首的都柏林民族主義者的反對，從而引起長
達十餘年的爭議。其間葛列格里夫人積極支持雷恩爵士，並為該計
劃奔忙，但收效不大，反而遭到反對派的攻擊。

2. 指以莫菲為代表的反對派輿論。

4. 葛列格里夫人出身於貴族。

9-10. 指葛列格里夫人和雷恩爵士等為之奮鬥的寂寞的藝術事業。

致一個幽魂（145 頁）

「幽魂」：指查爾斯·斯圖亞特·帕內爾（1846-91），愛爾蘭國民
黨和議會黨領導人，曾任大不列顛地方自治聯盟主席，號稱「愛爾蘭
的無冕之王」，在愛爾蘭民族自治運動中起過重要作用。由於與歐什
阿太太的私通關係，他遭到眾議，被開除出黨，免去職務。

2. 帕內爾死後，在都柏林歐康納爾大街為他建有一座紀念碑；現
該處為帕內爾廣場。

9. 指休·雷恩爵士。見〈致一位徒勞無功的朋友〉一詩註。

17. 指威廉·馬丁·莫菲，他曾組織攻擊帕內爾。亦見〈致一位徒勞
無功的朋友〉一詩註。

19. 帕內爾葬於都柏林格拉斯內文公墓。「被單」當指裹屍布。

海倫在世時（147 頁）

葉慈在 1909 年 7 月 8 日的日記中寫道：「兩天前我夢到這樣一

個想法：『如果人們虐待我們的繆斯，我們有什麼理由抱怨，既然海倫在世的時候，他們所給她的不過是一支歌和一句玩笑？』」(《自傳》)

山墓（151 頁）

4. 羅西克勞斯神父即克里斯蒂安・羅森克勞茨（1378-?），德國術士，祕術社團玫瑰十字兄弟會創始人。據說在他去世多年以後，他的屍體被發現在墓裡毫無朽壞。葉慈於 1890 年加入麥克格萊戈・梅瑟斯領導的在倫敦的玫瑰十字祕術社團「金色黎明祕術修道會」。

亡國之君（153 頁）

此詩寫茉德・岡，作於 1912 年，經過埃茲拉・龐德的修改。

東方三賢（153 頁）

基督教傳說，耶穌降生後，有三位賢哲自東方前來朝覲。葉慈認為基督的降生和受難並非預示一個新的不變的文明；在世界末日之前還會有更莫測的神祕，因為歷史是循環的。

6. 卡爾佛里山：耶穌受難處，在耶路撒冷。

一件外套（155 頁）

此詩作於 1912 年。

一位愛爾蘭飛行員預見自己的死（159 頁）

葛列格里夫人的獨生子羅伯特・葛列格里（1881-1918）在英國皇家空軍服役，於 1918 年 1 月 23 日第一次世界大戰期間在義大利前線陣亡。

3. 指德國人。

4. 指英國人。

5. 基爾塔坦：在庫勒莊園附近。

人隨歲月長進（159 頁）

此詩作於 1916 年 7 月 19 日，寫伊索德・岡的青春美貌對詩人的觸動。

所羅門對示巴（163 頁）

此詩作於 1918 年。所羅門（前 972-932）：希伯來人之王，象徵葉慈；示巴：阿拉伯南部（今葉門地區）一古國，此處特指示巴女王瑪格達，象徵葉慈之妻喬吉。《舊約‧列王記上》第 10 章第 1-13 節記敘有示巴女王訪問所羅門王一事。

學究（167 頁）

12. 蓋尤斯‧瓦勒琉斯‧卡圖魯斯（前 84?-54?）：古羅馬著名詩人，以善寫艷情詩著稱，死時年僅 30 歲。

他的不死鳥（167 頁）

此詩作於 1915 年 1 月，初題為「在中國有一位王后」。

4. 指麗達，見〈麗達與天鵝〉一詩註。
8. 不死鳥：指茉德‧岡。
9. 嘉碧‧戴斯利斯（1844-1920）：法國女演員、舞蹈家。
10. 露絲‧聖德尼斯（1879-1968）：美國舞蹈演員。
11. 安娜‧瑪特維耶夫娜‧帕夫洛娃（1885-1931）：俄國芭蕾舞演員。
12-14. 可能指茱麗葉‧馬婁（1866-1950）：生於英國，長於美國，以演莎劇著稱的演員。
17. 這些都是埃茲拉‧龐德的女友。龐德於 1914 年娶多蘿茜——葉慈的朋友奧麗薇亞‧莎士比亞的女兒——為妻。

得自普羅佩提烏斯的一個想法（171 頁）

塞克斯圖斯‧普羅佩提烏斯（前 50-16）：羅馬詩人。此詩是其作品第二卷（前 26）第二首詩的自由改寫。

4. 希臘神話中的智慧女神。
8. 希臘神話中的人頭馬怪貪酒好色，常強搶人間美女。

殘破的夢（171 頁）

此詩作於 1915 年 10 月 24 日，寫給茉德‧岡。

深沉的誓言（175 頁）

此詩作於 1915 年 10 月 17 日，寫給茉德‧岡。

1. 茉德‧岡曾發誓不結婚。

吾乃爾主（179 頁）

標題原文爲拉丁文，出自義大利作家但丁‧阿利蓋里(1265-1321)的詩集《新生》(1292-93)。但丁描述了一個幻景：「一個君主，在竟敢凝視他的人看來面目可畏，但同時又彷彿內心歡喜，可謂奇觀。他說著話，說了許多事情，其中我只能聽懂很少；我所聽懂的那些話裡面有這麼一句：吾乃爾主。」

1. 說話者的名字是拉丁文代詞，「希克」意爲「此、這」；「伊勒」意爲「彼、那」。前者爲客觀，後者爲主觀辯護。

26. 拉波‧蓋因尼(1270-1330)和基多‧卡瓦爾坎提(1230-1300)：均爲詩人，但丁的朋友。

30. 貝都因：阿拉伯語，意爲「帳篷居民」，指阿拉伯地區的遊牧部民。

37. 指蓓德麗采‧波爾提那里(1266-90)，但丁的愛人。

57. 約翰‧濟慈(1795-1821)：英國詩人。

入宅祈禱（185 頁）

4. 加利利：巴勒斯坦一地區，與耶穌的生平有關。

10. 「水手辛巴達」是阿拉伯傳說故事集《一千零一夜》中的一個故事裡的人物。

月相（187 頁）

葉慈〈麥克爾‧羅巴蒂斯的雙重幻視〉一詩原註云：「幾年前我寫了三個短篇小說，其中出現有麥克爾‧羅巴蒂斯和歐文‧阿赫恩這兩個名字。現在我認爲我用了兩個朋友的眞名，其中之一，麥克爾‧羅巴蒂斯，最近剛從美索不達米亞回來，他在那裡部分地找到，部分地悟出了許多哲學。我認爲阿赫恩和羅巴蒂斯——我曾經給他們的同名者賦予了一種動盪的生活或死亡——一直在與我爭吵。他們就位於一個幻景中，在其中我努力解釋我的有關生死的哲學。在某種程度上我寫作這些詩是作爲一種闡釋文本的」(1922；《葉慈詩集新編》595 頁)。

4. 康吶瑪拉：戈爾韋郡一地區。

11. 他：指葉慈。

14. 英國詩人約翰‧彌爾頓(1608-74)的長詩《沉思的人》(1632)中的

主人公。

15. 英國詩人珀西・比舍・雪萊(1792-1822)的長詩《阿他那斯王子》(1817)中的主人公。

17. 英國畫家塞繆爾・帕爾默(1805-81)為彌爾頓的《沉思的人》所作題為《孤獨的塔》的銅版畫插圖。

26. 沃爾特・佩特(1839-94)：英國作家、批評家。

28. 葉慈在短篇小說《東方三賢的禮拜》(1896)中寫到了羅巴蒂斯的死。

45. 雅典娜：見〈得自普羅佩提烏斯的一個想法〉一詩註 4；阿基里斯：希臘傳說英雄。

46. 赫克特：特洛伊國王普里阿摩與王后赫卡柏之子，在特洛伊戰爭中被阿基里斯所殺。弗里德里希・尼采(1844-1900)：德國哲學家。

67. 西奈山：在地中海與紅海之間的西奈半島上；在《聖經》中，是摩西接受十誡之地。

麥克爾・羅巴蒂斯與舞蹈者(203 頁)

此詩作於 1919 年，最初發表於《日晷》(1920 年 11 月)。他：代表葉慈的意見；她：代表伊索德的意見。

19. 雅典娜：見〈得自普羅佩提烏斯的一個想法〉一詩註 4。

26. 保羅・維若奈斯(1528-88)：義大利畫家。

32-33. 義大利藝術家米開朗基羅・波那羅蒂(1475-1564)於 1508-12 年在羅馬西斯廷教堂穹頂繪成壁畫《創世記》。《晨》和《夜》則是其在佛羅倫薩美第奇教堂的雕塑作品。

39-40. 指基督在最後的晚餐上分配飲食以像自己的血肉(見《新約・路加福音》第 22 章第 14-20 節)。

1916 年復活節(207 頁)

1916 年 4 月 24 日，即復活節翌日，愛爾蘭共和兄弟會在都柏林發動起義，宣告愛爾蘭共和國成立，約七百人的愛爾蘭志願者軍隊佔領了部分市區。至 29 日，起義被英軍鎮壓，15 位領導人遇害。

17. 指康斯坦絲・郭爾-布斯(1868-1927)，她出身名門，1900 年嫁給波蘭伯爵卡西米爾・約瑟夫・杜寧-馬凱維奇(1874-1932)，起義期間任愛爾蘭共和兄弟會志願軍軍官。葉慈認為她的熱衷

政治是美的喪失。

24. 指帕垂克·皮爾斯(1879-1916)，律師兼詩人，都柏林郡聖恩達學校創建者，曾任共和兄弟會主席，起義失敗後遇害。

25. 希臘神話中的飛馬珀伽索斯蹄踏之處有泉水湧出，詩人從中獲取靈感。

26. 指湯馬斯·麥克多納(1878-1916)，詩人兼評論家，都柏林大學學院教授，起義失敗後遇害。

31. 指約翰·麥克布萊德(1878-1916)，起義軍軍官，茉德·岡的離異了的丈夫，起義失敗後遇害。

33. 指茉德·岡。

68-69. 英國國會於 1914 年 9 月通過了愛爾蘭自治法案，由於第一次世界大戰爆發而延緩實施。又由於這次起義，遂有人謠傳英國政府打算取消該法案。

76. 詹姆斯·康諾利(1870-1916)：愛爾蘭工會領袖，國民軍創建者和總司令，起義失敗後遇害。

78. 綠色是愛爾蘭的國色。歌頌 1798 年起義的歌曲有《佩戴綠色》、《我的披風上的綠色》等。

關於一名政治犯(213 頁)

指康斯坦絲·郭爾-布斯·馬凱維奇伯爵夫人(1868-1927)。1916年復活節起義失敗後，她被英軍逮捕，關押在倫敦霍洛威女監。

再度降臨(217 頁)

《新約·馬太福音》第 24 章第 31-46 節載耶穌預言他將再度降臨人間，主持末日審判，開創新紀元。《新約·約翰一書》第 2 章第 18節載約翰預見到昭示天啓之獸或「反基督」將在世界末日之前到來，毀滅舊世紀。葉慈把二者揉合起來，結合新柏拉圖主義的歷史循環說，預言已歷近兩千年的基督教文明將在劇烈的暴力衝擊下終結，隨之將開始一種新的文明，因為他認為人類文明兩千年一循環。此詩寫於 1919 年 1 月，也反映了葉慈對第一次世界大戰和愛爾蘭的「黑褐戰爭」的態度。詩中的「再度降臨」是虛寫，實寫的是基督再度降臨前的破壞之神的降臨。

1. 螺旋：葉慈用兩個交相滲透的旋轉的錐體圖形來說明造成人類歷史循環的主客觀因素的相互作用。一個文明從其中一個錐體

的尖端開始，呈螺旋形旋轉到底部而「崩散」結束，然後又從另一錐體的尖端開始反向旋轉，開始另一文明的循環。

2. 獵鷹象徵人性；馴鷹人象徵人類。或說獵鷹象徵人類和現在文明；馴鷹人象徵耶穌基督。

5. 暴力之象。有感於俄國革命和愛爾蘭內戰或第一次世界大戰。

12. 「世界靈魂」：葉慈解釋為「一個不再屬於任何個人或鬼魂的形象倉庫」；亦稱「大記憶」；亦即柏拉圖所謂生命之源，或類似於榮格所謂「集體無意識」。

18. 又一次文明的循環即將結束。

20. 耶穌之搖籃。暗示基督教自誕生伊始就為自己準備了敵對者。

22. 伯利恆：耶穌降生之地。「反基督」亦來此投生，更添恐怖氣氛和諷刺意味。

為我女兒的祈禱(219頁)

安・巴特勒・葉慈生於 1919 年 2 月 26 日。

4. 此詩作於峇里鄺塔堡，葛列格里夫人的庫勒莊園附近。

26. 海倫因與特洛伊王子帕里斯私奔而引起十年特洛伊戰爭。

27-29. 希臘神話中的愛與美及繁殖女神阿芙羅黛悌誕生於海浪之中，嫁給瘸腿的火和鍛冶之神赫准斯託斯為妻。

32. 據希臘神話，母山羊阿瑪爾忒亞曾哺育主神宙斯，其雙角充溢著瓊漿仙釀。後一角脫落，充滿果實，宙斯將之送給女神們，即為豐饒角。為富饒之象徵。

38-40. 指葉慈自己及其戀愛和婚姻。

60. 指阿芙羅黛悌，亦影射海倫和茉德・岡。她們都錯選了男人。

戰時冥想(225頁)

4. 太一：新柏拉圖主義鼻祖普羅提諾(204-270)所謂的最高理念。他認為從「太一」流出「理性」，從「理性」流出「靈魂」，從「靈魂」流出「物質」。

航往拜占庭(229頁)

拜占庭是小亞細亞古城，經羅馬皇帝康斯坦丁一世(287?-337)重建，名為康斯坦丁堡(一譯君士坦丁堡)；公元六世紀時為東羅馬帝國首都，東西方文化在此交匯，繁榮一時；葉慈視之為理想的文

化聖地，藝術永恆之象徵；即現今土耳其之伊斯坦堡。

1. 指愛爾蘭及自然物質世界。

4. 繁殖之象徵。

18. 據葉慈記憶，義大利拉文那的聖阿波里奈教堂牆壁上有描繪聖徒受火煎烤的拜占庭風格鑲嵌畫。

22. 指人的肉體，靈魂暫時受難的牢獄。

30. 葉慈原註：「我曾在某處讀到，在拜占庭的皇宮裡，有一棵用金銀製作的樹和人造的會唱歌的鳥」(《新編葉慈詩集》595頁)。葉慈認為物質轉瞬即逝，只有精神和藝術才永恆不朽。

我窗邊的燕雀巢(233頁)

英愛條約於1921年12月6日在倫敦簽訂，1922年1月7日在愛爾蘭議會通過，但愛爾蘭共和派拒不接受該條約，於是爆發了1922-23年共和派與愛爾蘭自由邦政府之間的內戰。葉慈原註：「在愛爾蘭西部我們把歐椋鳥叫做燕雀；內戰期間有一隻在我臥室的窗戶旁的石洞中築巢。」

麗達與天鵝(237頁)

據希臘神話，斯巴達王廷達瑞俄斯之后麗達被變化成天鵝的主神宙斯強姦而生海倫(性愛的象徵)、克萊婷(亞格曼儂之妻)和狄俄斯庫里兄弟(戰爭的象徵)。葉慈認為這預示舊的文明(上古時代)行將終結，新的文明(荷馬時代)即將到來，而變化的根源即在於性愛和戰爭。

10-11. 海倫與帕里斯的私奔導致特洛伊戰爭和特洛伊城邦的毀滅；希臘聯軍統帥亞格曼儂(權力和尊嚴的象徵)在凱旋歸國後被其妻克萊婷夥同姦夫謀殺。

題埃德蒙·杜拉克作黑色人頭馬怪圖(239頁)

埃德蒙·杜拉克(1882-1953)：英國畫家，葉慈之友。

8. 據說是一種用在埃及底比斯古墓中木乃伊棺裡發現的麥種培育出來的小麥，在英國有種植。見《關於古埃及人的傳說》(倫敦，1854)。葉慈以此暗示隱祕的智慧在播種以後數百千年方能成熟。

10-11. 基督教傳說，在羅馬皇帝狄修斯(?-215)迫害基督徒時期，

七個殉道者被封閉在小亞細亞古城以弗所附近的一個山洞裡。兩百年後他們醒來,被帶到提奧多修斯二世(401-450)面前,他們的故事堅定了他的動搖的信仰。馬其頓國王亞歷山大大帝(前356-323)於公元前334年攻佔以弗所;他的帝國在他死後不久即解體。

在學童中間 (241 頁)

葉慈於 1926 年 2 月參觀沃特佛鎮的聖奧特蘭小學後作。

9. 見〈麗達與天鵝〉一詩註。

15-16. 柏拉圖在《會飲篇》中記,希臘劇作家亞里斯多芬(前450-385)論辯說,原始人是雙性的,類似一球體,後被宙斯一分為二,就像以頭髮切開煮熟的雞蛋。性愛則被視為企求重新合一。

26. 此詩初版指里奧納多・達芬奇(1452-1519)。

34. 葉慈原註:「我從潑爾菲瑞關於『山林女仙的洞府』的文章中取用了『生殖之蜜』,但是在潑爾菲瑞那裡沒有找到視之為破壞對出生前自由之『回憶』的『藥物』的根據。……」(《葉慈詩集新編》597 頁)。潑爾菲瑞(232/3-305):新柏拉圖主義哲學家。他在《關於山林女仙的洞府》一文中解釋說蜂蜜「恰當地象徵了降入迷人的生殖領域的快樂與愉悅。」

41. 柏拉圖(前429-347):希臘哲學家。

43. 亞里斯多德(前384-322):希臘哲學家,曾任亞歷山大大帝的私人教師。

45. 畢達哥拉斯(前582-507):希臘哲學家,音程的數理基礎的發現者。

初戀 (249 頁)

寫與茉德・岡的戀愛。

人類的尊嚴 (251 頁)

寫對茉德・岡的苦戀。

美人魚 (251 頁)

寫與奧麗薇亞・莎士比亞的私情。

野兔之死(253 頁)

寫對伊索德・岡的單戀。

12. 可能暗指她與弗朗西斯・斯圖亞特的不幸婚姻。

空杯(255 頁)

寫與奧麗薇亞・莎士比亞的關係。葉慈在 1926 年 12 月 6 日致信莎士比亞太太:「回顧青年時代就好像看渴死的瘋子留下的半嘗未嘗的杯子。」

他的記憶(255 頁)

寫 1907 或 1908 年與茉德・岡發生性關係。

5. 赫克特:特洛伊勇士,特洛伊王普里阿摩與赫卡柏之子,爲希臘英雄阿基里斯所殺。

15. 她:特洛伊的海倫,象徵茉德・岡。

三座紀念雕像(257 頁)

都柏林市歐康奈爾大街上有英國海軍大將霍瑞修・耐爾森(1758-1805)、愛爾蘭政治領袖丹尼爾・歐康奈爾(1775-1847)和查爾斯・斯圖亞特・帕內爾(1846-91)雕像紀念碑。三者私生活均欠檢點。

紀念伊娃・郭爾-布斯和康・馬凱維奇(263 頁)

伊娃・郭爾-布斯(1870-1926):詩人、社會主義者;康斯坦絲・郭爾-布斯・馬凱維奇(1868-1927):革命家。後者因參與 1916 年復活節起義而被判處死刑,後改判無期徒刑,1917 年 6 月遇大赦出獄,仍舊活躍於愛爾蘭政壇。葉慈自 1894 年起與該姊妹相識。

1. 利薩代爾:蓋爾語,意爲「盲人的庭院」,郭爾-布斯家族在史萊果郡的莊園。

16. 喬治時代爲 1714-1820 年。而利薩代爾建於 1832 年。

死(265 頁)

爲愛爾蘭自由邦司法部兼外交部長凱文・歐希金斯(1892-1927)被恐怖分子刺殺而作。

自性與靈魂的對話 (267 頁)

25. 元茂長舟備守 (譯音)：日本武士，活躍於應永年間 (1394-1428)。

象徵 (275 頁)

5. 日本外交官佐藤純造 (1897-) 於 1920 年 3 月贈給葉慈一柄家傳的寶劍。參見〈自性與靈魂的對話〉一詩。

十九世紀及以後 (277 頁)

葉慈於 1929 年 3 月 2 日致信莎士比亞太太：「我漸漸擔心世界最後的偉大詩歌時代已經結束。」

在阿耳黑西拉斯──沉思死亡 (277 頁)

阿耳黑西拉斯：西班牙南部一城市，位於直布羅陀對面。

11. 英國科學家艾薩克・牛頓爵士 (1642-1727) 曾經說：「我不知世人會怎樣看我；但我自己覺得我不過像一個孩子，在海灘上玩耍，不時地逸出常規，撿到比一般漂亮的卵石或貝殼罷了，而偉大的真理之海洋在我面前尚全然未被發現」(大衛・布魯斯特《艾薩克・牛頓爵士的生平、著作和發現》，愛丁堡，1855 年，第 2 卷 407 頁)。

12. 羅西斯：見〈被拐走的孩子〉一詩註 13。

16. 指上帝。

摩希尼・查特基 (281 頁)

葉慈於 1885 年在都柏林會見印度婆羅門摩希尼・莫罕・查特基 (1858-1936)，從此樹立了他對輪迴轉世學說的終生信仰。

拜占庭 (283 頁)

此詩作於 1930 年 9 月。拜占庭象徵藝術和靈魂的聖地。葉慈認為靈魂須不斷輪迴再生，逐漸達到不朽境地；而每次再生前，須經淨化。此詩即寫靈魂超脫輪迴，走向永恆樂土之前的最後一次淨化。

1. 物質世界的現象。

3. 妓女拉客聲。

4. 指東羅馬皇帝查士丁尼安於公元 532-37 年間在拜占庭修建的聖索菲亞大教堂。

9. 幻影：指超脫了輪迴之劫，無死無生的「精靈」。它引導靈魂走
向永恆。

11. 哈得斯是希臘神話中之冥王。哈得斯的線軸喻靈魂，它降生人
世而纏繞上「經驗」（屍布），因爲生對於靈魂意味著自由的喪
失、監禁或死亡。解開纏繞的「道路」（生命）則意味著脫離塵世，
回到永恆。

13-14. 無生無死的精靈召集靈魂回歸永恆。

16. 在活在世上的人看來，精靈的幻影是死的，但從永恆的觀點看
來，却正是它活著，而世上之人是死的。

17. 藝術品爲不朽之象徵，故它藐視自然物和人類。

20. 古羅馬人墓碑上刻有雄雞，爲再生之先導。

25. 康斯坦丁堡廣場上有鑲嵌圖案的甬道，爲藝術之象徵。

27. 傳說拜占庭街角有燐火，可滌除死魂靈身上的不潔。

30-32. 日本能樂劇中有少女在想像的罪惡之火中揮袖而舞的場
景。葉慈藉以指塵世之火。

33. 西方傳說，靈魂由海豚馱往極樂之島。

34. 藝術的創造者抵禦人欲的進攻。

36. 藝術之象徵。

39. 尚未脫離輪迴之劫的靈魂。

40. 人類情感之海。

老年的爭吵（287 頁）

此詩作於 1931 年 11 月，記與茉德・岡的一次爭吵，可能有關
絕食女囚事。

2. 指都柏林。

9. 輪迴觀念給老之將至的葉慈以希望。

16. 葉慈在《自傳》中寫初見茉德・岡的印象：「那時，她就像春天女
神的古典式化身，維吉爾的讚美『她走起路來好像女神』只是爲
她一人而寫的。」

對不相識的導師們的謝忱（289 頁）

2. 指葉慈太太「自動書寫」時下降附體的「神靈」們。

格倫達湣的溪水和太陽（289 頁）

格倫達湣：蓋爾語，意為「雙湖之谷」，位於威克婁郡拉臟鎮附近。

受責的瘋珍妮（291 頁）

5. 歐羅巴：希臘神話中的腓尼基公主，被宙斯化成白牛劫持到克里特，生彌諾斯和拉達曼堤斯。後嫁給克里特王阿斯忒里俄斯。

催眠曲（299 頁）

3-6. 據希臘神話，特洛伊王子帕里斯誘拐斯巴達王后海倫，從而引發十年特洛伊戰爭。

8. 據中古傳奇《崔斯坦與伊索德》，騎士崔斯坦奉命赴愛爾蘭護送美女伊索德回康沃爾與馬克王成婚，途中二人誤服巫藥而相愛。

14-18. 見〈麗達與天鵝〉一詩註。「神聖的鳥兒」即宙斯。歐羅塔斯河在斯巴達之東。

長久沉默之後（301 頁）

此詩作於 1929 年 11 月，寫給奧麗薇亞・莎士比亞。

像霧和雪一般狂（301 頁）

葉慈原註說：「1929 年春，生命復歸，猶如偉人的創造者們不可遏制的精力和勇氣的影響一般；彷彿除了新聞和評論，那所有的遁詞和解釋之外，這世界要被撕成碎片。我寫了〈像霧和雪一般狂〉，一首機械的小歌，隨後在那狂熱的幾周裡，幾乎《或許可譜曲的歌詞》那組詩全都湧入了腦海。然後又病了，我寫了〈拜占庭〉和〈維羅尼卡之帕〉，尋找適合我年齡的主題，從而得以把自己暖回生命。自那以後，我又給《或許可譜曲的歌詞》增加了幾首詩，但總是保持最初詩作的情緒和設計」（1933；《校刊本》831 頁）。

7. 賀瑞斯（前 65-8）：古羅馬作家；荷馬：古希臘盲詩人。

8. 柏拉圖（前 429-347）：古希臘哲學家。

9. 圖里：即馬爾庫斯・圖里尤斯・西塞羅（前 106-43），古羅馬演說家。

父與女（303 頁）

葉慈與女兒安妮的一次對話實錄，寫小女孩對男性美的最初印象；約作於 1928 年，其時安妮應為 9 歲。

5. 指葉慈。另說指一位名叫佛戈斯・菲茨傑拉德的朋友。

最初的表白（307 頁）

在為此詩及以下的〈所選〉和〈離別〉二詩所作註中，葉慈解釋說：「我把一個女人的愛情象徵化為黑暗試圖阻止太陽從它的大地床舖上升起的努力。在『選擇』〔後改為〈所選〉〕的最後一節，我把這象徵改為男人和女人的靈魂穿過黃道帶上升」（1928；《校刊本》830頁）。

她在樹林中的幻視（309 頁）

14. 希臘神話中的美少年阿多尼斯和愛爾蘭傳說中的狄阿米德都是被野豬所傷而死。

20. 安德瑞亞・曼特格納（1431-1506）：義大利畫家。

依譜重填的兩首歌（321 頁）

1. 葉慈劇作《一鍋肉湯》（1903 年初版）1922 年版所增補的一首歌。「派絲汀・芬」（蓋爾語，意義為「秀髮少女」或「芬的小女孩」）是一首流行的愛爾蘭民歌的標題。

2-6. 第 1 及 2-6 行最初發表於葉慈劇作《演員女王》（1922）中；第2-5行增入《三月的滿月》（1935）中。

瑞夫在波伊拉和艾琳之墓畔（323 頁）

葉慈原註說：「『超自然的歌』中的隱修士瑞夫是一個虛構的聖帕垂克的批評者。他的基督教信仰像許多早期愛爾蘭基督教信仰一樣，可能來自埃及，與基督教前思想相仿」（1935；《校刊本》857 頁）。聖帕垂克（385-461）是最早去愛爾蘭傳播基督教的羅馬傳教士，愛爾蘭的主保聖徒。波伊拉：愛爾蘭傳說中萊因斯特國王梅斯格德拉與北愛爾蘭女神布安之子；據葛列里夫人所著《繆阿瑟姆吶的庫胡林》，波伊拉「屬於茹德瑞格〔按：北愛爾蘭英雄群體之一〕一族，雖然他僅佔有極少土地，但他是北愛爾蘭王國的繼承者，無論男女老少，誰見了他都喜愛，因為他非常會說話，他們都叫他『蜜嘴波伊

拉』。」艾琳是他的愛人。據葉慈敘事詩《波伊拉與艾琳》,「波伊拉與
艾琳是一對戀人,但是愛神安格斯希望他們在他的國度,在死者中
間幸福,便給每人講了一個關於對方之死的故事,於是他們心碎而
死。」葉慈 1934 年 7 月 24 日致信莎士比亞太太:「我腦子裡還有一
首詩,說的是一個修士半夜在去世很久的一對戀人的墓上讀祈禱
書,那天正是他們的週年忌日;當夜他們〔的靈魂〕在墓地上空交
合,他們的擁抱不是部分的,而是全身起火發光;他就藉著那光亮
讀書。」

8.　波伊拉與艾琳死後,一棵紫杉樹和一棵蘋果樹分別從他們的葬
　　身之處生長起來;他們相戀的故事則寫在用紫杉和蘋果木做的
　　板子上。

15.　此說出自瑞典神祕主義者伊瑪紐埃爾・斯韋登堡(1688-1772)。

瑞夫在出神狀態(327 頁)

1.　葉慈曾在家裡對一些朋友朗讀〈瑞夫駁斥帕垂克〉一詩。讀畢,
　　他問他們懂不懂,其中一位(可能是茉德・岡)回答:「不,我一
　　個字也不懂」。

7.　此詩描寫詩人自己的交歡之感。葉慈於 1934 年接受回春手術,
　　性能力大大恢復。

那裡(327 頁)

　　「那裡」:葉慈《幻景》體系中之第 13 圓錐體,實為球形,為完美
自足之境界。普羅提諾用以指神聖球體:「太陽,那裡,是所有星星;
每顆星又是所有星星和太陽。」柏梅說,那裡,「生命向內纏繞趨向
太陽。」

2.　蛇頭銜蛇尾是神祕主義的完美之象徵。

什麼魔鳥的鼓噪聲?(329 頁)

　　此詩寫神人之交合。

它們從何處來?(329 頁)

　　此詩問個人情愛和一般歷史事件背後有什麼神祕的決定力量。

12.　查理曼(742-814):初為法蘭克國王(768-814),後由教皇列奧
　　三世加冕為西羅馬帝國皇帝(800-814)。

人的四個時期（331 頁）

在葉慈的哲學體系中，個人人格和人類文明可劃分成四個階段：1.地、本能、早期文明；2.水、情欲、中古騎士時代；3.風、理智、文藝復興至 19 世紀末；4.火、靈魂、文明被仇恨毀滅的時代。

會合（331 頁）

葉慈把星相學上的木星（朱庇特，亦爲古羅馬神話中的主神）和土星（薩圖恩，亦爲古羅馬神話中的農神）的會合與一種「相對立的或主觀的」天命，火星（馬爾斯，亦爲古羅馬神話中的戰神）和金星（維納斯，亦爲古羅馬神話中的愛神）的會合與一種「基督教的或客觀的」天命相聯繫。見阿蘭·韋德編《葉慈書信集》（倫敦，1954）828 頁。

2. 見〈題埃德蒙·杜拉克作黑色人頭馬怪圖〉一詩註 8。

3. 「他」指耶穌基督。

4. 「女神」指維納斯。

須彌山（333 頁）

1933 年，葉慈爲印度僧人師利·普羅希大師所著《聖山》一書作序。此詩可能作於那期間。在劇作《大鐘樓之王》的前言中，葉慈寫到：「一首關於須彌山的詩自發地來臨，但是哲學是個危險的主題……」（1934-35；《校刊本》855 頁）。

9. 須彌山：「須彌」係梵語「蘇迷盧」之訛略，意爲「妙高」。須彌山即西藏境內的凱拉神山，在印度教神話中是位於宇宙中心的金山，是世界之軸。天神居於此山，其餘脈即喜馬拉雅山，山南即婆羅多婆舍國。主要天神都在此山或附近有各自的樂園，信者死後在那裡與他們一起等待轉世再生。艾佛勒斯山：即喜馬拉雅山之珠穆朗瑪峰。1885 年英人主持的印度測量局以其前任局長艾佛勒斯（S. G. Everest）的姓氏命名該峰；1952 年中國政府將其更名爲珠穆朗瑪峰；尼泊爾則稱之爲薩迦-瑪塔。

天青石雕（337 頁）

1935 年 7 月 4 日，70 歲的葉慈收到友人哈利·克里夫頓贈送的一件生日禮物———一塊中國乾隆年間的天青石雕。翌日他寫信給女詩人多蘿茜·韋爾斯利說：「有人送給我一大塊天青石雕作禮物，上面有中國雕刻家雕刻的山巒、廟宇、樹木、小徑和正要登山的隱士

和弟子。隱士、弟子、頑石等是重感覺的東方的永恆主題。絕望中英雄的呼喊。不,我錯了,東方永遠有自己的解決辦法,因此對悲劇一無所知。是我們,而不是東方,必須發出英雄的呼喊。」葉慈最初的構思側重於東、西方對待悲劇的不同態度,但 1936 年 7 月 25 日詩成之後,它的主題更加豐富了。葉慈在寫給韋爾斯利的信中說此詩「幾乎是我近年來所作的最好的作品」(《致多蘿茜・韋爾斯利談詩書信集》)。

2-3. 調色板、提琴弓和詩人分別代表視覺藝術、音樂和文學,它們為熱衷於政治的人們所鄙棄,面臨毀滅的危險。葉慈作此詩時,歐洲正籠罩著對可能爆發的戰爭的恐慌。

6-7. 在 1690 年的波義尼戰役中,英王威廉三世擊敗詹姆斯二世。有民謠描述他使用炸彈的情景。在第一次世界大戰中,德皇威廉二世曾使用齊卜林飛艇空襲倫敦。比利是威廉的暱稱,故此處一語雙關。

10-11. 均為英國戲劇家威廉・莎士比亞(1564-1616)筆下的悲劇人物。

16. 葛列格里夫人說:「悲劇對於死者來說必定是一種快樂。」因為他們找到又失去了人們所追求的一切。

25-26. 指埃及人、阿拉伯人、基督教徒和伊斯蘭教徒。

28. 指古希臘人及其文明。

29. 伽里瑪科斯:前五世紀希臘雕刻家,發明以旋鑿雕刻衣紋,曾為雅典守護神廟製作一盞金燈及一個棕櫚樹形的青銅長燈罩。

39. 指仙鶴。

曼妙的舞女(341 頁)

瑪格特・儒多克(1907-51):英國演員、詩人,著有詩集《檸檬樹》(1937);葉慈為之作序。葉慈曾說她的詩藝越來越糟,勸她停止寫詩。她因此想自殺,那麼她的詩就有可能傳世。一天她冒雨跳進海裡,又想到她熱愛生活,遂開始在海灘上跳舞。翌日,她去了巴塞隆那,在那裡發了瘋。

三叢灌木(343 頁)

此詩是對多蘿茜・韋爾斯利(見〈致多蘿茜・韋爾斯利〉一詩註)所作的一首謠曲的改寫,其本事來源係虛構。

一畝草地(357 頁)

作於葉慈晚年在都柏林居住的河谷別墅。

15. 米開朗基羅：(1475-1564)：義大利畫家、雕塑家。
20. 泰門和李爾：分別是莎士比亞悲劇《雅典的泰門》和《李爾王》中的人物。
23. 威廉・布雷克(1757-1827)：英國詩人、畫家。

致多蘿茜・韋爾斯利(361 頁)

多蘿茜・韋爾斯利(1889-1956)：英國詩人、韋靈頓公爵夫人、葉慈晚年的朋友。

7. 多蘿茜・韋爾斯利曾購置了數英畝土地，把該地區原住居民連同他們的狗一起逐出。
10. 多蘿茜・韋爾斯利的愛犬布魯圖斯。
16. 希臘神話中專司懲罰犯罪之人的女神，爲克洛諾斯和夜女神的女兒。

刺激(363 頁)

此詩作於 1936 年 10 月 7 日，最初發表於 1938 年 3 月的《倫敦信使報》。葉慈 1936 年 12 月 4 日致信多蘿茜・韋爾斯利稱「我的詩全都出自憤怒或情欲」；12 月 9 日的信附以此詩，稱之爲他的「最後辯解」。12 月 11 日，葉慈又將此詩寄給艾瑟爾・曼寧，冠以「某些事情逼得我發瘋；我的舌頭失去了控制」句。

朝聖者(365 頁)

6. 德戈湖：多呐戈爾郡和費爾瑪納郡交界處一小湖，是愛爾蘭最重要的朝聖地，人稱「聖帕垂克的煉獄」，據傳聖帕垂克曾在那裡禁食齋戒，看見另一個世界的幻景。
7. 指表現耶穌受難的系列圖畫，通常爲十四幅，天主教會稱之爲「苦路十四處」。
13. 在天主教神學中，煉獄是註定要升入天國的靈魂死後滌除污穢的處所。

桂冠詩人的楷模(367 頁)

桂冠詩人是享受英國皇室薪俸而爲其慶典場合提供頌詩的詩人

的稱號。當時的桂冠詩人約翰・梅斯菲爾德(1878-1967)爲慶祝英王喬治六世(1895-1952)登基寫了一首〈爲國王的在位祈禱〉(《泰晤士報》1937年4月28日)。喬治之繼位是因其兄愛德華八世(1894-1972)爲娶瓦麗斯・辛普森太太而退位。

那些形象(369 頁)

7. 「乏味勞作」指參加政治活動。當時德、義法西斯主義的崛起令歐洲知識分子擔憂,而蘇俄的社會主義成就令他們興奮和幻想。

8. 九繆斯是希臘神話中藝術和科學的保護神。

布爾本山下(375 頁)

布爾本山位於愛爾蘭西部史萊果郡,史萊果鎮北。此詩被一般編輯者排在葉慈詩集的最後,是葉慈一生思想的總結,表達他對今生和來世的信念,帶有總結和預言性質。

1. 指古埃及救世主的傳道使徒。

2. 用雪萊《阿特拉斯的女巫》典故。女巫能洞察事物的眞實性,乃靈魂之象徵。

3. 今名厄爾馬亞湖,在埃及亞歷山大港南。

4. 傳說布爾本山上有超自然存在的幻影,愛爾蘭神話中許多事件也發生在此山上。此節與前一節代表葉慈信仰體系的兩個重要來源:一是東方的神祕宗教,一是愛爾蘭民間迷信。

25-26. 約翰・米切爾(1815-75):愛爾蘭民族主義者,因從事反英鬥爭而被捕。引語來自他的《獄中日誌》。

43. 希臘哲學家普羅提諾(205-269/270)據說生於埃及的呂科波利斯。他反對柏拉圖的藝術是摹仿之摹仿說,認爲藝術能直接回到萬物之源「理念」;藝術作品具有獨立性,能補自然美之不足。

44. 菲狄亞斯(前 490-432):希臘著名雕刻家。

45-47. 義大利畫家米開朗基羅・波那羅蒂(1475-1564)在梵帝岡西斯廷教堂穹頂繪製著名的《創世記》一畫,其中有裸體的亞當。

54. 十五世紀文藝復興初期畫家(或特指達芬奇)崇尙宗教美,這與前一節崇尙人體美的藝術風格形成對照,二者各代表傳統的一面。

64. 愛德華·卡爾佛(1799-1883)：英國畫家。理查德·威爾遜(1714-1782)：英國畫家。威廉·布雷克(1757-1827)：英國詩人兼版畫家。克勞德·洛蘭(1600-1682)法國畫家。他們代表傳統藝術的繼承者。

66. 塞繆爾·帕爾莫(1805-1881)：英國畫家。他曾評論布雷克爲維吉爾作品的英譯本所作的插圖說：「它們像那位卓越的藝術家的所有作品一樣，拉開了肉體的惟幕，窺見了所有虔誠勤勉的聖徒享受過的、那留給上帝的選民的安息之處」(《塞繆爾·帕爾莫傳及書信》倫敦 1892 年版，15-16 頁)。

79. 自 12 世紀愛爾蘭被諾曼人征服至 20 世紀。

84-88. 葉慈的曾祖父約翰·葉慈(1776-1846)在年間任史萊果郡竺姆克利夫(蓋爾語，意爲「柳焰之山脊」)教堂教區長。葉慈遺骸於 1948 年 9 月 17 日遷葬於竺姆克利夫，墓碑上鐫刻著此詩末尾的三行墓誌銘。

黑塔(383 頁)

此詩完成於 1939 年 1 月 21 日，是葉慈所作的最後一首詩。

7. P·W·喬伊斯在《古愛爾蘭社會史》(倫敦，1903)中解釋說：「有時國王和諸侯的屍體以直立姿勢入葬，全副武裝，面朝敵人的疆土。」

在塔拉宮殿中(387 頁)

塔拉：山名，在米阿斯郡境內，是古愛爾蘭尤伊內爾王朝歷代君王加冕之地和王國首都所在地。

作爲德爾斐神諭的消息(389 頁)

德爾斐是古希臘城市，其中的阿波羅神殿以神諭靈驗著稱。普羅提諾的學生潑爾菲瑞(223-304)在《普羅提諾傳》中敍述了他請阿彌琉斯求問神諭，以獲知普羅提諾的靈魂在死後的命運之事。神諭說他將象徵性地回歸，經過生命之海，受到冥界樂土判官們的歡迎，並受到柏拉圖、畢達哥拉斯和不朽的唱詩班的眾神的喜愛。此詩即描寫普羅提諾在樂土所見。

5-6. 古愛爾蘭諸神稱爲圖阿莎·德·妲南，即妲奴女神的部族。尼婭芙是妲奴部族中的美女。她曾把武士兼詩人烏辛誘引到她們

的國度『青春之鄉』。

7-8. 畢達哥拉斯（前 582-507）：古希臘哲學家、數學家，音程的數理基礎的發現者。

9. 普羅提諾（204-270）：希臘哲學家，生於埃及，是新柏拉圖主義創始人。

13-15. 見〈拜占庭〉一詩註 33。

26. 在希臘神話中，阿耳戈英雄之一珀琉斯捉住山林仙女忒提斯並與之成婚。愛爾蘭國家美術館藏有浦森的油畫《珀琉斯與忒提斯結婚》。

30. 潘：赫爾墨斯之子，山林、畜牧及繁殖之神，人身而羊腿，頭上生角。

長足虻（393 頁）

長足虻：雙翅目長足虻科昆蟲。形小，藍或綠色，有金屬光澤。捕食較小的昆蟲，見於陰濕的沼澤周圍。（《簡明不列顛百科全書》，中國大百科全書出版社，1985）。

5. 蓋尤斯・尤力烏斯・凱撒・奧克塔維亞努斯（公元前 63-公元14）：古羅馬第一位皇帝。

15. 指年輕時的特洛伊的海倫。

21-28. 指義大利畫家米開朗基羅・波那羅蒂（1475-1564）在羅馬西斯廷教堂穹頂繪製著名的壁畫《創世記》，其中有裸體的亞當。

一炷香（395 頁）

2. 聖處女即耶穌之母瑪麗亞。

3. 聖約瑟是瑪麗亞的丈夫。

約翰・金塞拉對瑪麗・穆爾太太的哀悼（397 頁）

均為虛構的人物。

21-22. 「給故事披上一層皮」是愛爾蘭成語，意為潤飾，使之可信。

26. 見〈亞當所受的詛咒〉一詩註。

高談（401 頁）

此詩作於 1938 年 7-8月間，最初發表於當年 12 月的《倫敦信使報》和《國民》上。

1. 葉慈曾寫道，當（十九世紀）九十年代結束後，「我們都從高蹺上

下來了」。他在致多蘿西・韋爾斯利的信中寫道:「我現在開始踩偷來的馬戲團高蹺了。」

9. 瑪拉基(「我的使者」)是《舊約・瑪拉基書》的假定作者;聖・瑪拉基(1095-1148)是愛爾蘭著名聖徒;瑪拉基・穆里根是詹姆斯・喬伊斯(1882-1941)在小說《尤利西斯》(1922)中給葉慈的朋友奧利佛・聖約翰・郭伽蒂(1878-1957)取的化名。但此處很可能是葉慈虛構的一個人物。

鬼影(401 頁)

此詩作於 1938 年 3-4月間,最初發表於 1938 年 12 月的《倫敦信使報》。標題:葉慈於 1938 年 1 月在馬約卡島病後做的一系列夢中所見死神。

人與回聲(405 頁)

1. 史萊果郡境內克塢克納瑞山腰上的一個峽谷。

11. 指葉慈劇作《凱瑟琳・尼・胡里漢》(1902)。在《愛爾蘭英語文學和戲劇簡史》(倫敦,1936)中,愛爾蘭作家斯蒂芬・桂因(1864-1950)寫道:「《凱瑟琳・尼・胡里漢》對我的作用是,我在回家的路上自問,這樣的劇本是否該上演,除非是準備讓人們走出去開槍或被槍殺的。」

13. 可能指瑪格特・儒多克,見〈曼妙的舞女〉一詩註。

16. 可能指庫勒莊園。葛列格里夫人 1932 死後,房子失修,後被賣給一承包人,1942 年被拆毀。

21. 自殺的象徵。參見莎士比亞《哈姆雷特》第三幕第一場:「他可能用一把出鞘的短劍/結果自己時」。

馴獸的逃逸(409 頁)

這是一首關於詩思枯竭的詩。馴獸喻指葉慈早期作品中的形象。

10-16. 葉慈早期敘事詩《烏辛的漫遊》(1889)中有英雄烏辛被仙女尼婭芙誘往青春之島、黑塔之島和遺忘之島的情節。

18. 葉慈早期劇作《女伯爵凱瑟琳》(1892)敘述女伯爵凱瑟琳為拯救愛爾蘭飢餓的人民而把自己的靈魂出賣給魔鬼,最終被上帝拯救的故事。

21. 指茉德・岡。

25-26. 葉慈早期劇作《波伊拉海灘》(1903)敍述英雄庫胡林因誤殺
　　 親生兒子而發瘋的故事。當庫胡林與海浪博鬥之時，劇中的傻
　　 子和瞎子却溜到烤爐邊偷麵包吃。

31-32. 葉慈在 1906-1914 年間任艾貝劇院經理，忙於日常事務，而
　　 忽視了精神生活。

40. 葉慈述及的形象都存在於精神世界，始於內心(情感)，因此無
　　 法接近。他於是被撇在經驗(理智)的垃圾中，不再有夢來救贖。

政治 (413 頁)

　　1938 年 3 月，《耶魯評論》刊登了美國詩人阿奇波爾德・麥克利
什的〈詩歌中的公共話語與私人話語〉一文。文中讚揚了葉慈詩裡的
「公共話語」，但暗示他應當把這種話語用於寫政治題材。葉慈即作
此詩作答。他說此詩所據並非「一個真實事件，而是片刻的冥想」。
原題作〈主題〉。作爲題記的德國小說家湯瑪斯・曼(1875-1955)的那
句話也轉引自麥克利什的文章。

英詩名索引

葉慈年表

1862 年： W・B・葉慈牧師(祖父)於都柏林桑地蒙堡逝世。

1863 年： 約翰・巴特勒・葉慈(父親)與蘇珊・波萊克斯芬在史萊果結婚。

1865 年： 6 月 13 日，威廉・巴特勒・葉慈出生於都柏林市桑地蒙特大道喬治大宅一號。

1866 年： 蘇珊・瑪麗・葉慈(麗麗)出生於史萊果附近。

1867 年： 全家遷居倫敦市瑞金公園菲茨羅伊路 23 號。經常去史萊果外祖父母家。芬尼亞黨人起義。「曼徹斯特烈士」殉難。

1868 年： 伊麗莎白・柯伯特・葉慈(蘿麗)出生於倫敦。

1871 年： 約翰・巴特勒・葉慈(傑克)出生於倫敦。

1871-75 年： 父親借助於司各特和莎士比亞的作品對葉慈進行「人格」教育。

1874 年： 全家移居西肯星頓區伊蒂斯住宅區 14 號。

1875-80 年： 就讀於英國漢默史密斯的郭德爾芬小學；回史萊果外祖父母家度假。

1876 年： 全家遷居契斯威克區貝德福公園伍德斯多克路 8 號。

1877 年： 查爾斯・斯圖亞特・帕內爾任地方自治同盟主席。

1879 年： 帕內爾領導的愛爾蘭民族黨建立愛爾蘭土地同盟。

1880 年： 因土地戰爭，全家遷回愛爾蘭都柏林市厚斯區，以照管基爾達爾的地產。入都柏林的埃拉斯姆斯中學。

1882 年：　　自認爲愛上了遠房表姐勞拉・阿姆斯特朗。開始寫
　　　　　　　詩。弗・卡文迪什勳爵和柏克遇刺於鳳凰公園。愛
　　　　　　　爾蘭土地聯盟被鎮壓。

1884 年：　　入都柏林首府藝術學校。與喬治・拉塞爾(AE)同
　　　　　　　學。父親因葉慈拒絕上三一學院而失望。

1885 年：　　兩首抒情詩發表在《都柏林大學評論》3 月號上。創
　　　　　　　立都柏林祕術學會，任主席。結識凱瑟琳・泰南。

1886 年：　　棄畫從文。初遇約翰・歐李瑞。開始閱讀愛爾蘭詩
　　　　　　　人的作品。初次體驗降神會。格拉茲通與帕內爾爲
　　　　　　　爭取地方自治而聯合。第一個地方自治議案失敗。
　　　　　　　貝爾法斯特發生暴動。

1887 年：　　全家遷回倫敦。加入布拉瓦茨基夫人通靈學會理事
　　　　　　　會。初次在英國雜誌上發表詩作。成爲兩家美國報
　　　　　　　紙(《神意星期日報》和《波士頓導航報》)的文學撰稿
　　　　　　　人。會見前拉斐爾派藝術家。母親兩度發病。

1888 年：　　會見威廉・莫瑞斯、喬治・蕭伯納、威廉・亨利和
　　　　　　　奧斯卡・王爾德。編寫《愛爾蘭民間傳說故事集》。
　　　　　　　在史萊果外祖父母家度夏。家裡賣掉地產。

1889 年：　　輕度虛脫。第一本詩集《烏辛的漫遊及其他》出版。
　　　　　　　在牛津大學出版社做編輯、抄寫工作。與埃德溫・
　　　　　　　艾利斯合編《威廉・布雷克詩全集》。經歐李瑞之妹
　　　　　　　介紹結識茉德・岡。

1890 年：　　〈湖島因尼斯弗里〉發表於《全國觀察家》雜誌。被通
　　　　　　　靈學會勸退。加入「金色黎明」祕術修道會。結識弗
　　　　　　　洛倫絲・法爾。

1891 年：　　在倫敦創立詩作者俱樂部和愛爾蘭文學會。在都柏

林創立民族文學社，由歐李瑞任社長。小說《約翰‧舍曼》發表。向茉德‧岡求婚。

1892 年： 《凱瑟琳女伯爵及各種傳奇和抒情詩》出版。外祖父母逝世。

1893 年： 《凱爾特的曙光》和三卷本《布雷克作品集》出版。格拉茲通的第二次地方自治議案在英國下院通過，在上院被否決。道格拉斯‧海德創立蓋爾聯盟。

1894 年： 2 月：遊巴黎，同阿瑟‧賽蒙斯會見魏爾倫。奧斯卡‧王爾德被捕。3 月：短篇小說集《隱祕的玫瑰》出版。詩劇《心願之鄉》在倫敦上演。經萊奧內爾‧約翰生介紹結識其表妹奧麗薇亞‧莎士比亞太太。秋：與舅父喬治‧波萊克斯芬在史萊果做法術實驗。二訪利薩代爾莊園。冬：帶慰問信訪王爾德。

1895 年： 《詩集》出版。編輯《愛爾蘭詩選》。移居「聖殿」（倫敦法學學會會所），與阿瑟‧賽蒙斯合住。

1896 年： 移居沃本住宅樓。與奧麗薇亞‧莎士比亞私通。爲《卷心菜》雜誌撰稿。與阿瑟‧賽蒙斯遊愛爾蘭西部。結識葛列格里夫人。遊阿蘭群島。在巴黎遇見約翰‧辛。加入愛爾蘭共和兄弟會。

1897 年： 《隱祕的玫瑰》出版。盤桓於庫勒莊園；與葛列格里夫人一同採集民間傳說。籌建愛爾蘭民族劇院。與茉德‧岡在英國巡迴講演，爲紀念伍爾夫‧透吶募捐。寫作《斑鳥》（未發表的長篇小說）。都柏林發生抗議維多利亞女王在位 60 週年慶典騷亂。

1898 年： 遊巴黎、倫敦、都柏林、庫勒、史萊果。在都柏林茉德‧岡家遇詹姆斯‧康納利。與茉德‧岡訂結「靈

婚」。

1899 年： 愛爾蘭文學劇院首次演出綵排。上演《凱瑟琳女伯
爵》。詩集《葦叢中的風》出版並獲當年最佳詩集「學
院」獎。訪茉德・岡於巴黎，再度求婚。布爾戰爭爆
發。阿瑟・格瑞菲斯創立聯合愛爾蘭人（新芬）黨。

1900 年： 母親逝世。與梅瑟斯發生齟齬，另組「金色黎明」倫
敦分會。向茉德・岡求婚。退出愛爾蘭共和兄弟會。
維多利亞女王巡幸愛爾蘭。

1901 年： 與喬治・穆爾合寫的《迪阿米德與格拉妮婭》在都柏
林快樂劇院上演。在庫勒莊園會見休・雷恩。向茉
德・岡求婚。

1902 年： 愛爾蘭民族戲劇社成立，葉慈任社長，茉德・岡、
道格拉斯・海德、喬治・拉塞爾（AE）任副社長。茉
德・岡主演《凱瑟琳・尼・胡里漢》。在倫敦會見喬
伊斯。

1903 年： 詩集《在那七片樹林裡》、文論集《善惡觀》出版。詩
劇《王宮門檻》寫成。開始在美國麥克米蘭公司出
書。率民族戲劇社劇團訪倫敦，演出《沙漏》、《一鍋
肉湯》和《凱瑟琳女伯爵》。到美國講演（40 講），在財
經上獲成功。伊麗莎白・葉慈創辦敦・埃默出版社
（後改名為夸拉出版社）。茉德・岡與約翰・麥克布
萊德結婚。

1904 年： 艾貝劇院開張，任經理兼舞台監督。《在波伊拉海濱》
和《王宮門檻》上演。在庫勒莊園寫成詩劇《黛爾
德》。

1905 年： 《蔭翳的水域》在倫敦上演，旋即被改寫。

1906 年： 愛爾蘭民族戲劇社改爲有限公司，與葛列格里夫人
和辛一起被提名爲董事。《詩集 1899-1905》出版。

1907 年： 在《西部世界的浪蕩子》風波中爲辛辯護。與葛列格
里夫人及其子羅伯特同遊義大利北部。父親去了紐
約。

1908 年： 8 卷本《詩與散文匯集》出版，早期作品皆經修改。
12 月：訪已分居的茉德・岡於巴黎。學習法語。

1909 年： 約翰・辛逝世。編輯辛格的《詩和譯作》。遇識埃茲
拉・龐德。

1910 年： 接受英國王室年金津貼（每年 150 英鎊）及自由參加
任何愛爾蘭政治活動的免罪權。辭去劇院經理職
務。在倫敦講演，爲艾貝劇院籌資。5 月：訪茉德・
岡於諾曼底。《綠盔及其他》出版。與梅寶・狄金生
的性關係出現危機。喬治・波萊克斯芬逝世。

1911 年： 《爲一愛爾蘭劇院所作劇》出版。經莎士比亞太太介
紹結識喬吉・海德-李斯。同葛列格里夫人訪巴黎。

1912 年： 率艾貝劇院演出團訪美；因上演辛的《西部世界的
浪蕩子》，演員在費城被捕。在哈佛大學作題爲「美
的戲劇」的講演。散文集《瑪瑙的切割》在美國出版。
在都柏林成立第二個艾貝劇團。與泰戈爾合作翻譯
孟加拉文《吉檀迦利》。龐德追隨葉慈，教他擊劍術，
並一起朗誦作品。冬：休・雷恩贈畫風波。

1913 年： 8 月：龐德作爲葉慈的秘書同住於蘇塞克斯的斯通
別墅。關於休・雷恩贈畫風波《沮喪中所作詩》發表。

1914 年： 1-3月：在美國和加拿大旅行講演。同茉德・岡一起
調查米爾波奇蹟，寫出未發表的調查報告。龐德與

莎士比亞太太之女多蘿茜結婚。詩集《責任》出版。
開始對家族史發生興趣。完成《自傳》第一部。第三
次地方自治議案得到英國王室批准。8月4日：第
一次世界大戰爆發。

1915年： 受龐德影響對日本能樂劇發生興趣。《在鷹之井畔》
寫成並上演，由日本舞蹈家伊藤道男主演。拒絕英
國騎士稱號。休・雷恩在「露西塔尼亞」號事件中遇
難。

1916年： 4月：都柏林爆發愛爾蘭共和兄弟會領導的復活節
起義。5月：15位領導人遇難（包括茉德・岡的丈夫
約翰・麥克布萊德）。寫成〈1916年復活節〉。訪茉德・
岡於法國。購置峇里麗塔堡。向茉德・岡求婚。在
茉德・岡之女伊索德幫助下讀法國詩。

1917年： 向伊索德求婚，遭拒絕。10月20日：與喬吉・海德
李斯在倫敦結婚。葉慈太太在蘇塞克斯度蜜月期間
開始扶乩活動。詩集《庫勒的野天鵝》出版。

1918年： 1-2月：偕妻在牛津。詩劇《埃瑪的唯一嫉妒》寫成。
《穿過寧祥的月光》出版。同妻子監修峇里麗塔堡。
羅伯特・葛列格里殉難。11月11日：一戰停戰協定
簽署。新芬黨在大選中獲勝。

1918-21年：「黑褐之亂」。

1919年： 2月：安・巴特勒・葉慈出生。夏：遷入峇里麗塔
堡。拒絕去日本講學的邀請。

1920年： 偕妻子去美國旅行講演。最後一次見父親於紐約。
閱讀歷史和哲學，爲寫作《幻景》作準備。詩集《麥克
爾・羅巴蒂斯與舞蹈者》出版。

1921 年： 麥克爾・葉慈出生。《四舞劇》、《晚近詩集》出版。
12 月：英愛條約簽訂。內戰爆發。

1922 年： 愛爾蘭自由邦憲法使內戰加劇。第一任總統阿瑟・
格瑞菲斯逝世。2 月：購置都柏林梅里昂廣場 82
號。峇里鄽塔堡前橋樑被共和軍炸毀。父親在紐約
逝世。自傳第二部《面紗的顫動》出版。9 月：應邀出
任自由邦參議員。接受都柏林大學名譽文學博士學
位。

1923 年： 〈麗達與天鵝〉寫成。11 月：獲諾貝爾文學獎。寫作
《瑞典的厚贈》。德・維列拉下令共和軍停火。自由
邦加入國聯。

1924 年： 組詩《內戰期間的沉思》發表。《隨筆集》出版。閱讀
歷史和哲學。患高血壓。偕妻子遊西西里、卡波里
和羅馬。

1925 年： 訪問米蘭。在瑞士講學。在參議院發表關於離婚問
題的演說。《幻景》出版。

1926 年： 自傳第四部《疏遠》出版。寫成〈航往拜占庭〉和〈在學
童中間〉。爲艾貝劇院改編《伊底帕斯王》。艾貝劇院
演出歐凱西的《犁與星》風波。6 月：出任新愛爾蘭
貨幣委員會主席。

1927 年： 完成《伊底帕斯在科羅納斯》。在西班牙和法國南部
患肺充血。健康狀況惡化。7 月：愛爾蘭司法部長凱
文・歐希金斯遇刺。

1928 年： 2 月：移居義大利拉巴羅。參議員任期既滿，由於
健康原因，拒絕連任。
7 月：詩集《塔堡》出版。寫作組詩《或許可譜曲的

詞》。

1929 年：　　夏：在峇里鄜塔堡最後一次逗留。冬：修改畢《幻
　　　　　　　景》。寫成〈拜占庭〉。《旋梯》出版。12 月：染上馬耳
　　　　　　　他熱病於拉巴羅。

1930 年：　　春：在熱那亞休養。11 月：《窗玻璃上的字》寫成並
　　　　　　　上演。

1931 年：　　獲牛津大學名譽文學博士學位。最後一次與葛列格
　　　　　　　里夫人在庫勒莊園度夏。在 BBC 貝爾法斯特台做廣
　　　　　　　播講演。

1932 年：　　5 月：葛列格里夫人逝世。創建愛爾蘭文學院。10
　　　　　　　月：最後一次旅美講演，爲文學院籌集資金。《或許
　　　　　　　可譜曲的詞》出版。

1933 年：　　獲劍橋大學名譽文學博士學位。寫成詩劇《大鐘樓之
　　　　　　　王》。《旋梯及其他》、《詩匯集》出版。對歐達菲的藍
　　　　　　　衫運動發生興趣。

1934 年：　　接受回春手術。6 月：在拉巴羅。初遇多蘿茜·韋爾
　　　　　　　斯利夫人。《輪與蝴蝶》、《劇作匯集》出版。

1935 年：　　喬治·拉塞爾(AE)逝世。肺出血復發。編輯《牛津現
　　　　　　　代詩選》。劇與詩集《三月裡的滿月》、自傳第三部《出
　　　　　　　場人物》出版。七十誕辰慶祝宴會。11 月：同師利·
　　　　　　　普羅希大師去馬約卡島過冬，協助他翻譯《奧義
　　　　　　　書》。

1936 年：　　哮喘。6 月：在都柏林拉斯凡漢「河谷」別墅。在英國
　　　　　　　廣播公司(BBC)作關於現代詩歌的廣播講演。編輯
　　　　　　　《牛津現代詩選》。共和軍被宣佈爲非法。

1937 年：　　當選爲文藝協會會員。四次在 BBC 播講。《幻景》修

訂本出版。《散文 1931-1936》出版。德・維列拉的新
憲法通過。

1938 年：　《鷺鷥蛋》出版。移居法國南部。隨筆與詩集《在鍋爐
上》寫成。1 月：《新詩》出版。8 月：出席艾貝劇院
《煉獄》首演並講話（最後一次公開露面）。奧麗薇
亞・莎士比亞逝世。茉德・岡來訪。完成詩劇《庫胡
林之死》。寫作最後一首詩〈黑塔〉。

1939 年：　羅病。1 月 26 日逝世於法國開普馬丁。28 日葬於羅
克布呂吶。6 月：《最後的詩和兩個劇本》出版。9
月：第二次世界大戰爆發。

1941 年：　庫勒莊園被夷平。

1948 年：　遺體由愛爾蘭海軍巡洋艦運回愛爾蘭，受到隆重禮
遇，遵照〈布爾本山下〉一詩所囑，葬於史萊果竺姆
克利夫墓園。新的聯合政府組成，宣佈愛爾蘭退出
英聯邦，成爲共和國。

譯者簡介

傅浩 (1963-)，祖籍武漢，生於西安。畢業於北京大學英語系、中國社會科學院研究生院外文系，獲文學博士學位(1990)。現任中國社會科學院外國文學研究所副研究員。曾以高級訪問研究員身分赴英國劍橋大學、香港大學、香港中文大學、荷蘭國際亞洲研究所、愛爾蘭都柏林大學三一學院等學術機構研修或講學；應以色列外交部邀請赴耶路撒冷出席國際希伯來文學翻譯家會議；應聘爲英國米德爾塞克斯大學名譽客座教授。獲尤金·奈達翻譯獎 (1985)、《文化譯叢》譯文獎 (1987)、梁實秋文學獎譯詩獎 (台灣，1991; 1992; 1994)、世界大學生繪畫展參加賞(日本，1985) 等。著譯有《英國抒情詩》(1992)、《詩歌解剖》(1992)、《耶路撒冷之歌：耶胡達·阿米亥詩選》(1993)、《葉芝抒情詩全集》(1994)、《英國運動派詩學》(1998)、《約翰·但恩：艷情詩與神學詩》(1999)、《葉芝評傳》(1999) 等。

書林詩叢／詩集／譯詩／詩論